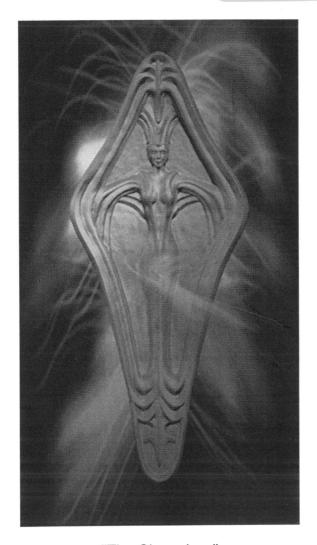

"The Chrysylyss"

Talisman-Pendant available @ theMermaidStory.com

The Mermaid Story
Epyphany

by

Don "Sev" Severance

For more info visit

www.theMermaidStory.com

cover art and design by *Sev*

To Karen

Welcome to the world of
"Oojai"

Dun
"Seu"
Scream

For Mom and Dad the original DIY-ers

PROLOGUE

If you were gliding through the clouds somewhere over a remote section of the Indian Ocean and you happened to look down at just the right moment, you would be one of a very few to get a glimpse of a mysterious and magical place. It is an island of less than 10 square miles, ringed completely by extensive coral reefs and numerous sand-fringed small islets, which serve to frame a beautiful lagoon. At the center of the lagoon a mountain rises up into the clouds—the quiet volcano, Tigress Baku.

You won't find it on any maps. It is a whispered secret, a myth, the birthplace of the Siren's song, a story handed down... it is a place that only music and laughter can truly describe.

This small, magnificent island shall be known forever as...

OoJai - The Island of Blyss.

To walk on the warm black sands of OoJai
a beautiful waking dream
enchanted by the scented breeze
soothed by the sound of the tide
sliding up and down the sandy beach
teasing smooth stones that line the gentle curving inlets
gaze up at the hills behind the cliff
trees bent over as if holding their sturdy trunks
aching with laughter
some private joke
between the trees and the smiling winds

In the first year of the new millennium, a child was born. A strange, beautiful, and powerful new creature. The child of Chrysylyss, born to the ocean. Her name is . . .

Epyphany.

TWILIGHT MYSTERY

It is twilight. The sun has slipped below the horizon shooting gold and purple rays into the darkening sky. The glowing columns cast a shimmering hypnotic reflection across the bay; the warm night air vibrates with the gentle sound of the evening surf as it dances lazily along the black sand. Something surfaces with a gasp, then . . . silence. The water ripples. Bubbles rise to the surface. Two creatures fly out of the water . . . a scream accompanied by a low moan and a high whistling sound . . . then quiet again as they plunge back into the sea. A few moments pass, then suddenly the strange dance resumes.

There seems to be a woman. Her naked body glistens in the eerie twilight as she skims along the surface, one long leg bent at the knee, toes pointing up out of the water . . . how can she move so fast in that position? A large sleek tail fin slices through the waves. The sounds grow louder and the quiet moments grow shorter until the bodies appear as a single blur breaking through the surf. Is she crying? No she is laughing. Then she moans, let's out another little scream, gasps for air, and they are gone.

20 YEARS LATER

The morning sun peeked out over the horizon, sprinkling gold tinted diamonds across the bay. The stars faded away and the sounds of the night grew faint as the small seabirds scurried along the shore trying to outrun the ceaseless waves. A slight breeze arose and whispered in her ear, *a new day*. Epyphany stirred, then opened her eyes. As she slowly awoke, she smiled and thought, I will never grow weary of this view. If I could greet this sparkling vista every morning for the rest of my life, it would be a life well lived.

She wondered briefly, what will this day bring? A small shiver ran through her. She decided to ignore it, slid off the smooth warm stone that was her bed and dropped quietly into the bay. She barely made a ripple as she swam slowly towards the shore. Epyphany tried to ignore the low-frequency hum being transmitted from an unknown source several miles distant, rolled effortlessly onto her back and stared up at the sky wondering . . . when will they come? Lost in this unpleasant thought, she failed to see Reefer flying from the shore to meet her. He swooped down passing low over her head and squawked in delight at her startled gasp.

"It's not very often that I can sneak up on you! You must have been far, far away."

"Yes, I was. I was as far away as that sound. Can you hear it?"

"No. Remember, no one can hear like you do."

"True. Well never mind. Could you do me a favor and swing out past the barrier reef? I'm picking up an odd vibration.

Reefer quickly returned. "There's something I think you should see on the other side of the reef."

HUMAN CONTACT

With a returning sense of apprehension, Epyphany swam out of the bay. Reefer flew ahead as she made her way around the barrier reef into the open sea, she stopped cold at what she saw — about one half mile from the reef in the deep water a very large yacht was drifting slowly.

Epyphany had seen a fair number of ships in her travels but none that approached the beauty and elegance of this machine. It seemed more like a creature of the sea than a mere boat. It's long slender hull simulated the streamlined curves of her dolphin friends. The front was raised slightly by two sleek silver pontoons giving it the illusion of speed though it was moving less than 10 knots. This was undoubtedly the source of the hum Epyphany had noticed upon awakening. But now she perceived an additional secondary vibration leading her to believe that the ship must have some alternative means of propulsion. It seemed unattended, almost as if it were waiting for orders. There was no sign of the presence of anyone on board.

In all her years on Oojai, Epyphany had never seen a boat this close to her island. With her mind full of questions, she swam closer, and then instructed Reefer to head out farther and scan the area. She felt that shiver again and this time she couldn't ignore it.

Circling the boat several times Epyphany tried to get a sense of who the captain might be and what this ship was doing here. About a half an hour passed and Reefer finally returned.

"There's a man."

"Where is he? Is he alone?"

"Yes, he seems to be. I think he's barely treading water, he definitely needs help."

When the need arose, Epyphany could skim across the water faster than Reefer could fly. As soon as she was in deep water she could sense his distress and weariness. She came upon him in minutes and only then did she stop to think about the results of what she was about to do.

Epyphany had been taught the seriousness of underestimating humans' lack of compassion for any creature that they didn't understand. Blyss had related several personal experiences that confirmed those lessons. So the few times that Epyphany had been in close proximity to humans, she had made sure that she wasn't discovered. This moment felt different, something was compelling Epyphany to ignore those lessons.

FIRST GLIMPSE

Thurrow was really getting tired. After treading water steadily through the night, he was starting to lose hope. He thought, "How could I be so dumb? After all these years and experience on every kind of boat through every kind of weather, I fall off this incredibly stable boat in a dead calm!" Recognizing that he was probably delusional by now, he could still swear that something or someone had pushed him.

Before checking on the pontoon hydraulic system, Thurrow had set the ship's auto pilot to idle slowly around the perimeter of the atoll. He was extremely excited about this recent discovery but somewhat puzzled. This coral island had not turned up on any maps and he had found no record of it anywhere. It was curious that he should just happen to be nudged off course overnight. He thought perhaps one of the pontoons might be out of line. Though he knew that was unlikely, he could not come up with any other explanation. The more he'd thought about it the more mysterious it became. One minute he was making his way across the pontoon, the next minute he was in the water.

 Once he got his bearings he immediately began a valiant attempt to reach his ship. Though the boat only had a couple of yards on him, it was moving slightly faster than he could swim. As he continued in his olympic effort, the ship drifted steadily away from him. Thurrow watched sadly as his beautiful vessel was swallowed by the evening haze. He moaned out loud and held back tears of frustration as the purr of it's turbine faded in the distance. He was many miles from any shipping lane, there was little chance that anyone would ever find him.

Once he reconciled his fate, Thurrow switched into survival mode, quickly figuring out how to use the least amount of energy to stay afloat, he somehow managed to hang on through the dark night. As the sky lightened, he was surprised that he had lived to see another day. Thurrow knew that he was strong enough to tread water for a few more hours but he was also aware that the blinding sun, hunger, and dehydration would soon destroy his resolve . . .

Something in the sky caught his attention, a large bird was headed towards him. In that same moment he also felt a strange presence. Thurrow sensed an odd variation in the current around him and he immediately thought of sharks. Laughing to himself he thought "and here I was afraid that I might drown". Then suddenly the water around him became calm. An inexplicable sense of peacefulness enveloped him. This mystifying calm continued even as he saw something break the surface of the water a few yards away and move slowly towards him. The surrounding water seemed to vibrate in tune with his heart beat. He felt like he was one with the ocean and the sky — he closed his eyes for a moment.

When Thurrow opened his eyes he was looking directly into the eyes of another, not more than 6 feet away. He was instantly confused, he felt he should be afraid though he was not, he felt that he should scream or try to swim away but his instinct to flee was overcome by his curiosity. The eyes of this creature continued to look at him, he felt something like a voice in his mind. Not really words, more like music. It was not just in his mind, he felt the message vibrating gently through his whole body informing him that he was not in danger.

He was hypnotized by the power and gentleness in the glistening gold green eyes of this beautiful creature. She moved closer and he struggled to break the bonds of her gaze. Sensing his struggle she simply closed her eyes, turned away then reached back and held out one hand toward him.

He recoiled slightly at the sight of her hand. There were three long elegant fingers and an elongated thumb, connected by a thin membrane, the fingernails were long, tapered and slightly curved like talons. He anticipated an iron grip. Quickly realizing that he had no choice he reached out to her.

When their fingers touched Thurrow knew his life would never be the same. Something inside him was released. Some unnamed fear melted away and was replaced by a conscious desire to understand. He thought "This mysterious creature exists, she has decided to save my life". Then he lost consciousness.

RESCUE

As she approached Thurrow, Epyphany was surprised that a man near drowning would hesitate to accept assistance. In her limited encounters with humans Epyphany had managed to remain undetected, so she was quite sure that this one was likely the first to get a good look at her. She hesitated for a moment trying to imagine the future consequences of meeting this human face to face. If she let him drown her world would stay unchanged a little while longer. She almost swam away.

Holding Thurrow under one arm, Epyphany swam effortlessly back to the bay and toward the lagoon. Looking up to signal Reefer, she noticed Blyss standing on a cliff high above the cove entrance. Though her stature was small, framed by the glow of the morning sun, Blyss had the appearance of a much larger woman — more in keeping with her majestic spirit and mysterious abilities.

Epyphany thought, "What now? What will I do with this human? Blyss has warned me repeatedly against making contact with humans." Anticipating what Blyss would have to say, Epyphany hoped she could postpone that conversation for as long as possible.

Distracted by these thoughts, she didn't notice that Blyss wasn't the only one who had been watching her swim into the bay with her mysterious companion. As she approached the entrance to the lagoon, Dali and Magnum swam up on either side of Epyphany. Although their curiosity was almost palpable, they managed to hold their questions. She acknowledged her friends, then she continued to wonder if she had done the right thing. In the fog of her self doubt she felt the heat and light of a small fire illuminating her path. She didn't know why but she felt there was really no other choice. There was something she and this man were meant to do. The trio swam silently into the lagoon.

Swiftly crossing the lagoon into a small bay, Epyphany, Dali, and Magnum approached the narrow inlet and waterfalls that masked the entrance to the hidden cove. Surrounded by the sound of falling water, they disappeared into the shadows of overhanging branches, lush vegetation and flowering vines. Once inside the cove, the trio and guest were welcomed by a few more members of the Tribe. Having little experience with humans, her new audience kept a safe distance while she made her way toward the Cavern.

A KISS?

With Thurrow passed out under her arm, Epyphany wasn't quite sure how to manage the underwater tunnel to the Cavern Temple. Under normal circumstances, a well-trained swimmer could make the distance on a single breath of air, but she had no way of knowing what condition this weakened human might be in. She decided her only choice was to inject some extra oxygen into his system.

Epyphany had never been this close to a human male. From a distance, they had appeared light and fragile. Blyss was the only human she had ever touched and Blyss was not a typical human.

Holding Thurrow so firmly against her body resulted in a feeling very different from the affection she had known with Blyss. This man was as big as she was if one didn't count her long, powerful tail. He was solid. He had a wonderful steely yet elastic quality to his skin. For a land creature, this one seemed well proportioned for swimming, probably the reason he survived the long hours adrift. Now she must push air into his lungs, nourish his brain with oxygen, and hope he survives the brief underwater journey.

Spinning in and out of consciousness, Thurrow had been aware of being propelled swiftly through the water. He could sense great strength and tenderness simultaneously. It was as if his confused mind was being massaged and lightly probed. Feeling strange delight, he thought he might be smiling but doubted the message had made it to his lips.

Suddenly he felt the grip shift. Through his swollen eyelids he could see an alien, yet beautiful, face coming towards him. He wasn't frightened—just overwhelmed. In the next instant he felt his mouth engulfed completely by the most sensuous lips he had ever known. Large and soft and moist with an ineffable taste. Like sweet fruit and chocolate and lime, like pop rocks and butterscotch . . . How could such a combination entice? These were not thoughts exactly. The term 'thoughts' implies a process much too slow to describe what he was feeling. If you added the speed of light to earth's distance from the sun and multiplied it by the velocity of electricity you might get an idea of the crackling speed of these multiple sensations. He wondered who or what was kissing him . . . and why?

Epyphany moved him gently in front of her and placed her mouth over his. Thurrow's eyes opened. He twitched slightly then relaxed in her arms. Their eyes met, their tongues touched, Epyphany exhaled, Thurrow gasped, then she pulled him close and disappeared behind the waterfall and down into the dark tunnel.

THE CAVERN TEMPLE

Still holding Thurrow firmly at her side, Epyphany virtually flew out of the tunnel and across the surface of the Temple Pool. Heading straight for the center of the pool, she gently propelled him up the ramp at the base of the Gold Tower. She then took one slow lap around the pool in order to clear her head and regain her composure. Epyphany tried to imagine the potential consequences of her decision. She had broken the most important rule that Blyss had been pounding into her head since she was a child. Human contact! Not only contact but physical contact . . . a pleasant shiver ran through her at the thought of her mouth on his, and she quickly tried to bury the feeling. Worst of all, she had brought him here, to the most sacred and secret Temple on earth.

Before Thurrow could comprehend what had just happened, he felt himself flying out of the water and sliding on his stomach up a smooth stone ramp. As he came to a gentle stop he opened his eyes, rolled onto his back, and gazed up in total wonder. Some kind of enormous cave, a tower of light? He thought he heard a voice but once again he couldn't tell if it was real or in his head. The facts did not compute . . . his body shuddered, he coughed twice then passed out from exhaustion.

Epyphany could not imagine what she was going to tell Blyss. How could she explain it when she couldn't even understand it herself? At that thought, she turned back to look at Thurrow. She froze . . . Blyss!

For twenty years Blyss had been educating, guiding, and training Epyphany in the ways of the modern world. Hardly a day went by that she didn't warn Epyphany about direct contact with humans. In preparation for the inevitable, Epyphany was introduced to the cruel realities of the so called "civilized world" and taught the necessary skills to deal wonders of Oojai. To start, you must understand that you are not in danger from any of the tribe – that is unless you should try to harm any of us."

Q&A

Thurrow didn't quite know where to start; his world and the way he had always perceived it had been completely altered. A less intelligent, less rational man would have become unhinged by now. His experience and scientific training were his saving grace. He needed to organize his thoughts – find the most important question. He sat down with his feet dangling in the warm pool, leaned forward and looking directly into Epyphany's enchanting eyes he spoke,

"Is this reality?"

Epyphany was startled by his question. She was raised here and had grown to know and love Oojai, Blyss, and the entire Tribe. She awoke everyday to a world of beauty and sounds so familiar they felt a part of her. She had never questioned her reality. Her quick mind grasped the situation as Thurrow must be experiencing it.

"If you mean, 'Is this a dream?' or if you're wondering if you are hallucinating, the answer would be no. Although this island may be like nothing you've ever imagined, it exists as part of the same world you know. It's just that circumstances and powers beyond my understanding have allowed you to awaken to us."

"Then can you tell me where I am? Why it has never been discovered? How you and Blyss came to be here . . . what you plan to do with me?"

Epyphany replied, "These are all understandable questions and I will try to answer those that I can. You are still in the Indian Ocean. We have never been discovered because the world wasn't ready. Blyss rescued me when I was a newborn infant and brought me here. I'm still not sure exactly how Blyss ended up here and I'm not sure what Blyss has in mind." Then she paused, with a sly smile she said, "One of the first things I want from you is another oxygen exchange."

Thurrow was glad he was sitting or he might have fallen down. He had been listening closely but had to ask her to repeat the last statement. He thought he knew what she was referring to and had a flashback to the moment her mouth had engulfed his, but her tone was so matter-of-fact it didn't quite compute.

"You want a kiss?"

Before Epyphany could answer, Blyss suddenly appeared and suggested they introduce Thurrow to a few of the tribe.

Thurrow followed Blyss over the bridge with Reefer waddling awkwardly behind, his large webbed feet slapping the damp stone. When they reached the perimeter, Thurrow could now see a series of paths and walkways that surrounded the entire pool. They made their way out to the end of a narrow stone pier that extended into the deep water. He heard some familiar sounds as the water in front of them began to stir. Blyss reached behind her back and as if removing an arrow from a quiver, she pulled some sort of instrument out of a shiny black case that he had somehow failed to notice.

When Blyss raised the instrument to her lips, Thurrow could see it was an elongated spiral shaped shell. He recognized the shape and variety but this was sleeker and larger than anything he had come across in his studies. It's smooth translucent surface both reflected and transmitted light with a prismatic effect. As she blew gently the sound and the changing color were hypnotic. Thurrow gazed out at the pool as though in a trance. Ripples broke the smooth surface of the pool and a variety of shapes slowly emerged and surrounded the pier.

As she placed the Swhorl back in its case, Blyss spoke:

"Thurrow, I'd like you to meet a few members of Epyphany's and my exceptional tribe."

Still feeling slightly drugged from the music, Thurrow tried to connect each creature with their name.

"Dali" – a large bottle-nose dolphin with bright piercing eyes.

"Magnum" – this menacing looking alligator must have been over 20 feet long… with a forked tail!

"Yew" Thurrow stifled a laugh – this large round manatee seemed to be grinning.

"Cheeks" Blyss explained, "Yew's wife." Thurrow thought he heard this gentle creature giggle.

"Speed" Thurrow recognized this one as a leather-back sea turtle. He knew this endangered species. They truly were built for speed. With his streamlined carapace and oversized flippers there was no way this big guy would be left behind.

"Zip" A splash, then an iridescent greenish-blue flash of light, caught Thurrow's eye. In sharp contrast to the other members of the tribe, this one was a little flying fish. He wondered what special powers this little creature held.

"Irie" A gorgeous blue sailfish swam slowly by, sensuously raising her sail fin.

"You'll meet Storm soon. He's a bit too large to hang out with us in the Cavern."

On Oojai, "large" had new meaning. Thurrow looked forward to seeing Storm.

Blyss asked Thurrow, "Are you feeling strong enough for another tunnel dive back to the cove?

You can hitch a ride with Dali if you have any doubt."

"I don't remember much about the first trip, so I guess I'll take a ride with Dali if he doesn't mind."

"Wise."

Dali was fine with the idea. He sensed a change in Epyphany and he was glad to keep a close eye on this human.

Thurrow waded into the pool. He was no stranger to swimming with dolphins. Part of his marine biology training had been living and working with them. He had developed a true love and respect for these intelligent, friendly, ocean people. Thurrow grabbed Dali's dorsal fin, took a deep breath, and along with the rest of the tribe, they dove under water.

With Dali towing him swiftly through the tunnel, Thurrow's short trip was memorable and joyful experience. The walls of the tunnel were formed by a dark green stone, relatively smooth except for slight indentions that could serve as hand or foot holds. If swimming was not an option, an athletic human or dextrous creature could climb horizontally along the walls. It was dimly lit by the same natural lighting phenomenon he had seen in the Cavern. Thurrow marveled at this strange and wonderful tribe of creatures swimming around him and he realized he hadn't had this much fun since he was a child. What an amazing journey!

Approaching the end of the tunnel, Thurrow braced himself for the blinding light of day. He was surprised as they came splashing through the waterfall into the gentle light of a setting sun. The cove was hidden deep in a short canyon so the view above him was a magical mix of color and shadows. The moon and the stars were peeking through the fading golden sunlight. A vaporous mist rose from the jagged shoreline, adding even more mystery to Thurrow's continuing adventure.

THE CHANCEL

Epyphany swam up next to Thurrow and Dali as they continued through the cove into the lagoon. She asked Thurrow, "How are you feeling?"

"Physically, never better. Mentally, a little overwhelmed. If I haven't told you this already – thanks for saving my life."

"You're welcome. Are you up for a short swim?"

"Sure." Thurrow said thanks to Dali then let go.

Dali reluctantly swam away wondering where Epyphany was taking Thurrow. He wasn't concerned for her safety; he'd seen Epyphany handle herself in some incredibly dangerous situations. It was just that he was feeling something he'd never felt before, something like an uncomfortable curiosity.

Epyphany led Thurrow to a small natural jetty on the shore not far from the cove entrance. She motioned him toward a cluster of interesting rock formations at the end of the breakwater.

"This is where I often sleep. It's the first image in my earliest memory of Oojai. I love to fall asleep here looking at the sky reflected in the lagoon and wake up to the brilliant sunrise. The Tribe knows not to bother me here unless it's very important.

I call it the Chancel . . . a church word Blyss taught me when I was very young. Oojai feels like a religion to me – a pure religion without rules, with no demanding Gods. If one opens themselves to this place, they realize it is more than just beautiful landscapes and breathtaking sunsets. There is a calming, nourishing spirit here. If you quiet your mind, Oojai will share her secrets and guide your better nature. When I travel great distances from here, her power weakens slightly, but I feel she is connected to and accessible from any place on this planet."

Epyphany suddenly paused.

"Wow! Sorry! I didn't intend to babble on like that. I didn't realize how much I longed for human connection."

Thurrow was mesmerized. He had forgotten where he was, forgotten the impossibility of this creature, and lost all sense of apprehension or foreboding. It wasn't just her singular alien beauty or the wonderful effect the vibrations of her voice had on his entire skeletal system. It was her words and her passion. She was so unaffected, so incredibly disconnected from the follies of mankind.

Her voice found him again. "Have I put you to sleep?"

"No. In fact, quite the opposite. You have awakened something in me which I barely recognize and would be hard-pressed to explain. I could listen to your voice and your words all night."

They were silent for a moment, then Thurrow spoke.

"Do you still want to exchange oxygen?"

Epyphany laughed. "I do know the term. I don't know why I couldn't say it. I have no experience with human intimacy. When you were floundering in the ocean struggling to survive, I felt an incomprehensible attraction that clouded my reason. I feel that now. Blyss has told me that I am unique to this world, and I sense that uniqueness in you as well. I am not fearful by nature, but I have never simultaneously feared and desired anything more . . . but yes . . . please kiss me."

Thurrow followed as Epyphany made her way into the shallow water and in a single graceful movement spun around towards him then gently propelled herself up onto a smooth, low stone shelf. It was less a shelf and more like a couch carved in alabaster, a translucent white sculpture of subtle curves designed to cradle the most significantly beautiful creature on earth.

Though he had been aware of her long slender tail he hadn't really considered it. Most of the time he'd seen her she had been up to her neck in the water. He had only been thinking about her in terms of her total presence without quantifying the sum of her parts. Her saw her complete now for the first time.

Semi-reclined, hands placed firmly behind her, palms down, elbows locked, supporting her weight evenly, head tilted back and cocked slightly to her right, gazing up at the stars, she was muscular like a dancer, with full firm breasts and a long narrow waist blending into the alluring curve of her hips. The curve tapered gently into a long powerful tail. Her tail was partially submerged, then curled out of the water exposing the wide sleek tail fin which undulated slowly.

She was a vision, a living sculpture. Framed by the glowing alabaster she seemed to be suspended in time and space. Since he was a child, Thurrow had been interested in the sea, including the legends and lore as well as the science. Looking at her and knowing she fit the mythological description, he still had a hard time thinking of her as a "mermaid." Through the ages in every type of media, the image was more a decoration, an accessory to a story, a graphic depiction of a sailor's lonely desire or the symbol of our dream to commune with the mysterious ocean. Epyphany was so much more. She was not just a woman with the tail of a dolphin. She was some extraordinary being, an evolutionary link from what the world has been to what the world could be.

Epyphany motioned him with her tail.

"Have you slipped into another trance?"

"You have that effect on me."

"Good, come sit next to me. I think I may have dreamed you here. I need to to touch you."

"I was thinking the same."

Thurrow waded closer and slid up next to her. This time when she held out her hand to him there was no hesitation. He reached up with his other hand and turned her head toward his. Her skin was so smooth. Not completely dissimilar to a human but a different kind of smooth. But for the fact of the warmth and softness it was as if she actually had been carved in marble then precisely machined and polished.

Those eyes! For a moment Thurrow felt like he was falling.

Epyphany had leaned in close and looked him directly in the eyes. He felt like she was inside his head seeing everything he had ever thought or felt or seen. Until now, Thurrow had thought Sadjah possessed the most beautiful eyes on the planet, but with Epyphany it was not just beauty. This was a soulfulness beyond life experience, an empathy so pure and love so raw he felt his heart stop. He couldn't breathe. At that moment he would have welcomed death.

He pulled her close and they clung to each other under the Oojai moon. They couldn't stop kissing. They were matched in strength and desire – they could have devoured each other. Lost in time, they were deaf and blind…

They didn't hear or see what was undoubtedly the largest whale on the planet as it swam slowly into the cove under a full moon with Blyss, a tiny silhouette, standing on his head ridge. Storm stopped about 50 feet from the Chancel where Epyphany and Thurrow were enraptured. Blyss gave him the signal and he blew out a spectacular single-column spout of water, thousands of gallons, the likes of which would be sufficient to douse the fires of hell.

Unharmed, the lovers were washed quickly and efficiently into the sea. When they came up for air and recovered some sense of equilibrium, they saw Blyss and Storm heading out to the lagoon. Thurrow and Epyphany looked at each other and laughed, both secretly thankful for the interruption. Still chuckling from the incident, they decided to take a short swim in the moonlight. When they returned, they slipped back up to Epyphany's stone bed, curled up in each other's arms, and fell into a deep sleep.

DARKNESS

It is so dark. Darker than either of them had ever experienced. A total absence of light. With no source, there are no reflections and no shadows. The brain beseeches the eyes for information, they open wider . . . nothing. And quiet, total silence, not a single perceivable vibration. They turn their heads from side to side, scanning . . . panic! Face to face, they can't even hear each other's frightened breathing or feel their own hearts beating. Floating . . . flying . . . suspended . . . weightless, they are being absorbed, they are ceasing to exist.

Something envelops them, squeezes them together, extracts their essence and crushes the flesh and blood container that defined their physical presence. Their souls contract . . . one millisecond of unbearable pain!

Release!

A soundless scream inside their heads.

Then . . . nothing.

Thurrow and Epyphany awoke at exactly the same moment. Each slightly dazed by a nightmare too horrifying to remember.

Warmed by the morning sun as the waves lapped gently against the Chancel bed, they smiled and spoke at the same moment, cutting each other off. They laughed, then Epyphany said, "Want a tour of the island?" Thurrow nodded and they slid into the water.

EXPLORATION

That morning was the beginning of a month of joy and discovery beyond anything that Thurrow and Epyphany had ever known. Thurrow was a powerful swimmer, but without his water sled there was no way he could keep up with Epyphany. She had abilities that surpassed any technology he had invented or even conceived. Her world was the antithesis of his high-tech world. So he often opted for simply sliding up next to her and holding onto her dorsal fin as they glided smoothly through the bay.

Touring the island with Thurrow's voice in her ear and his body close to hers, Epyphany saw Oojai anew. She felt the wonder and beauty of her home magnified by his child-like awe and she was delighted by his unrestrained outbursts of joy. Though Epyphany had shared incredible adventures, boisterous celebrations, and years of enriching friendships with Blyss and the Tribe, she had never enjoyed herself as much the days with Thurrow. He made her laugh. He showed her a different view of the world she thought she knew. He noticed details; the artist in him saw shapes where she saw things, he saw color in shadows where she had seen only darkness. He was full of wonder; his scientific curiosity and thirst for knowledge led them into places on Oojai she had never noticed. When they were exploring some random inlet he would point to vegetation or rock formations and exclaim or explain.

Some days Thurrow would venture alone into the jungle or hike the green tropical slopes and mountain valleys bringing back samples of exotic fruits that even Blyss had overlooked. Thurrow was intrigued by Tigress Baku, an extinct volcano rising one half mile into the sky near the center of the island. He would show Epyphany specimens and theorize as to their origins. She was smitten.

It was no accident that most days they would end up swimming with one or more members of the Tribe. Since their passions had been doused that first night at the

Chancel, they had accepted the fact that Blyss wasn't about to give them much privacy anytime soon. As a result, Thurrow was able to get to know these wonderful creatures on a first name basis. He had been anxious to learn how it could be that so many diverse species were able to communicate. It took him awhile to wrap his head around the explanation.

To begin with, each tribe member was a highly evolved member of their own species with some special talent or ability that set them apart from their own kind. They were mutants, misfits—shunned, ignored, often exiled, or by their own choice distanced from the society of their natural habitat. The second connection was Oojai, or more specifically, the Gold Tower. Among its many mysterious powers, it was a beacon of sorts. All these various mutants had been drawn to Oojai by a vibration, the frequency of which only they could sense. It was this language of subtle tones that they all shared, including Blyss and Epyphany. Living in close proximity to the Tower, they all soon developed the ability to interpret as well as emit variations of these tones.

When they spoke, it wasn't in words as humans think of them. It was a combination of vibrational deciphering, tonal interpretation, and telepathy. The tones were received along with a mental picture of the thought which was instinctively decoded, then translated into something like a little mind movie. That movie could communicate the idea or phrase. The net result was that they could "speak" to each other. Within days, Thurrow was starting to pickup some of the transmissions, and with concentration, succeeded in limited "conversation." He had never considered himself a mutant or misfit, but he realized he felt more alive in their company and completely at home living among this tribe.

Epyphany related some of her childhood memories to Thurrow and he shared stories of life in the modern world. They were both enthralled. It seemed Blyss had never given Epyphany a clear picture of her actual birth. Thurrow didn't fully understand why she hadn't pressed Blyss on the subject. There were references to this demi-goddess named Chrysylyss. It was implied that this mysterious and revered figure was Epyphany's mother. Thurrow had seen the image depicted in several locations around Oojai. There was an enchanting, larger-than-life-size statue rendered in silver and set into one of the walls in the Cavern Temple. When Thurrow had first encountered it, he had felt compelled to kneel down at her feet. He was not religious in the traditional sense and certainly not given to iconic worship, but this statue seemed more than a symbol. He had always felt there was a secret place in his heart and mind – a room of forbidden knowledge locked and barred from rational thought. Kneeling before Chrysylyss, he felt he had found the key to that room.

EDUCATION

Thurrow was surprised to find that Epyphany possessed a well-rounded understanding of the world he lived in. She understood the sciences of math, physics, and chemistry better than many of his peers. It seemed she had read the classics and knew her way around various religions and philosophies from around the globe. Her understanding had a child-savant quality—a bookish knowing rather than a lived experience. When he questioned how she could learn so much about the world and its history while living on a secluded island in the middle of the Indian Ocean with no library or obvious means of electronic communication, he shouldn't have been surprised when she replied, "the Gold Tower."

For Thurrow, the Gold Tower was the biggest mystery of all, but for Epyphany, it had been so much a part of her reality, she had ceased to question its existence. To her it was like the sun; it was just there—glowing, radiating pure energy and knowledge. Without taking it for granted, she simply accepted it and gave it her respect and appreciation.

Since her early childhood, Epyphany had spent untold hours in the presence of the Tower. She and Blyss would share a couple evenings a week sitting back to back at the foot of the Tower, heads touching, each with one palm touching the wall of the bottom tier and the other hand splayed flat on the smooth stone base. Blyss would tell Epyphany stories or Epyphany would ask whatever questions came into her mind. In this way, Epyphany gained unparalleled knowledge and insight into the past and present of earth and its inhabitants. Still, there was much Epyphany didn't understand about the hearts and minds of humanity. She was baffled by the constant conflict and the violence humans inflicted upon one another. They had achieved so much but seemed to have learned so little.

Thurrow was at a loss trying to explain. He empathized with Epyphany. Through his work, Thurrow and the incredible team of experts he collaborated with had found solutions. With the use of technology, conservation, and teamwork, the entire population of the planet could live a healthy and happy life. He was baffled at the short-sighted policies of the world leaders. He was saddened by the greed, both corporate and individual, that was woven into the fabric of society. Humans were steadily and efficiently rendering their own planet uninhabitable.

He managed to keep his conversations on the lighter side, emphasizing the wonderful imagination and innovation humans were capable of. There was a shadow of doubt in his heart, but he told Epyphany he hadn't lost hope.

Epyphany's connection to the Tower was not only cerebral, but recreational as well. The Cavern had been her playground, and as she grew, the Tower became her jungle gym — when she was big enough, she learned how to "climb" it. The Tower was a fountain. There was a gentle stream of water steadily streaming down and around the tiered shelves and cascading over the extruded steps, forming small waterfalls. As her strength and dexterity grew, Epyphany was able to twist and turn around the steps like an aquatic gymnast, sliding up the steep terraces that formed the Gold Tower. Once at the top, she would stand on her hands, then take a breathtaking flip into a death-defying dive, penetrating the deep pool below with barley a splash. Even Blyss, with her unflagging faith in Epyphany's abilities, was astounded every time.

Thurrow spent many of his nights on Oojai mediating and sleeping in the Cavern. The sound of falling water was like a never ending symphony. At times, Blyss would blend complex rhythms with her drum or play beautiful haunting melodies with the Swhorl. Thurrow had experienced several of those intoxicating concerts. The music itself was a spiritual education. Every thing Blyss did served to educate and enlighten.

One evening after a somewhat exhausting yet exhilarating day of diving out along the barrier reef, Epyphany surprised

Thurrow with an unexpected inquiry.

"Would you tell me about some of the women in your life? Have you been married? Is there someone waiting for you to return."

For some reason, these questions threw him totally off guard. That life seemed far removed from the timeless world of Oojai. He was still coming down from the incredible visual high he experienced viewing the diverse and exciting sea life in and around the reef. His world right now was Epyphany and Oojai. He felt like a different man than the person she was asking about.

Thurrow could fully understand Epyphany's curiosity but it certainly was a buzz kill! The first name that came to mind was Sadjah. When he had left for this voyage, their relationship was in a gray area. They had decided to give it a break for a while. He believed that she was under the impression things would be just fine with a little time apart. There was a lot about Sadjah that appealed to Thurrow but in his heart he felt like it could never work.

He tried to give Epyphany the short version.

"I married my high school sweetheart before either one of us had a clue about who we were as individuals. It lasted a little over a year. There were no children, and we had an amicable divorce. I confessed my love a few times over the years; it was either the wrong reason, or the right person but the wrong time, or the right reason but wrong person . . . I'm kind of married to my work and that usually means when I'm in a relationship, there's always three in the room. I haven't met a woman for whom I've felt a mutual balance of love, tolerance, and empathy."

He tried to ignore the last question but she persisted.

"So there's no one waiting for you?"

"Well, she's not exactly waiting . . . that is . . . well it's . . . it's difficult to explain. We didn't officially break up. In her mind it's a temporary separation."

Epyphany tilted her head, staring intently, concentrating on every word, feeling she was missing something.

Thurrow continued, "We disagreed on some key issues, then her work became very demanding and I needed to get back to my research, so we never truly resolved the issues. My ship was ready so I told her I needed to go. We had a frosty bon-voyage dinner, then I left the next day." Thurrow left out the part in which after a couple of bottles of champagne, the frosty dinner turned into very hot night in Sadjah's penthouse apartment.

"Do you miss her"

He responded truthfully. "I really haven't thought too much about her since I hit the open sea."

This seemed to satisfy Epyphany for now and the conversation moved on to planning further exploration and the days to come.

Every day on Oojai was magical. This was truly heaven for beings such as Thurrow and Epyphany who shared an unquenchable thirst for knowledge and truth. The Tribe came to accept him as one of their own. It was an unimaginable gift for a marine biologist to actually "talk" to the creatures he had been studying. Thurrow was able to gain incredible insight from these animals through their lengthy conversations.

He was saddened to hear the stories of the increasing hardships for those living in or near the oceans. So far, Oojai had not been directly affected by the chemical pollution in the air and sea or by the over-fishing and the sonic pollution destroying the hearing and communication of dolphins and whales. The busy shipping lanes were disorienting all types of sea mammals and destroying breeding grounds. Under the banner "we will feed the world," they were wreaking havoc on the planet.

Thurrow couldn't stop thinking about sharing all this great research, and how much this first-hand data would increase the odds of success in convincing the scientific community, as well as the world leaders, that direct action was needed immediately—that is if he could first figure out how to convince them that he was not a certified nut job.

Setting these thoughts aside, Thurrow swam up next to Epyphany and said, "I have to tell you once again, I have never been so happy. I can't imagine my world with out you and Blyss, the Tribe, and this island." Treading water, he faced Epyphany, reached out and pulled her closer, then looking straight into her eyes he said, "You are the most beautiful and intelligent and mysterious creature on earth and I am in love with you."

DEPARTURE

Epyphany felt a connection with Thurrow beyond words. Together they were music and dance, each moment a fresh note as they composed the symphony of each day, moving through her world of water and sunshine in synchronized motion like untethered souls racing through the heavens. It was an incredible month of joy and laughter, intense conversation and a continuous undercurrent of bridled passion. Thirty days of of a life she had never imagined with a man like no other. Every minute with Thurrow was an inspiring excursion into the heart, mind, and soul. He had told her he loved her and she felt the same. The depth of her love for Thurrow was a completely new experience—so different than the love she felt for Blyss, the Tribe, or even Oojai. Their spirits were intertwined.

With three words, her world unraveled. Blyss had come to her and said, "He has gone."

Epyphany couldn't believe what she was hearing. At first she thought Blyss meant he had gone for a swim with Dali or gone to meditate in the Cavern.

Blyss tried again. "He has left Oojai. He has gone back to his world."

Blyss

This was the most difficult decision Blyss had ever faced. She had dedicated her life to the care and welfare of Epyphany. She loved her as if she were a daughter, and the last thing she wanted was to cause Epyphany pain. But Blyss knew beyond doubt that this was not the right time for Epyphany and Thurrow. There was no way to convince her that this was best. The planet's future was at stake and sacrifices would have to be made. Blyss couldn't predict the outcome, but she had felt the truth of her decision. Epyphany was strong and intelligent; she would bear the burden of lost love and she would transcend her loss. She would fill the void with a renewed sense of purpose.

Blyss had secretly helped bring Thurrow to Oojai. At the time she wasn't sure he was the one the Tablets had foreseen but his stay had convinced her that he was a likely candidate. With Storm's help, she had nudged Thurrow's ship off course, and the following day, used a subtle energy displacement technique that she had mastered to put him off balance and into the water. The day Epyphany rescued Thurrow, Blyss knew there would come a time when she would have to figure out a method to deliver him back to his world. She hadn't foreseen how quickly they would connect or the strength of their bond. Watching them grow together those few weeks was one of great joy and sorrow. Blyss had no way of warning Epyphany to the plan without arousing suspicion in Thurrow. Their passion was growing daily. Lost in the magical world of Oojai, they had become completely oblivious to the obstacles their love must overcome. She knew she couldn't keep their passion at bay much longer, so Blyss implemented an exit strategy.

Thurrow

Epyphany and Thurrow had evolved a tradition of ending each day with one last relaxing swim around the cove. They grudgingly accepted the fact that one of the tribe was always reporting their whereabouts or activities, so they were not surprised when Dali joined them and asked if he could talk privately with Thurrow. Epyphany was slightly annoyed, but she agreed and told Thurrow to meet her back at the Chancel.

Dali asked Thurrow to follow him. Somewhat mystified but curious, Thurrow followed Dali out into the lagoon. When they entered the lagoon, Thurrow was surprised to see Blyss moving slowly toward them, seemingly walking on water. When they got closer, Blyss invited Thurrow to join her on what turned out to be Storm's partially submerged back.

"There's something I need to show you."

Thurrow thought, Blyss is not her usual self. His instincts were telling him that something was not quite right. She had been completely honest and forthcoming throughout his entire visit and he had no reason to suspect otherwise, but this scenario was highly unusual. As they left the lagoon and headed out into the open sea, Thurrow's suspicion turned into apprehension.

Blyss turned to face him and spoke.

"I know you and Epyphany are deeply in love. And I also know that even in the height of your passion for her, you have not forgotten your differences. Lost in the joy of the moment you may have suppressed your fears and doubts, but unlike Epyphany, you are aware of the "real world." You are older and wiser and you should not deny that hard-won wisdom. Do you think the world outside of Oojai is ready for a couple such as you and Epyphany? Are you ready to entertain the thought of living the rest of your life in the confines of Oojai? Do you deny your nature, your desire to help humankind? These past weeks were not a vacation from reality, they were a sample of a different way of living, a glimpse into an alternate path for the inhabitants of this planet. Whether you like it or not, you are now a potential link in the evolutionary chain. At this precise moment in time perhaps you are the most important man on earth, or maybe just a pawn in a scheme destined to fail—I don't know. What I do know with certainty is that Epyphany is not yet ready for you, and you need to discover with certainty what you are willing to give up to be with her.

Before Thurrow could respond, Blyss raised both palms toward him then directed his attention to the horizon.

"Your ship is ready."

Thurrow had lost track of the speed and distance they had traveled. He was overwhelmed by everything that Blyss had said, his heart was racing and his head was spinning. So many questions! She had read his mind. She had seen deep into his heart. She was exactly right; he was conflicted and confused. Thurrow had no doubt about his love for

Epyphany, he had never felt so completely in love, but now he couldn't deny that he had succeeded in avoiding the nagging issues of reality. When he saw his ship, the life he had known and loved came rushing back to him. So much had happened, time had stopped on Oojai. He felt so alive there, so at home with all those wonderful magical creatures. Now with his ship in view, he was reminded that his world held it's own brand of magic and mystery as well. There was so much to discover. He was on the cutting edge of the science that was finding solutions to help save the ailing planet and years of research had been starting to pay off. He didn't want to give that up.

The Samudra Hantu

Thurrow had named his ship "Samudra Hantu." It was Indonesian for Ocean Ghost. He simply referred to her as Samu. She was more than just a ship to him — she was the total extent of his material wealth — his home, lab, workshop, music studio, art studio and his gallery. A floating facility full of all the important gadgets, tools, and toys he had invented over the years. An original design, Samu was the culmination of years of research, millions of dollars, and thousands of hours of labor. He had designed her with the help of the world's top computer experts, software developers, engineers, and technicians. Experts from all schools of science, math, art, and design had contributed to his concept. There was nothing like her on earth. She was more than a machine to him. Using cutting edge Artificial Intelligence software, Samu was capable of original thought. She had developed a personality of her own. He was not ashamed to admit it out loud . . . he thought of Samu as a true friend.

Blyss had decided to be straight with Thurrow. Initially she thought she might just drug him and send him on his way, but immediately saw the folly of that choice. He was smart and he was honest, and Thurrow and Epyphany both deserved as much truth as she dared to share. She explained to him that she had developed the special ability to create what she called a "mind cloud." When he boarded his ship, his confusion would disappear. He would head to the galley, enjoy a healthy meal, then go straight to bed where he would sleep for 24 hours. Blyss had hacked Samu's mainframe and programmed her to get back on course and to erase all information related to the journey to Oojai. When Thurrow woke up, he would have no memory of the last 30 days. This lost time would remain a mystery to him until time or fate allowed him to reconstruct it. He would continue on his quest to save the planet from human desecration.

Thurrow knew what Blyss was doing. She was letting him make the choice while giving him no choice. He wanted to talk to Epyphany, but recognized the painful futility. As he approached his floating home, he wondered if he was just a coward?

Epyphany

Epyphany had experienced loss. She had witnessed death. She had known grave disappointment and pain. Blyss had always been there, with the right words, silent empathy, hugs and reassurance, and unconditional love. Now her heart was broken. She was feeling emptiness and loss greater than ever before, and she couldn't turn to Blyss. Though she was trying to understand, her pain was twofold. She had lost Thurrow and there was now a wall between her and the most important person in her life.

When Blyss had come to her with the news of Thurrow's departure, she almost passed out. She felt her heart slamming against her ribs, an electric shock of pain passed through her, and her head felt like it would explode. That was followed instantly by complete numbness, body and mind. If at that moment Dali hadn't arrived she would have simply sunk to the bottom of the lagoon and drowned. It took all her remaining strength to hold onto Dali, wide-eyed, tearless, and blind, as he towed her back to the Cavern Temple.

RETURN

When Thurrow woke up he felt exceptionally good. He was looking forward to another day in his lab. The present voyage had been surprisingly productive so far, both in research results and personal satisfaction.

For some reason an image of Sadjah popped into his head. He realized he hadn't thought of her for weeks. He actually missed her. She could be abrasive and demanding at times, but he had to admit she got things done. He liked that in a woman. As the head of a multibillion dollar international corporation, she didn't have time for slackers or small talk. These months away from her had weakened his resolve to break away from her. They definitely had disparate views of the problems facing the world. She justified her accumulation of massive wealth with the fact that her companies were improving the quality of life for millions of people, creating jobs, and financing research. She was proud of the company slogan, "Pisces Corp. We Feed the World." He knew that Pisces Corp. did more than feed the world, but right now his attention was on the woman, not the conglomerate.

Though his mind was alert and already considering his list of projects, Thurrow felt a little confused. Suddenly it dawned on him that he had no idea what day it was.

He addressed the ship.

"Samu"

"Yes, Thurrow"

"What day is this?"

Thurrow was completely dumbstruck by Samu's response.

"Samu, what have I been doing for the last few weeks?"

"I presume the usual—sleeping ,eating, and working."

"Do you have records?"

"There is no new data; you haven't logged in for over 30 days. Now that you ask, I understand your concern. I really hadn't given it much thought since I've been quite busy processing your long list of requests. You have been known to go analog from time to time. Remember that little computer hiatus you took, relying only on paper and pencil and hand tools? Or perhaps I have had a malfunction."

"What about the GPS archives?"

"We have been on on a steady course home since you reset the co-ordinates."

Thurrow had no memory of resetting their course. He should have felt more concern, but for some reason his good mood prevailed. In fact, he was pleased to think that they were on their way home. He had gathered plenty of new information and he looked forward to a little human contact. If he could become so immersed as to lose track of a month, he guessed he needed a little taste of humanity. At that, he dove into his day and the days that followed with a renewed energy as Samu speedily carried him back to civilization. Thurrow didn't give the lost time another thought.

Two Weeks Later

The harbor lights shone in the distance as Thurrow reduced the speed of the Samudra Hantu. He was excited. He hadn't seen or talked to Sadjah for months. They had left on reasonable terms although it had been an ambiguous bon-voyage. He knew he had been a little harsh judging her, and now he felt the need to try to see things from her perspective. She had so much to offer and his urge to be with her was undeniable. There was much to miss about her.

In spite of all the attributes that made Sadjah one of the most desirable women on the planet, he suddenly felt something calling him back to sea. But at this moment it made no sense! He hadn't even docked yet. Thurrow guessed he was just anticipating the inevitable adjustment every sailor must make when they face life back on dry land. His foggy memory just couldn't shake that longing feeling, it was as if a mysterious spirit had touched his heart.

"I need to shape up," he thought. "Pay attention old boy or you'll slam this ship into the pier."

One Year Earlier

Thurrow met Sadjah at one of those dreadful fundraisers where he had to kiss up to the very people who were the problem. Like most of these extravagant events, it was designed to attract and impress. In this case, it took place on the penthouse roof of the celebrated Pisces Corp. headquarters overlooking the Seattle seaport. He was there to help them ease their collective guilt. He would take their money and do the best he could to solve the problems their greed and myopic world view had created. While working the room full of jabbering tuxedos, he experienced the "Hollywood" moment . . .

After excusing himself from an intolerable and fruitless conversation, he turned to head for the bar, then stopped, immobilized as if he had run into an invisible forcefield. He stood there gazing at the most strikingly beautiful woman he had ever seen. She was standing alone at the bar, in profile, looking up at an invisible presence as if privy to a quiet conversation with some ethereal deity. As he followed her gaze, it became evident that she was anticipating something.

In the next instant the sky was filled with swaying columns of colored search lights criss crossing the heavens. The DJ slowly raised the volume and the entire crowd simultaneously looked up. The air filled with an hypnotic pulse of bass and percussion. The slightly inebriated partiers were swaying and staring into the sky when several skydivers sliced through the towers of light. The crowd scattered and made room as the paragliders landed gracefully on the roof. They gathered their chutes, formed a large circle, and quickly inflated a brightly decorated rescue cushion. A helicopter then descended through the lights and hovered over the crowd while lowering a long silk ribbon. A beautiful aerial contortionist slid smoothly down the silk. She performed for several minutes to a mesmerized audience. For her finale, she leaned back into a inverted bow and simply released her legs from the silk, curving her body into a perfect dive. She landed in the center of the cushion as the stunned crowd gasped, then exploded into cheers. Still moving to the music, the ribbon dancer made her way through the awestruck crowd and joined Sadjah on a small stage near the bar. The dancer then pulled a check from the folds of her costume and ceremoniously handed it to Sadjah.

With a voice as rich as dark chocolate and as smooth as honey coated silver, Sadjah simply said, "Ladies and Gentlemen, concerned citizens, on behalf of the stockholders of The Pisces Corporation, I would like to present this check for one hundred million dollars to GORU, the Global Oceanic Recovery Utility." Once again, the audience erupted with joyous approval.

As generous as that number sounded, Thurrow knew that photos of the spectacular donation ceremony would grace the cover of every newspaper and magazine across the globe. He would also expect to see a professionally edited YouTube video going viral. Pisces Corp. would recoup a good share of their donation in free advertising alone. He wasn't unappreciative of the sizable donation, but instantly recognized Sadjah as a shrewd and imaginative leader.

Everyone gathered around her, the press loved her, men and women alike practically bowed in her presence. Through it all, she was calm and funny, relaxed and casual. She was skilled at dismissing the rude drunks as well as the arrogant millionaires. To her credit, when anyone had something worthwhile to contribute she was focussed and attentive. She was a woman who knew the value and power of information.

As one of the driving forces of GORU, Thurrow knew that he

would eventually meet Sadjah. He was looking forward to it. He just wasn't the type to wait in line.

Thurrow made his way to the perimeter of the rooftop gardens to enjoy the incredible view of Seattle's diverse skyline. When he wasn't flying or sailing around the world, Thurrow always seemed to end up back in Seattle. Puget Sound offered him the best of both worlds. When he was moored at Seattle's seaport, the excitement of the city was at his doorstep — or with the flip of a switch, he could take Samu on a quiet cruise though the beautiful inlets and waterways of the Sound.

PHASE TWO

The crowd around Sadjah finally thinned; she made her excuses and found a spot back at the bar. Scanning the roof top, she was disappointed to find that Thurrow was nowhere in sight. Sadjah seldom made a move without a plan and this occasion was no exception. "Phase One" was a resounding success now it was time for "Phase Two."

This night had been marked on her calendar for quite some time. Under the heading GORU/Spectacle was the subheading THURROW/Yes! It was no coincidence that she was solo this evening. More than a few people had commented on the fact but she had simply brushed them off with a sly smile. Everyone knew she could have any one of the world's top ten richest and most powerful men at her side with a wink.

She and Thurrow had crossed paths several times in the past year but had never been formally introduced — in fact she was somewhat surprised he had never made a move. Sadjah had to admit that his quiet, somewhat aloof demeanor made him even more desirable. During those months, she had been involved with several men. She had used them to further her education or connections, or as means to economic gain, and enjoyed their rapt attention only to ditch them when she got bored. Sadjah was well aware that her beauty opened a lot of gold-plated doors, but what most men didn't count on was the incredible intellect that lay behind every calculated response. The seductive moves she could make on the dance floor and in the bedroom were mere smoke and mirrors compared to the intricate tactics she employed maneuvering within the secret confines of the corporate world.

Even as she had burned through her "A list" of lovers, she had kept Thurrow on her radar. Sadjah had read most of the articles printed about him or written by him. He had made the news quite often, and recently there had been several in-depth specials about his life and his work. His education, experience, and skill set would have been daunting to most women, but only enhanced Sadjah's curiosity. He had a reputation for unwavering honesty and an unflagging dedication to preserving the environment in general and the oceans specifically. She looked forward to seeing the cabin of his legendary "Samudra Hantu." Just saying the name made her smile in anticipation.

Thurrow's immediate absence suited her fine, affording her a little more time to fine tune "Phase Two." With her virtually unlimited resources, Sadjah could find detailed information on just about anyone. Unfortunately, she had given her ubiquitous assistant the night off. Right now she simply wanted to know Thurrow's cocktail of choice. So she whispered his name into the latest iThing. She had to laugh, knowing Thurrow had helped design the device she was using to carry out her plan.

Sadjah motioned the enthusiastic young bartender who was instantly at her service. She leaned in close and they spoke softly for a moment. She moved away from the bar as the young man spoke to another bartender then scurried off. She had a little time to kill so she walked slowly around the party working the prosperous crowd, all the while looking for evidence of Thurrow's whereabouts. Just when Sadjah was beginning to think he may have have grown tired of the affair, she caught a glimpse of him standing alone at the far side of the terrace.

Right on cue, her new favorite young bartender came trotting up behind her. Almost out of breath and grinning widely, he handed her a small silver tray holding two small ice filled glasses and a beautifully etched crystal decanter filled with rich gold liquid. Sadjah reached into her purse and handed him a delicately embossed card, then said, "Your timing is perfect."

Lost in thought, Thurrow didn't hear Sadjah approach. He was pleasantly surprised when he felt a light touch on his shoulder. Not quite speechless, he enjoyed an extra beat or two of silence while he took her in.

Thurrow had met a lot of attractive women in his travels, but Sadjah's beauty spoke to him in a unique voice. Standing close to her that first time was like seeing a rainbow as it might appear on another planet; with a different atmosphere refracting light into strange and wonderful shapes, a refreshing new spectrum of color. She was tall, and with her high heels she barely tilted her head to look him in the eye. She moved as if defying space and time. Her long legs carried her swiftly to her destination though she appeared to saunter. Her unhurried conversation belied the undercurrent of urgency to make her point.

Framed by random length shocks of jet black hair, her face seemed to glow. The gray-green eyes sparkled under the shadow of the longest eyelashes Thurrow had ever seen. She was a masterpiece of contrasts. She was slim and curvaceous, slender but strong, controlled yet spontaneous, soft within her armor of implied indifference.

Sadjah introduced herself and added, "It's odd we haven't met before; we seem to travel in some of the same circles. I was hoping you might be interested in sharing a cocktail."

He nodded and smiled. "I'd be honored."

Thurrow held the two small glasses in one hand as Sadjah removed the stopper and handed him the decanter. He recognized the aroma immediately and said, "Cruzan Single Barrel Rum, my favorite. Did you break into my ship and raid my liquor cabinet?"

"It just took a little high-tech research and a highly motivated bartender."

Thurrow laughed and said, "That was quite an entertaining spectacle you arranged. Oh yes, and thanks for your generous donation."

"I am the queen of spectacle and you are very welcome. I'm a big personal fan. I think you are doing some amazing work." She raised her glass. "The world could use more people with your skills and dedication."

He returned her toast, and as the glasses clinked, their fingers touched briefly . . .

Reunion

With the ship successfully docked and secured, he made his way to the gangplank. Taken completely by surprise, Thurrow stopped mid-step.

Sadjah!

"Hey Baby, didja miss me?"

Thurrow sighed audibly and thought, "God she is gorgeous!"

In the months he had been gone, it seemed she had grown even more radiant. They both picked up their pace as they moved toward each other.

Sadjah panted . . . "You can't even know how much I've missed you."

Thurrow dropped his gear and lifted her in his arms. "Wow, you feel sooooo . . . "

She cut off his words with a long deep kiss. All of Thurrow's second thoughts evaporated. Sadjah took his hand and they headed back to the Thurrow's cabin.

MEANWHILE

The first weeks after Thurrow's abrupt departure were filled with a sadness that permeated the whole tribe. Epyphany spent much of her time curled up on her Chancel or shunning the daylight floating listlessly in the Temple Cavern. Occasionally she would swim off to some secluded inlet and just stare out at the horizon.

One question maintained a continuous debilitating loop in her mind — Why?

One question blotted out the sun and laughter and music — Why?

One question took away her appetite, blinded her to the beauty of Oojai . . .

It haunted every waking moment and kept her from her dreams. What had Blyss told Thurrow? Why had he listened to her? How could he profess his love so sincerely then turn and leave without a word? Epyphany had a powerful intellect and a quick rational thought process. Historically, she could look at the facts and come up with solutions instinctively. This unimaginable situation had left her stunned. She felt hollowed out. Thurrow had unleashed the boundless love within her. He had expanded her universe and opened her heart and mind to limitless possibilities. When he left, a cold blinding fog descended and all the beauty and love in her world dissolved into the icy mist.

Blyss was worried. There was a dark cloud over Oojai. Though she had no doubts about her decision, she had underestimated its effect on Epyphany as well as the Tribe. Dali, Reefer, and all the others had accepted Thurrow and had been enriched by his presence, but Blyss hadn't grasped the intensity of their growing dedication to him. Looking at it now, it was easy to see that Epyphany's love for Thurrow only increased the Tribe's respect and admiration for him.

Since that sad night when she sent Thurrow away, Blyss had

been unable to make her case to Epyphany. There was no clear answer to give. The future was a riddle, even for Blyss. Epyphany went out of her way to avoid Blyss. The pattern of their existence had been shattered. She had to admit that her role in Epyphany's life had changed. Blyss decided that the only way to resuscitate Oojai and its inhabitants would be to create some kind of distraction. She was pleasantly surprised when the distraction came from within the Tribe.

Dali had always been tuned into Epyphany's wavelength at a deeper level than the rest of the tribe. Epyphany was biologically part of the dolphin family, and Dali could literally feel much of what she felt. There were human aspects to those vibrations that were beyond his comprehension, but lacking that filter sometimes gave him insight that was uncluttered by the inconsistencies of human emotion. Where Epyphany's human DNA and lack of experience just led to confusion, Dali's survival instinct led him to action. Feeling her pain, he instinctively knew she needed activity — something to demand her attention and override the negative mantra ruling her mind and heart.

Dali kept a discreet distance from Epyphany while monitoring her moods and waiting for the appropriate time to approach. One day as she was taking one of her solitary swims in the Lagoon, he swam up next to her and said, "You must follow me." Startled by an uncharacteristic command from Dali and too mentally exhausted to argue, she acquiesced.

Smiling to himself, Dali pulled slightly ahead of her and slowly increased his speed as they made their way though the barrier reef and out to the open sea. By the time they entered the deep water and before Epyphany realized it, she was practically chasing Dali. As they approached full speed Dali hurled himself into the air then dove straight down as fast as he could. Under normal conditions, he knew he would be no match for Epyphany, but he was sure her recent malaise had weakened her physically as well as emotionally. At this stage of the race, Epyphany was beginning to think

Dali had either lost his mind or had something really important to show her. Her curiosity kept her on his trail and she dove.

Dali had come to Oojai over ten years ago. He had the unique ability to communicate to lower life forms. Like the rest of the Tribe, he was also hyper-intelligent and physically evolved. He had become bored with the dolphins in his pod and they were finding his intellect and "artsy" temperament tedious. They wanted to eat and play, he wanted to create. They found his actions suspect as they watched him use his power to manipulate the crawling creatures into designs on the white sand of the ocean floor. It was a fascinating combination of colors and shapes slowly morphing into abstract patterns and unlikely juxtapositions. It wasn't as if he could "talk" to them, he simply had the ability to influence their reflex and response systems. At times he could actually stop the movement of an entire group of diverse species simultaneously, momentarily achieving a living mural. His peers just didn't get it. When he finally made his home on Oojai, Dali found himself in a paradise of advanced thinking. Some of the Tribe still didn't get his "art" but at least they were open to the concept. Some of them would even volunteer to assist occasionally. He was inspired by Epyphany and she encouraged his artistic explorations. Dali evolved a method of designing three dimensional work using natural underwater settings and repositioning sunken objects.

When Epyphany caught up with Dali she found him poised in front of a steep rock wall rising from a long, ragged ocean shelf that dropped off sharply into a pitch black abyss. There was just enough light penetrating this depth to cause an eerie spotlight effect. Epyphany was awestruck. She swam closer in order to see how he had accomplished such unique artistry.

Before them, rising sixty feet or more, was a stylized relief of Chrysylyss. In this light it appeared to be carved in the rock wall, but on closer inspection, she could see it was a combination of natural formations, plants, sea life, found objects, light, and shadows. ⸳

Dali said, "It only works at specific times of the day, subject to weather conditions and the cycle of the seasons."

"It's beautiful, it's a masterpiece." Gazing at this incredible monument to her mother and feeling Dali's love and dedication, she became overcome with emotion. Epyphany's could hear her own heart beat loudly in her head. She could feel the rush of blood surging through her body, filling her brain with oxygen. She realized for the first time in weeks she had just spent more than an hour without thinking of Thurrow, free from the unrelenting weight of sorrow and grief.

Before she could thank him, Dali zoomed in close to her and asked, "Think you can catch me?" At that he spiraled straight up toward the light. Her instinct kicked in and she took off after him. Epyphany spent the rest of that afternoon with Dali racing around the barrier reef. She had forgotten how much fun it was just to swim fast and fly through the breakers with no agenda. She and Dali had spent a lot of time like this throughout her youth. She felt like she was reuniting with long lost friends—Dali and Oojai.

Scattered around the island and going about their individual routines, Blyss and the rest of the Tribe simultaneously stopped whatever they were doing. They could sense the change. It was as if an invisible tear soaked cloak had dissolved or melted away, leaving each heart lighter. The dull gray pall gave way to a clear crisp perspective. There was a buzz of hope and purpose vibrating throughout the island.

With the setting sun, Blyss made her way to her favorite perch on Tigress Baku high above the lagoon. Looking down on the rolling green hills and the sparkling bay with the waves breaking gently on the reefs, she took out the Swhorl and played the haunting melodies of the ancient songs of Oojai. Her hope was renewed.

PISCES CORP

Thurrow and Sadjah didn't leave his ship for three days. Much to Thurrow's surprise, Sadjah had cancelled meetings with some of the most influential people on the planet. He had never seen her so relaxed. There was so much to tell her, but while sharing stories of his days at sea, Thurrow found his memory a little cloudy. Having gathered most of what he needed to finish his research and with the completion of a few promising designs, he counted this trip a resounding success. Still slightly mystified as to the source, Thurrow was pleased to have gained real insight into the ocean's bio-rhythms. He retained a very hazy sense of connectivity, something like an epiphany — a strange awareness that he couldn't readily articulate. Babbling enthusiastically to Sadjah, he came off like a drunken sailor who claims he has danced with the Sirens or dined with Poseidon.

Sadjah just nodded and smiled as Thurrow spoke, she liked the sound of his voice. She had no idea what he was rambling about but she knew he was happy, and more than that, he seemed truly happy to be with her. She was hoping they could avoid some of the topics that had split them apart. Thurrow amused her on multiple levels, she could picture them together . . . Thurrow fit nicely into her plan. With his connection to the technical and scientific community and her web of corporate and political ties they could rule the world. She smiled at the thought, a pleasant tingle awakened her sleeping tiger and Thurrow found himself pleasantly silenced once again.

During Thurrow's absence, Sadjah had put her career into overdrive. She finally lined up the necessary players and put together a deal that placed her in total control of the Pisces Corp. She had not been voted in but her power now eclipsed the current CEO. She had become the company's youngest majority shareholder. With that kind of power Sadjah didn't need to be chairman of the board.

The Pisces fleet of fishing vessels was expanding as the company swooped down and swept up most of the smaller companies. Pisces' tentacles were reaching into every facet of food production, as well as cruise lines and the shipping industry, including the support technologies. Sadjah's plan to control the entire seafood supply chain was on track. The new ad campaign was getting results and whatever press they couldn't win they simply bought. They already owned over 40% of the major media markets. With Thurrow on board, it would buy them the credibility they needed to grab the hearts and minds of the masses. It would be "clear sailin' matey" as her father liked to say using his very lame pirate impression.

The bonus in this whole plan was that Sadjah actually cared for Thurrow. She couldn't quite admit it to herself but she had started to fall in love with him before their latest separation. She seldom mixed love and business, but this relationship had potential beyond any she had ever imagined. She would do her best to not alienate him this time.

On the fourth morning after Thurrow's arrival, he and Sadjah woke up early, both ready to get back to business. Thurrow enjoyed being with a woman as engaged in her work as he was. Although he knew they were motivated by different goals, these last three days gave him hope of a mutually beneficial compromise. She seemed to have softened since they had last spoke. Sadjah was in such a unique position to do good. If he could sway her toward a more visionary business model perhaps she could start to define profits in terms broader than just dollar signs. She wasn't blind to the damage her company was doing to the oceans and he knew she couldn't deny it. For three days they had avoided the topic, but when they caught their breath, when the music stopped, when the sweat dried and the smoke cleared there was a big elephant in the room. Its name was The Pisces Corp.

DISTRACTION

Several weeks had passed since Thurrow had left Oojai. After Dali's intervention and some intense discussions with Blyss, Epyphany was finding it progressively easier to leave thoughts of Thurrow behind. When she did think about him, it was with a sweet sadness. She had come to appreciate the experience as a valuable lesson. She was thankful for what they had shared and she accepted the harsh truth of their opposing realities. As a result of her loss, Epyphany had come to appreciate her friends and her life on Oojai even more. The days passed, pleasant, calm, and uneventful. Epyphany was not unhappy, but she needed a change or a challenge. If she could not have love, at the very least Epyphany would have to find purpose.

The day started like any other day. It was cool and quiet. A gentle luminosity washed the Cavern Temple walls with a soothing soft glow. The Tribe was relaxing and floating aimlessly in the rejuvenating pools surrounding the Gold Tower, soothed by the songs of Blyss and comforted by the shimmering reflection of the Chrysylyss. Eventually, they grew restless and collectively agreed to make their way through the tunnel to the Lagoon.

Revitalized by the warm sun, they started swimming the perimeter. As they slowly picked up the pace, a leisurely swim turned into a spontaneous competition. Blyss watched from the shore, Reefer circled overhead, and Yew and Cheeks enjoyed the race while relaxing out in the middle of the lagoon. The rest of the the tribe were exceptionally fast. Just to keep it it interesting, the quickest among them hung back for the first lap, giving everyone the joy of competition. Though Epyphany wasn't designed as aerodynamically as the others, she compensated with pure power. Magnum was faster than any other alligator in existence, but he was built for sprinting, not for distance. He was the first to quit the race. On the third lap they started to pick up the pace. Surprisingly, tiny Zip hung in for another lap, skipping over the top of the the wake left by Speed's streamlined carapace as he sliced through the surf. If Thurrow had been there, he would have laughed at the sight of this tiny flying fish racing a giant leatherback sea turtle. The Tribe was seldom surprised by the outcome of these races, but that knowledge never dampened the fun. Dali consistently hung on to third place, while Epyphany and Irie ended up in the final lap, both moving so fast it looked like two streaks of color and spray circling the lagoon. As usual the event ended with Irie proudly displaying her beautiful sail fin as she made a slow victory lap.

The impromptu race was a nice temporary distraction, but with Thurrow gone, the Oojai vibe was slightly subdued. They decided they all could use a little change of scenery. The adventure started with a plan to visit a nearby island.

The idea was to journey to one of the neighboring islands and do some recreational exploring. Blyss, Yew, and Cheeks were glad to stay behind as guardians and caretakers of Oojai. With the help of Blyss and the Gold Tower, Epyphany and the Tribe plotted a route that would keep them out of the shipping lanes and off the sonar of any known military operations. They knew there was always a chance of an unexpected sighting from private vessels or drug runners, but with Epyphany's unique hypersensitivity to sound and motion, they were confident of avoiding discovery. It had been over a year since any of the Tribe had ventured far from Oojai, and the anticipation was palpable. Thurrow and the mixed emotions left in the wake of his departure were far from everyone's thoughts. They were all looking forward to experiencing the vast open sea and the mystery of adventure.

The day was calm and clear. Storm was waiting outside the lagoon with Reefer perched comfortably on his back. The Tribe made their way enthusiastically past the reef. Epyphany had to remind everyone to slow down and conserve their strength; their destination was three or four days away under good conditions, and the ocean weather was as unpredictable as human behavior. Along the way, they were sure to find some tiny, uncharted islands where they could rest, and if not, Epyphany knew she could always hitch a ride with Storm.

Two days into the trip the weather had remained pleasant and they were able to cover several hundred miles. The journey was serving them well both mentally and physically, an antidote to the island life which had made them all a little soft. Ocean travel demanded an awareness crucial to survival. The Tribe's bond was strengthened and they fell into efficient patterns of communication and teamwork. Occasionally they would run into varied schools of fish, some of which would serve as reminders of their heritage, and others which would serve as lunch. As a group they had no worthy opponents—the larger carnivores could sense the power of the pack and so steered clear.

Around midmorning on the third day, Epyphany signaled an unscheduled stop. She had started her day with an uneasy feeling of unknown origin. She didn't mention it early on because it was such a subtle shift in her consciousness, a slight change of mood. But as the morning wore on, it turned into a nagging sensation of discomfort, then into an actual vibration. She still couldn't determine the origin, but it was undoubtedly a faint distress signal. It turned out that she wasn't the only one affected. A few of the others were experiencing a similar, albeit more subtle, version of the vibe. It crossed her mind that Blyss might be trying to get a message to her. Then as she was pondering the source, the entire tribe felt a pulse. It was as if a bomb had exploded underwater somewhere in the distance. It wasn't enough to be disorienting, but it was followed by a secondary thought wave that was definitively distress. Epyphany, Dali, and Storm were most affected by the second wave. They now understood the source. A single dolphin could never generate a signal that powerful. Somewhere out there, a large pod of dolphins was in real trouble.

AN APPOINTMENT

It had been a couple months since Thurrow's return, and he and Sadjah had been taking full advantage of their limited time together. He had visited several major cities around the world making a case for the Global Oceanic Recovery Utility (GORU). Convincing the world leaders that the health of the ocean and its inhabitants was in serious decline, proved to be a difficult job. Though the entire scientific community agreed that the planet was facing an impending environmental disaster, it was just one more unpleasant issue for which corporate and political leaders had little motivation to solve. Thurrow was aware of several tragic events and a large amount of unassailable negative data, none of which was making the news. When he mentioned this fact to Sadjah she just nodded and changed the subject. He had begun to notice that whenever he referred to the environment she would steer the conversation in another direction. He wanted to share his deep concern with her, to try to engage and enlighten her, and possibly convince her to join him in his crusade to save the oceans. He couldn't understand how such an intelligent person could ignore the facts. Since his return, he had been hopeful that their rekindled affection would bridge the gap in their divergent political and cultural viewpoints, but he just couldn't find a way to break though to her. Thurrow decided to schedule a meeting.

Sadjah was enjoying another challenging day working in the stark luxury of her penthouse office. Although it had been over a year since she had acquired the most sought after real-estate in the Pisces Tower, she was still in awe of the amazing view of downtown Seattle and Puget Sound. Her brief reverie was interrupted when her assistant buzzed. "Your next appointment is here." She looked at the calendar and saw GORU. "Oh no, I'm not in the mood for this. I gave them one hundred million dollars. What else do they want?" When the door opened, she was taken completely by surprise. In walked Thurrow, smiling, wearing an uncharacteristic suit and tie, and carrying his ubiquitous shiny aluminum attaché case. He seldom left home with out his laptop.

"This is a pleasant surprise." Her voice betrayed a slight irritation. Sadjah didn't like surprises when it came to business, plus she sensed Thurrow was a man on a mission.

"I'm here on official business, I hope you'll forgive the ambush. I have some things I'd like to discuss that have nothing to do with our relationship and everything to do with Pisces Corp. I know you have people to handle such things, but I feel there are corporate issues that would be better addressed from the top down. I know you can't deny that you are the one who makes the final decisions."

"Well, this all sounds very formal. Since you've scheduled the time, you have my full and undivided attention." She tried to keep some warmth in her voice, but she was already on the defensive.

"Thank you. I know you are a busy woman so I'll get right to my point. Where can I plug this in?"

Thurrow opened his laptop and Sadjah synced it to her office projection system. "I have put together a short presentation to bring you up to speed on some unsettling events that have been occurring throughout our ocean's global ecosystems. For obvious reasons, the powers-that-be haven't found it in their best interest to report these events."

For ten minutes they sat there quietly watching. Occasionally Thurrow would sneak a sideways glance at Sadjah, searching for some reaction.

Sadjah did her best to remain unmoved by the diverse footage. She was not unaffected by what she saw, but as a hardened professional business leader, she knew she must appear neutral. When the video presentation ended, Thurrow immediately moved to phase two of his mission.

"I'm not here expecting you to change your entire business model on the merits of a ten-minute-video. With the help of some of the best brains in atmospheric sciences, geologists at the forefront of natural hazards, economists, and my own personal investment gurus, I have put together a brief prospectus outlining possible scenarios for both prevention and adaptation. It seems we have passed the tipping point relative to the rise in ocean temperature. That fact rules out complete prevention, but we still have time to implement several helpful programs. I have outlined a series of steps designed to lessen the impact of the inevitable results of our current misuse of the earth's resources.

"These programs and innovations are the results of extensive research and a methodical study of current data. They are based on a consensus from the global scientific community. This is not about politics, it is about survival. I'm hoping that you will find the time to personally read this."

Thurrow went on, "I can tell you from personal experience, there is money to made from doing the right thing. It's not the kind of money that accumulates in quarterly cycles, but like all worthwhile investing, it is the long view that serves the corporation, consumer, and the community equally. In the very near future, we will be facing a global disaster of catastrophic proportions. On behalf of GORU and the planet, I'm seeking your help to turn the tide of public, political, and corporate opinion."

Somewhat defensive now, Sadjah asked, "Are you implying that it is up to Pisces Corp. specifically?"

"It is up to all of us — individuals, communities, countries, and corporations. I believe that as one of the world's largest companies, Pisces Corp. could lead the way and be the catalyst for a complete turnaround in the global attitude toward climate change."

"It was very clear that some of the vessels in your video wore the Pisces logo. Do you intend to use this in your propaganda campaign? Is this some subtle form of blackmail?"

With Sadjah's tone and use of the words "propaganda" and

"blackmail," Thurrow felt like she had slapped him in the face. He stopped for a moment and looked her directly in the eyes.

"Sadjah, I'd like to believe that by now you know me well enough to know I am truthful at all costs. I am not making this up — nothing in this video is staged or taken out of context. I'm not pointing at any single entity. It's not just Pisces, it's a global mindset of greed and short term gain, oblivious to future consequences. This video is just a small sampling of the misuse of our planet's rich resources.

Sadjah stepped around her desk, and in an attempt to relieve the tension, took his hand in hers. "I know you are a truthful man and I love you for it. I respect your passion and I admire your genius, but I think you might be overestimating my influence on a company as large as Pisces. I will do what I can. If you leave the video and prospectus, I'll put it in the hands of all the right people.

Thurrow shook her hand and thanked her for her time. When he closed the door behind him, Sadjah turned and stared out at the incredible panorama. Low clouds dropped a gentle rain on the foggy scene below.

DOLPHIN RESCUE

Without hesitation, the tribe fell in behind Epyphany as she led them toward the source of the signal. A moment later, two more explosions occurred, and this time the whole group felt the sonic pressure. They were immediately aware of a continuous stream of distress signals — the audible variety of clicks, whistle-like sounds, and other agitated vocalizations seemed to increase as they got closer to the source.

Flying slightly farther ahead, Reefer reported the first sighting. "There are three big ships. I've never seen anything like these. They form a triangle . . . must be a couple of miles apart . . . slowly closing in."

Swimming at top speed with Irie by her side and Storm close behind, Epyphany instructed Dali to hang back, then she sent a "thought bundle" up to Reefer and the Tribe as they did their best to keep up. "We need to focus this bundle back to Blyss. When I hit the transmission note, concentrate and project with me. I hope Blyss will know what to do." At that, Epyphany started singing a strange musical scale, an alien sound that started so low the Tribe could feel it in their bones. The note quickly ascended to a pitch no human could hear. When she reached her highest note she held it until she was sure they were in sync, then they all let go of the thought. Each member of the tribe felt the strange and powerful shock, a split second of a singular electric connection between themselves, Blyss and the Gold Tower.

Under normal conditions, they would be perfectly still throughout this process and allow for a minimal recovery time. Epyphany knew she was taking a chance trying a group projection with everyone swimming at full speed, but she felt there was little time to spare. Something horrific was about to happen and she needed to stop it at all costs. Checking back with everyone, she asked,

"Still with me? Still moving?" It took a minute or two, but soon they were all accounted for and all in motion.

As they closed in on the scene Reefer spoke again. "Epyphany, this is hard to describe . . . it looks like the explosions killed . . . there have been some losses. On the perimeter, the water is discolored and there are some floating carcasses. Within the triangle it appears as though dozens of pods are converging. The water is churning with confused dolphins. The ships are turning ninety degrees and starting to move slowly in a circle. They're dropping nets! There must be one thousand or more dolphins out there! What can we do?"

Epyphany pushed herself even harder, within minutes she could see the ships. They were huge. When she and Blyss had plotted the course for their trip, there was no record of activity for this area. She had kept herself informed of human behavior, most notably the ocean related news, and she knew that this was illegal. How could such large scale slaughter be taking place? She hoped Blyss got her message.

Epyphany instructed Irie and Zip to monitor the perimeter and keep her informed. She told Dali, Magnum, and Speed to place themselves about half way between two ships, to stay together and to stay clear of the nets until they got her signal. With Reefer reporting from above, she and Storm headed towards the closest ship.

By the time she and Storm were close enough to the ship to suit her purpose, she could see the vessels had nearly completed connecting their nets. Without hesitation, she gave Storm the most dangerous mission. She asked him to dive and approach the rear side of the ship as close to the propeller as he dared. On her signal he would swing his tail around as hard and fast as possible, close enough to the hull to cause serious turbulence. At that moment, she would attempt a trick she had never successfully completed. She would use the mind cloud technique Blyss had been trying to teach her. Epyphany would try to confuse and instruct the captain in hopes that he would over compensate and lose control of his ship. She waited for news from Reefer . . .

Epyphany had to believe they weren't too late.

Meanwhile Zip and Irie reported that the dolphins were ninety percent enclosed and close to panic. If something didn't happen soon, many of them wouldn't have room to surface for air. They would drown.

Thankfully at that moment, she heard Reefer's voice practically screaming in her head. "Blyss came through, the ships are turning, they seem to be heading away from the dolphins." At that she gave the signal to Storm then focussed all her energy on the Captain. He didn't know what hit him. The ship had started turning on it's own, then began to rock violently. Bewildered, he watched his hand grab the throttle and gun it. His ship almost capsized and several men were thrown into the bloody water. The net separated from the ship and slowly drifted away.

At the same time, Magnum ripped a hole in the net, and with Speed's help, opened up a large exit. Dali was using all his mental strength trying to keep the pod from mass panic while urging the dolphins toward the opening. At all three corners of the killing triangle, the vessels were headed in opposite directions ripping the net apart. The frightened dolphins scattered as they attempted to find the surviving members of their pod.

Epyphany was relieved to see Storm had made a safe get-away. Before she had time to worry, the rest of the tribe were at her side unharmed, exhausted, but elated. Watching the frustrated captain gain control of the distant ship, she noticed the large, bright red logo painted on the bow — an image and words she would come to fear and hate — "Pisces Corp, We Feed the World."

TWO MASTERS

Thurrow left the meeting with a strange feeling of apprehension. He had noticed that although she tried to hide it, Sadjah was moved by some of the images in the video. At one point, she stifled a small gasp and she managed to blink away the tiny hint of a tear. One would have to be emotionally impaired to remain unaffected by some of the scenes. He hadn't edited the video for gratuitous shock value, he simply wanted to show the harsh realities and the rampant cruelty that was being systematically inflicted on several species. There was a callous disregard for the fragile eco system that needed to be brought to light. It wasn't just about preserving the beauty of the ocean's flora and fauna – – these systems were the foundation of the entire food chain, without which we would find ourselves unable to sustain the growing population of the planet. He knew he was taking the chance of being perceived as an alarmist or fanatic, but it was too late to take the middle ground.

Sadjah had been polite and had made a token effort of warmth and understanding, but Thurrow didn't think he had furthered his cause by much. He knew she had worked hard to gain credibility and power in the company, and one meeting wasn't going to change the world overnight, but he was hoping to gain at least a little empathy. By the end of the presentation, he had perceived a slight chill in the room, and he was afraid his effort might have only served to gain a stronger adversary.

Sadjah

As Sadjah gazed out at the muted gray clouds blanketing the Seattle skyline, images from Thurrow's video were haunting her thoughts. She had a peripheral awareness of the various Pisces Corp. companies and their activities, but she had consciously ignored the actual means by which they contributed to her wealth. She could still hear the sounds —

the laughing men herding and slaughtering, hatchets hacking flesh, screeching dolphins, the sad song of whales tangled in nets, slowly drowning while they struggled against the weight. Images of stranded penguins, starving polar bears, streams turning to rushing rivers as the ice caps melt, underwater footage of pristine coral reefs being shredded by drag nets, cruise ships openly dumping their garbage at sea, islands of discarded plastic choking seabirds and poisoning the oceans, the homeless villagers rowing away in overcrowded boats as they evacuate their flooded island homes . . .

For the first time in many years Sadjah wept openly. Then her sadness slowly turned to anger. "How could he do that to me? What does he think I can do about it? It's very sad, but it's not my fault! Sure, Pisces may be a little shortsighted, but the world needs food . . . and we're supplying that food. People have to eat — does he want us to stop production, let millions starve? Then she softened. He does have a point, and his heart is in the right place, but it's all so complex . . . Where do we start?"

Sadjah had never been more conflicted. She wondered how she was going to serve her two masters. She was ruled by a seemingly unquenchable thirst for power. Her father had instilled in her his warped value system. He had built his empire from the ground up. She had grown up hearing whispered stories of his ruthlessness, but he had always favored her with encouragement and kindness. The family name and wealth had opened a lot of doors for her, but he always insisted she would have to work to prove her worth. For Sadjah, power and wealth was the yardstick of her worth, and with success came her father's approval, the closest substitute for his love. Without the trappings of wealth and power she feared she was just vapor. A hollow ghost of a woman. She had studied and worked hard ever since her childhood trying to live up to her father's image of her, and she had come to define herself by it.

Her other master was lust. In her middle teens she had

come to terms with her sensuality and her sexuality. It too served as a surrogate for love, but unlike love, she could control the circumstances. At the very least, it took her out of herself, gave her mind and soul a vacation from the pressure of her tremendous corporate responsibilities. At its best, it transformed her and allowed her to be soft and loving and lovable. Sex was a world unto itself; she felt safe and free, she could share the power, and even let go of the power occasionally. She could give or take pleasure without reservations. She could fly above it all.

Thurrow had become a key component in her plan to further her wealth and power, but he was also the singular person in her life that gave her a true feeling of contentment. Thurrow fulfilled something in her. His touch brought her to a place she had only imagined; it was so pure. Since his return, it was as if he was incapable of lies. His sincerity translated to a tactile experience bordering on spiritual communion. And he was a truly good man. She felt that their relationship could be the closest she would ever get to real love. Sadjah feared she would have to choose between Pisces and Thurrow.

Sadjah was not a woman who settled for less. She resolved to have them both, whatever the cost.

That night as they ate a quiet dinner together, there was no mention of the meeting. They both did their best to act as if the day's event had nothing to do with their personal relationship. At the same time, neither could deny an underlying sense of distrust. A crack had developed in the smooth veneer of their romance.

A DECLARATION

Upon returning from the battle, the exhausted yet elated Tribe swam directly to the Cavern Temple. Blyss was waiting for them. As they entered the tunnel, she could sense the confused thoughts and the sad images of their short battle. The Tribe gathered at the foot of the Gold Tower and Blyss waited for them to quiet their minds.

Then she spoke. "We have entered a new era. I'm sad to tell you that what you witnessed and thankfully prevented is just one small part of what appears to be an unprecedented escalation in the wholesale slaughter of dolphins and sea mammals of all varieties. The world's human population has grown so fast and so large that they are unable or unwilling to feed themselves without resorting to extreme and thoughtless measures.

In the past few decades, the civilized world has systematically depleted our resources and polluted the environment to the point where it is nearly impossible to sustain the populace. Rather than re-examine their methods and choose a course of conservation and innovation, the leaders have decided to ignore the facts and continue down the road to extinction. They have forgotten that this planet belongs to all creatures. That without balance, every system will eventually topple. You and I and all the innocent creatures of this planet are the victims of human abuse and disregard. There is a good chance that it may be too late, but your brave act proves that we don't have to lay back and watch as our beautiful oceans and our brethren species are ravaged. Not all humans are blind to the madness that prevails, but those who care are a minority. Most have been lulled into a false sense off security and raised to expect a life of comfort and consumption far beyond the realities of sustainability.

"We have lived simply, joyfully, and respectfully, connected to the systems that support and feed us. Greed and ego have no place in our world. Our wealth is the healthy environment that supplies us with the necessities. Earth was designed to supply for the needs of all it inhabitants. Humans have tried to alter that design to fit their selfish desires. In doing so they have ruined it for the rest.

"We must slow them down. We must show them a different path. There is a change coming, and though I'm not sure how it ends, I am sure we are part of the beginning.

"The Tablets tell a story — a prophecy that I have been trying to unravel for many years. In recent years, I've had some success and have seen some predictions manifest. We are part of that prophecy and we have reached the pivotal point. Until recently, it was nearly impossible to send humans a clear message without endangering our lives and our mission. Now I believe the survival of earth and all its creatures, relies in the most part, on the genius, the bravery, and the choices of one man, our link to the modern world. He is a champion of reason and innovation, a seeker of truth and he is our friend . . . Thurrow."

Epyphany flinched at the mention of Thurrow. She hadn't given him a thought throughout the entire journey and the ensuing events. In that moment it all came rushing back. What has become of him? Where is he living? Does he remember anything?

Soon after Epyphany had emerged from her deep depression, she and Blyss had a difficult but enlightening conversation. Blyss had been somewhat successful in convincing Epyphany that Thurrow's departure was in everyone's best interest. She had told Epyphany about the "mind cloud." It would be up to Thurrow. There was no sure way to know if he had the ability to reconcile a subconscious memory of Oojai with the reality of modern life.

A major point that Blyss had left out of her monologue was the crucial role Epyphany would have to play in their battle. She needed Epyphany to act on her well-honed instincts and she didn't want to confuse Epyphany's judgment with any preconceived notions of responsibility. Epyphany and

Thurrow had a strong bond. The question remained, would they have the desire and strength to survive the trials that lay ahead? Epyphany and the Tribe were deeply affected by Blyss' speech. They felt the undeniable truth and the deep sadness underlying her words. How could one man make that much difference? Their odds seemed overwhelming. Where would they start? They couldn't know that Blyss had seen this coming for a long time and that the recent events had allowed her to set the plan in motion. Blyss couldn't see an exact picture of the future, it came to her as a series of riddles or pieces of a puzzle that served as a roadmap to what may lay ahead. Like a map, it had alternate routes and detours. Blyss could only make informed guesses and intuitive decisions as they moved along any given path toward the unknown.

IN THE BEGINNING

The Gold Tower is that which has always been.

Before creatures crawled or swam or flew or thought or laughed or cried.

Before the wind and sea, the rumbling volcanoes and rushing rivers.

Before the sun and moon.

Then there was Blyss.

She awoke at the foot of the Tower knowing all and knowing nothing.

She awoke with a Silver Tablet in her hand.

She awoke to the breathing earth, the sighing moon, the laughing sun.

Blyss inhaled deep . . . exhaled complete . . . inhaled again . . . gathered and composed . . . solidified . . .

She smiled, then looked down at the tablet in her hand. Blyss knew so much . . . yet there was so much she didn't understand . . .

AN OFFER

Days later with the unsettling images of Thurrow's video still disrupting her corporate karma, Sadjah tried her best to concentrate on a strategy. She knew Thurrow was equally as dedicated to his cause as she was dedicated to Pisces profits. She wished to be more like Thurrow — he was indeed a visionary — but she was a realist. She had vision, but it was a narrow, focused beam shining on her bright future. Sadjah knew from experience that everyone had their price, but Thurrow was not like everyone. For one thing, he was already rich. When it came to the material world, he had very little interest in acquiring things unless they were truly useful. He would always take tools over toys, efficiency over luxury, and progress over profits. What could she possibly offer him? Sadjah suddenly thought, if he can't be bought maybe she could just rent him. She could create a new research facility to study and implement some of his recommendations — and put him in charge. She would give him a generous budget, he could staff it with all his egghead buddies . . . how could he turn it down? In this way, she could monitor his findings and appear to be working with him. Who knows? Maybe he could save Pisces some money while he tried to save the world. Knowing Thurrow's personal aversion to publicity, she would promise to maintain a low profile and simply leak the news to the press after everything was in place.

In Sadjah's mind it was a win-win. He gets to do his thing, she gets to use his good name and keep him under her thumb and . . . in her bed. Looking down, Sadjah caught a glimpse of her own smiling reflection in the black polished ebony desktop, she thought out loud, "Now, that's one talented, beautiful, foxy lady!"

Sadjah had her staff crunch some numbers, gather some facts, and put a proposal together. Within hours she had a general outline of what it would take to create an entirely new division, and within days she had everyone on the board ready to champion her cause. Between Thurrow's international reputation and her winning streak at the company, it wasn't hard to convince them. Now it was her turn to ambush Thurrow.

Thurrow had left town for a few days after his presentation in Sadjah's office. On his way home, he spent some time considering his future with Sadjah. She had been quiet and a little distant when he left, but he wasn't sure if it was his imagination. As a result, he was slightly apprehensive and unsure of his next move. Thurrow didn't want to pressure her, but he felt that every day of indecision was one day closer to disaster. The governments around the world were spinning their wheels; he felt that Sadjah with her influence at Pisces was his last hope.

Upon arrival, he received a text with her apologies. She was tied up in a meeting and would have to meet him later for cocktails at her place.

 Sadjah was sure he would head directly to his ship. He would go straight to his lab, catch up with Samu on her research processing and all that scientific voodoo that bored Sadjah to tears. Then he would go back up to the bar, grab a snifter of Cruzan, his favorite aged rum and make his way around the deck to the pool. After a short swim, he would change into some casual clothes, then head to the galley for a light supper. By now Sadjah knew Thurrow's routine fairly well. Sometimes she caught herself actually getting jealous of the Samudra Hantu, but it was in her best interest to let him relax on his beloved Samu for a short time.

After checking in with Samu and a relaxing swim, Thurrow was feeling more at ease. He thought he might put business aside for the evening and enjoy a pleasant night with Sadjah. His stomach reminded him that he hadn't eaten since that morning, and he headed to the galley. Just as he was about to check the fridge, the lights dimmed and some smooth retro funk music started playing through Samu's state-of-the-art sound system. The screen on the fridge switched from inventory mode to a colorful pattern of abstract designs, then words started floating into view. "I thought I'd surprise you.

Your dinner is ready on the upper deck." Thurrow was surprised. Samu didn't usually presume anything. Although she was like a friend, she was still a computer and usually stayed within the parameters of her programming. He would address that later, right now he was thankful and hungry.

Sadjah had decided to keep things casual. It was a warm night so she wore a simple short cotton romper with halter straps and a low neckline. She didn't want it to look like she was trying to seduce him into a decision, but she knew it was an outfit that would keep her assets on the bargaining table. Sadjah had hired a chef to work up a simple but diverse menu that was sure to please no matter what mood Thurrow might be in. She had just one shot to present this proposal in the best of circumstances, and she was leaving nothing to chance.

When Thurrow reached the upper deck, he saw Sadjah and just stopped. He shook his head and laughed out loud. "I should have known. Well, if you were going for the element of surprise, you succeeded. And a very nice surprise at that! What's the occasion?"

Sadjah said. "Let me see . . . it's a beautiful summer evening, I was a little off when you left, and I missed you. Is that enough?"

"That works for me. You look beautiful and I'm hungry — in more ways than one."

Sadjah just smiled thinking, "So far so good!"

They enjoyed an incredible meal and kept the conversation light, sprinkling it with laughter and a little flirting. Sadjah was having so much fun, she wondered if she should take the chance of ruining the mood, but thought, "If not now, when?"

They had thanked the Chef and were now alone, enjoying an after-dinner drink. Sadjah began to tingle with desire. She had all but given up on business. She was staring at Thurrow while he gazed at the sky. She wanted to feel his hands on her neck, she wanted to press her body against his, to feel him inside her!

She was about to ask him to dance when he turned to her and said, "This is such a lovely evening, and I hope I don't completely destroy the mood. I feel so close to you right now. One of the many reasons I care for you is that I can be totally honest with you. I have been wondering if you've taken any time to consider some of the recommendations I presented several days ago."

SNAP! It was as if a bolt of lightening hit her. Sadjah did her best to hide the shock. She should have been glad for the opening this gave her, but she had been so lost in the magical fog of longing that it took a few moments to get her bearings.

Sadjah stuttered. "ye yes . . . yes I have. I have given it a great deal of thought. I have had some of my brightest associates put together a proposal for you.

DANCE WITH THE DEVIL

Though she was somewhat disappointed and mildly frustrated, Sadjah knew this was the perfect opportunity to make her case to Thurrow. After all, this was exactly what she had planned. She just didn't plan to get caught in her own net of subtle seduction.

Sadjah had Thurrow's undivided attention, he was in a very good mood and he was the one who broached the question. Sadjah was prepared; she knew that this was not her typical business environment, so she had done her homework. No laptop, no charts and graphs. She had studied the proposal and had committed the facts to memory. It was very important that Thurrow should perceive her as an enthusiastic partner in this venture. She must convince him that the video had affected her deeply. Sadjah could not deny that she was moved, but not to the degree Thurrow had hoped.

Thurrow leaned into the conversation as Sadjah began her response. He was impressed with the speed and efficiency with which she had gathered so much information, with her obvious interest in the task at hand and her understanding of the urgency. He wished he hadn't had that second drink, but he was still able to follow most of what she was saying. Thurrow caught himself staring at her as she spoke. He was mesmerized by her intensity, her focused intelligence, and, most of all, her dazzling beauty. He could see the full moon reflected in her sparkling grey eyes. He was jolted out of his trance when he heard the words "working for Pisces."

Thurrow had to interrupt. "I'm sorry. I got a little distracted by the glowing moonlit countenance of the most beautiful woman I know. What were you saying about Pisces?"

Sadjah smiled. "Maybe we should have this conversation tomorrow. It is such a gorgeous evening." Inside she was hoping he would agree. Sadjah knew that with just the slightest touch from Thurrow, she would have her legs wrapped around him in an instant.

He said, "No, let's continue. This is really important."

As she explained her plans to create a special, highly funded environmental division within Pisces Corp. Thurrow started to sober up. When she got to the part about autonomy and hands-off, he found he was getting apprehensive. It was beginning to remind him of past conversations where the woman in his life ended up proposing. He knew she wasn't talking about getting married, but he was almost afraid to let her continue. Thurrow had to admit that Sadjah seemed genuinely committed to this idea of reevaluating Pisces' role in the future of the planet. As he listened, he got sucked into her enthusiasm.

Finally, almost out of breath, she came to the point. "I have the full agreement of the board and a 100% vote of confidence from the shareholders. We are offering you the position of Chief Scientific Officer, head of our new environmental-impact division with full authority to design, implement, and oversee the division. Wait — before you respond — the position comes with a very significant compensation and benefit package, including shares in the company. I know it's not about money for you, but as I have said, you could affect real change for both Pisces and the planet. You and me, Thurrow. We could change the world!"

Thurrow's first thought was, "I was right — marriage — in bed with Pisces!"

As she reached into her pocket to find the joint she had rolled earlier, Sadjah said, "I suggest you take a few days and give it some thought." She lit the joint and handed it to Thurrow. He took a long, slow toke, allowing the smoke to fill his lungs, holding his breath for maximum effect. He was thankful for the brief silence. Sadjah refilled their glasses then stood. She walked around the table, and standing behind Thurrow, began to rub his shoulders. Still silent and doing their best to stay in the moment, they both gazed at the moon. For the next few hours, they had no trouble separating business from pleasure.

Ten Days Later

Thurrow was bothered by his doubts about Sadjah's sincerity. As far as he knew, she had never lied to him, but he had witnessed several situations in which she manipulated the truth in order to achieve her goals. Pisces had a reputation as a ruthless entity when it came to acquisitions, and now Sadjah was at the helm of that behemoth corporation. How could he separate the woman from her business? Would he be working for Sadjah or Pisces? After examining the details of the proposal, he found himself tempted but still hesitant. Why did they need him? Why would they spend so much? There were plenty of other capable people to choose from who would jump at the chance for a third of what they were offering. Was his name worth that much to them or did they just want to own him and control his influence? He knew he would have to decide soon; Sadjah wasn't known for her patience and it was starting to affect their personal relationship.

It had been over a week and still Sadjah had no idea what was going through Thurrow's mind. She couldn't stand it much longer. Thurrow would be a fool to pass up such a lucrative deal. Perhaps she had overplayed her hand. She wanted this so badly, she may have lost perspective. Had she underestimated his independent nature? A slave to her own value system, Sadjah naturally assumed the offer would be too generous for anyone to turn down. She hadn't really considered his viewpoint. He might be thinking, "So much money, they must need me — but do I need them?" She had broken her own rules by rushing into this plan.

In the meantime, Pisces was having some problems of its own. Some mysterious occurrences were being reported from several of the fleet captains. Three of the super-trawlers had lost a record breaking catch due to a navigational dysfunction, and other vessels in both the fishing fleet and cruise lines were reporting similar experiences. Billions of dollars in revenues were at stake if this wasn't cleared up soon. Sadjah didn't need this right now. It was not in her plan!

Back on his ship, Thurrow listened as Samu briefed him on current events. She was programmed to scan for any news relating to the environment with a priority for ocean-related events. He knew Sadjah had been on edge for the last few days, but he had assumed it was related to the proposed partnership. Listening to the news, he learned that several ships in the Pisces fleet were experiencing some unexplained and unprecedented technical malfunctions. There were rumors of espionage. Pisces' latest additions to the fleet were state-of-the-art factory vessels. He couldn't imagine how anyone could have hacked those systems, at least not this early in their development. He could however think of plenty of reasons why. It was a controversial method of indiscriminately surrounding and herding thousands of fish into a massive net. They would then just scoop up the catch, sort, process, and pack nonstop until the net was empty. Often they would rendezvous with a shipping vessel, off-load, then continue "fishing."

Upon hearing of these events, Thurrow was reminded of the harsh realities of Pisces' business model. Sadjah must be in the thick of this right now. At that moment, he knew he couldn't possibly accept her offer. He was saddened to think of what that might mean for their relationship. With Sadjah, if you weren't with her, you were against her. Thurrow didn't want to lose her, but he couldn't reconcile her devotion to Pisces.

THE DECISION

Thurrow stopped off at a bar on his way to Sadjah's office. It was around three in the afternoon, so the place was pretty quiet —just a few businessmen unwilling to finish their liquid lunch and face the race. He ordered his Cruzan Single Barrel Rum. Thurrow needed to rethink this decision one last time. He had rehearsed at least ten versions of his rejection speech while trying to anticipate all the variations of Sadjah's reaction, but it was useless. There was no easy way to do this. He would keep it simple and brief, then politely excuse himself, allowing Sadjah to process in private. Thurrow truly hoped that they could salvage something of their relationship, but knowing Sadjah, he was doubtful.

Sadjah had been on edge all day. With all the recent turmoil in the company and the unknown future of the new environmental division she had foolishly proposed, Sadjah was feeling the pressure. She still had no idea where Thurrow stood. They hadn't had much time together since the evening she made her offer, and what little time they did have was spent in bed enjoying each other and avoiding discussion. So when her assistant showed Thurrow into her office, she was wound as tight as those trapped whales in Thurrow's video.

As Thurrow approached her desk, Sadjah picked up a hint of the sweet scent of rum. Her heart started pounding in her chest and she felt the moisture gather under her arms and on her upper lip. She knew it was over. She thought, "I must keep it together. I can, I will keep it together."

Looking at Sadjah, Thurrow knew she knew. "God, this is bad," he thought. "This is the hardest thing I've ever done." Just as that thought entered his mind, it was as if a far-away voice answered, "No it's not."

"Now what does that mean?" An image of an exotic and beautiful woman popped into his head. "Who is that? Shit! Am I losing my mind? I shouldn't have had that drink. Damn! Pull it together, man!" Thurrow felt that if he opened his mouth, he would just stammer. A door in his mind had opened a crack and a sliver of blinding light escaped. It was so confusing, this moment was pivotal, he needed clarity.

In the final seconds of Thurrow's awkward approach, Sadjah managed to gathered herself temporarily.

"Don't speak. I know what you're going to say and I can't bear to hear it right now. You need to leave. You need to leave right now! We will talk, but not now. I . . . I just can't . . .

Without saying a word, Thurrow turned as if in a trance. He silently opened the door and, failing to close it, stepped into his unknown future.

Sadjah quietly traced his steps, violently slammed the door shut, stomped to her desk, and kicked the chair out of her way. She then picked up the miniature gold replica of a Pisces cruise ship and hurled it across the room. It crashed through the face plate of her built-in aquarium. Hundreds of gallons of water and thousands of dollars worth of exotic fish flooded the room.

Her thoughts raced. "He must be out of his mind! What a fool! Doesn't he understand that this is a once in a lifetime opportunity? Did someone feed him some inside information? No! . . . No! . . No! This can't be happening!

Sadjah knew she had lost and she hated to lose.

ENLIGHTENED STRATEGY

During the rescue Blyss had received the Tribe's distress signal in the form of a powerful thought bundle — she was not surprised. In her protracted study of the silver tablets secreted in the narrow slots along the terrace walls of the Gold Tower she had discovered a similar scenario prophesied. The tablet design was not a detailed depiction of the event, but a simple low-relief of men standing in boats surrounding and herding dolphins. It was a primitive, stylized version in which some of the boats were being overturned by a whale, the men flailing and falling overboard. A mermaid, followed by some mysterious sea creatures, circled the scene.

Blyss instinctively relayed the the signal to the Gold Tower, but in retrospect she realized she wasn't precisely transmitting information to the tower. In those tense moments, Blyss lost track of time, came close to passing out, but instead she ended up "passing into." For the first time Blyss consciously became one with the Gold Tower.

Her experience was similar to projecting a focused beam of light, comparable to the flick of switch instantly lighting up a scene. Blyss felt as though she was witnessing the slaughter first hand. She could feel the scene in real time, not seeing, just doing. It was similar to a long distance "mind cloud" technique but on a much grander scale. She became a force of nature managing physics and electricity in unimaginable ways. But unlike the wild random force of a hurricane or a tornado, this was a sentient spiritual force with intention.

This powerful union was not without its price. After dealing with that huge factory ship, Blyss was left physically and mentally exhausted. This was not activity she could participate in on a daily basis. She would need a strategy, an organized way of incurring as much chaos for the adversary as possible while maintaining the health and welfare of both herself and the tribe.

Blyss realized that with Epyphany and the Tribe, and

hopefully with help from Thurrow, finally there was a real possibility of combatting the negative impact that humans were having on the Earth's ecosystems.

Thurrow would be key to a successful campaign. But at this point she had very little information about his current status. Thurrow's love for Epyphany was true, and so displacing his memory had been a challenge. Although Blyss knew that her mind cloud had been successful — she hoped it wasn't too successful.

Excited by the prospects of her enhanced connection to the tower, Blyss could now consider a campaign she would have never imagined possible. Perhaps she could nudge Thurrow's subconscious. Maybe she could loosen the chains that bound his memories of Oojai and Epyphany. After all, he had been a remarkable student with an undeniable aptitude for the language of Oojai, and he enjoyed a true connection to their world. Maybe the sound of the swhorl would trigger some memories. She thought "music is zooming around the atmosphere, bouncing off satellites and making it's way around the world every waking moment. I just need to figure out a technique to deliver my music to Thurrow."

The dolphin slaughter, the ensuing events, and the emotional urgency had been a trigger for the intense symbiotic union of Blyss with the Gold Tower. It was a mystical merging of flesh and earth's most precious element, a magical amalgam of spirit and pure energy. Blyss was determined to find the key to recreating the phenomenon at will.

Not long after addressing the tribe, Blyss found herself alone in the Cavern Temple. Time lost it's meaning leaving her with no idea if the sky held the sun or the moon. At once weary and restless, Blyss walked slowly toward the tower, she felt it's power beckoning. She decided to climb. Blyss had been climbing the tower regularly since the day of her awakening. It wasn't an easy climb, even with her skills and strength. The problem lay in the fact that water trickled steadily in every direction, covering the surface with an invisible film of moisture. The combination of the smooth gold and water made for an extremely slippery surface. There were no actual footholds or handles. In order to make any progress at all, one had to pick a destination, and through momentum and sheer willpower, just go for it. Blyss had long ago learned to approach it more like a dance than a climb. As a result of this difficulty, she seldom set her sites on the top tier.

But at this particular moment, in spite of her weary condition, she felt it was very important to go to the top. Without another thought, Blyss sprung from a squatting position at the base and landed on the top shelf of the first tier. In two more leaps, she found herself standing on the top. She spoke out loud, "I've never done that before!" The top of the Gold Tower was a very small, smooth, triangular space with just enough room for someone of small stature to stand or sit. It was the only dry spot on the tower. In order to sit, Blyss crossed her ankles then slowly sank down into a lotus pose. She had no plan, but once in that position she removed her Swhorl from it's case and began to play softly.

The Gold Tower began to glow, the intensity rising and falling with the music. Blyss was faintly aware of a small vibration. As the vibration increased, it set up a low frequency tone. This was followed by a secondary oscillation, which in turn sustained a middle note. With both tones harmonizing every note and texture of her improvised melody, Blyss became lost in the music and soothed by the subtle motion of the tower. The Temple Cavern reverberated with a haunting, uniquely beautiful and soulful sound. Hours passed, but Blyss was in a timeless state.

She didn't know it then, but Blyss had found both the key and the doorway — the key to communion with the tower and the doorway to Thurrow's buried memories.

Thurrow

On the other side of the planet, Thurrow had been alone listening to some late-night rhythm and blues. A week had passed since he rejected Sadjah's offer and he still hadn't spoken to her. There was no doubt in his mind about his choice, he could never be a pawn in Pisces deadly game, but he missed her. Thurrow was about to ask Samu to switch the station when the R&B mix faded into some very strange exotic music. He found it vaguely familiar, though he couldn't place where he had heard it. It was odd . . . he was instantly soothed. Laying back in his chair, he put his feet up and began to truly relax for the first time in weeks.

Thurrow closed his eyes as the music massaged his weary soul. His mind drifted, a sliver of a smile formed as all the muscles in his face loosened. With his head tilted back and his arms draped over the sides of the chair, he felt like he was floating in a warm sea. He could almost hear the sound of the distant surf.

Images began to drift into his semiconscious mind. He was surrounded by sea creatures, a huge whale surfaced near him, a beautiful sailfish sliced through the waves, a dolphin playfully nudged him, there was a menacing-looking alligator circling, an amusingly large pelican swooped down, and then suddenly the face of a strangely beautiful woman appeared. Large green and gold eyes held his gaze; sad and pleading, they pierced his soul. She was trying to speak but he couldn't hear her. As he reached out to her, he thought he heard his name echoing . . . Thur . . row . . row . . row . . row . . .

The vision faded. He woke from his trance.

THURROW . . . THURROW . . . wake up!

Samu was paging him. "You have a visitor. Sadjah is boarding the ship."

THE LAST STRAW

His tension returned as Thurrow watched the monitor while Samu tracked Sadjah's progress with the on board security cameras. He spoke softly, "Samu, close up please." The camera zoomed in. Seeing the expression on Sadjah's face only served to confuse Thurrow. He wondered aloud, "Is that a smile? If so what could it mean? Am I forgiven or forsaken?"

In the week that followed Thurrow's disappointing response to her offer, Sadjah found herself unable to concentrate or focus on a new plan. She missed him terribly, but every time she thought about seeing him she was overcome with rage. Accustomed to getting her own way, Sadjah had never developed the tools to deal with rejection. She knew her anger was unhealthy and often led to more bad decisions but frustration clouded her reason. Her first reaction was to fight. She knew it wasn't rational, but she took it personally – – in rejecting Pisces, Thurrow was rejecting her.

One minute she wanted to destroy his career, the next minute she longed for his touch. On one hand she thought maybe she could win his trust and push Pisces into the new direction of responsible stewardship of the oceans. She would then consider the quarterly profits and decide to let the markets dictate policy. She knew he was good for her and he had been so . . . very fine in bed. It was driving her mad.

When Thurrow met her on deck, Sadjah started the conversation the same way she had ended their last. "Don't speak! Please don't say a word."

Thurrow thought, "She certainly didn't come dressed for a fight." Sadjah was wearing a light, translucent, full-length sweater jacket. The hauntingly beautiful hand-painted design fell in long soft lines as peacock feathers trailed off to the sides. It opened wide in the front to show off the revealing neckline of a shimmering silk halter top. The skin-tight mini skirt wrapped low on her hips was little more than a wide leather belt. He could see the firm muscles of her incredible long legs flex in the dim light as she made her way toward him. Sadjah's ample breasts swayed freely as she came to an abrupt stop directly in front of Thurrow. Throwing both arms back, Sadjah shamelessly shook her smooth shoulders, letting her jacket fall to the floor. By this time, Pisces Corp and its environmental policies were far from Thurrow's thoughts.

Standing almost eye level in six inch stiletto heels, Sadjah tilted her head to the side while she took Thurrow's hand and placed it inside her halter top. He felt the familiar curve of her breast, and like a smooth hard beach pebble, her nipple grazed the palm of his hand. A shiver of animal lust ran up his spine. He cupped her firm ass in his other hand and pulled her roughly off her feet. One of her high heels fell to the floor. His hand slid from her breast to the back of her neck. As Sadjah wrapped her legs around his waist, the other shoe clunked on the teak deck. She turned her head to look him in the eyes. Her mouth was open and waiting.

Thurrow kissed her . . . a long deep kiss that made her moan with pleasure. With Sadjah clinging tightly, he walked slowly to the bedroom. Hours passed and they made love several times. Not a single word passed between them. Thurrow finally dozed off. He woke suddenly, and when he opened his eyes he saw Sadjah's silhouette in the morning sun. She was getting dressed. He lay there quietly for a moment watching her slender outline move gracefully through the rays of sunlight. As the fog lifted from his sleepy brain, he started to remember the evening's events. Still watching and thinking how strange it was that they hadn't spoke, he began to hum a strange melody. Sadjah froze.

She didn't know why, but the sound of Thurrow humming that odd tune somehow frightened her. Sadjah had planned to leave unnoticed, but now it was too late.

Thurrow was puzzled. He remembered relaxing to some exotic music just before Sadjah's late night visit, but he still couldn't place its origin. He was even more perplexed by

Sadjah's reaction to the humming. She appeared to be trembling.

Thurrow needed to talk. Once again he tried to break their silence, and once again she silenced him with a wave of her hand.

Sadjah thought, "I guess I'll have to change my plan and do this in person." In a steely cold voice, Sadjah finally spoke. "I have considered my options and I have made my decision. There are only two viable paths for us. Either you join me at Pisces and we continue to grow our partnership, or you lose this unique opportunity and you throw away this beautiful relationship. It's all or nothing."

After an intense and stimulating night of such erotic intimacy, Thurrow was stunned. "How could she give herself to me so lovingly and so completely through the night, then in the morning light deliver this cold-blooded ultimatum?" He thought, "It's not that simple; there must be some middle ground." He hated the thought of losing her. She was complex and driven, but he could live with that. In fact, he enjoyed that about her. Why couldn't she see this was not about business?

Her voice grew louder. "Go ahead Thurrow, choose . . . choose now! Without me what have you got? Your research? Your travels? The geeky dimwitted fan girls? I know you and you need me! Someone to challenge you — an equal. Don't throw this away on principles, Thurrow!"

"You're right. I want you! I love all that we are together, but why must you try to own me? You are lost, Sadjah. You have lost your identity. You can't separate yourself from your Company. And if you and Pisces are a package deal, I have to say no! You and I could do great things, but you've got it backwards. If you follow your heart, you might loose your standing in the company, but there is so much to gain. Are you afraid to loose your title? Your status? Your corrupt father's approval? Well that is the cost of principle over profit and you're not willing to pay that price. Sadjah . . . you . . .

we . . . we are lost."

Sadjah finished dressing in silence. Then she spoke. "Samu?"

"Yes, Sadjah?"

"He's all yours."

"I believe he holds my title, therefore — technically — I am all his."

"Hear that, Thurrow? Looks like you found the perfect woman. Good luck screwing your robot!"

Sad and angry, Thurrow responded weakly. "She's not a robot, she's a magnificent ship. And she probably has a warmer heart than you!"

"You will see just how cold my heart is." Sadjah turned and walked out of his life.

Thurrow sunk back into his pillow and closed his eyes. The haunting melody returned like a gentle ocean breeze soothing his anger. Listening to the mysterious lullaby, he surrendered to the melody and fell into a peaceful sleep.

DREAMING

Lost in the sound of the beautiful melody, Thurrow continued to sleep into the late morning. The vibrations of an unfamiliar instrument from a far-away place had broken through time and space. The music engulfed him and so he dreamed.

When he awoke from his dream, he felt refreshed and excited. He felt like he had been living in a fog and now the fog had lifted revealing a world bright with possibilities. With Sadjah gone, Thurrow knew that he should feel remorse or at the very least, conflicted, but instead he felt incredibly light hearted and energized. Thurrow knew what he must do, although he wasn't sure why.

Sitting in his control room, Thurrow prepared for a long voyage. He had no idea how long he would be gone so he instructed Samu to double check the complete list of inventories in every category and to double the normal supply levels. His ship was equipped with a small scale, fully automated hydroponic system that could grow a healthy supply of vegetables almost indefinitely. With the Samudra Hantu's state-of-the-art energy resource and recycling capacity, Thurrow figured he could stay at sea for over a year if he needed to.

As Thurrow prepared for his extended excursion, he found himself drifting off into short daydreams. Scenes of waterfalls and tropical forests would float into his consciousness. He would picture himself swimming in a beautiful lagoon or scaling rocky cliffs with breathtaking views. Occasionally he was startled out of his reverie by the faces of three uniquely beautiful exotic women—faces both familiar and alien. His heart would race and he would experience a mix of anticipation and anxiety. It was as if his mind had knowledge that his rational nature could not accept.

With only a few loose ends to tie up, he would be ready for departure within a couple of days. Thurrow had recently fulfilled his speaking engagements, and his split with Sadjah released him from a long list of social commitments. He thought, "Funny how a commitment to one person ties you to so many strangers. You don't think, 'I have fallen for this woman and now I have to talk with all these people with whom I have nothing in common.'" He smiled, "I guess there are some upsides, but for now I'm free of distractions with a new world to discover." This time the mysterious far-away echo in his head sounded much closer . . .

Blyss

Dripping with sweat and completely out of breath, Blyss abruptly stopped playing and slid the swhorl gently back in its case. She blinked several times and looked around the Cavern Temple. She knew where she was but for a moment she didn't know "when" she was. Blyss was reminded of that first day when she had found herself sitting at the base of the Gold Tower with a silver tablet in her hand. Slowly it came back to her — being drawn to the tower, the leaps to the top, the music and the vibration. Now she remembered everything. It was like a flying dream — untethered and floating in the music. She had seen Thurrow, tense and conflicted on his ship, trying to sort out his feelings. Then momentarily, the music found him . . . but the connection broke . . . she felt Sadjah's anger . . . heard the sound of their passion as it drowned out the swhorl. Blyss didn't stop; she kept playing. The Gold Tower fueled a spiritual passion in her, equal to the couple's ill-fated and forlorn desire . . . Blyss persevered. Her music had broken through and she would regain the connection at all costs. She would not stop. When Sadjah left, the music filled the void and Blyss was able accomplish her task. She found the key to his memory. The door was unlocked — she could slowly guide him back to his real home.

NEW MISSION

Physically drained and mentally depleted, Blyss slept though an entire day. Two days later, fully rested and recuperated from her intense out-of-body experience, she began to consider the next step in her loosely formed plan. She wasn't sure how soon and to what extent, Thurrow would regain his memories of Oojai, but she was hopeful. In the meantime, she needed to initiate some direct action against those industries most responsible for the unrelenting destruction of the fragile ocean habitat.

She linked to the tower and began honing her skills. The Gold Tower had always been a mystical source of information, but now Blyss was able to manage and manipulate her amplified abilities. Among it's mystical powers, the tower served as an infinite source of information capable of collecting and storing data 24/7. As she grew more comfortable with this mystical symbiotic relationship she learned to relax and conserve her strength, gaining insight as she experimented with her new found powers. Blyss was able to focus and control beams of light, sound, or bundles of pure energy at great distances, and had succeeded in disrupting a few small fishing operations. The media was starting to pay attention. Blyss decided it was time to make some headlines.

Using her newly acquired power, she found what she was looking for. The Pisces Corp had recently commissioned the first of what was to be a fleet of Super Factory Ships. The "Silver Finn" was one of a new generation of freezing trawler factory ships. Over 600 feet in length, this behemoth was able to process 500 tons of fish a day, could carry 4,500 tons of fuel, and store 10,000 tons of graded and frozen catch. The monster ship was currently fishing off the coast of Mumbai, India.

Blyss was outraged when she discovered deep-sea bottom trawling was doubtless one of the most destructive fishing practices. The facts were appalling. The process involves targeting fish stocks that are already overexploited; the bottom trawl nets smash the seabed, taking everything in its path, including species that are not targeted. Deep-sea bottom trawling scoops up 30% to 60% of wasted fish — ocean life that is discarded overboard, dead or dying. Along with the obvious problem of unsustainable fishing levels, bottom trawling has a devastating effect upon the ocean floor eco-system. The drag nets stir up the sediment at the bottom of the sea. The suspended solid plumes can expand several miles from the source of the trawling. These plumes cloud the water and lower light levels at the bottom, adversely affecting kelp reproduction. Ocean sediments often contain many sunken organic pollutants, usually toxins like DDT, PCB, and PAH. Bottom trawling mixes these pollutants into the plankton ecology where they can move back up the food chain and into the planet's food supply. Phosphorus is often found in high concentration within the soft, shallow sediments. Re-suspending nutrient solids like these can introduce oxygen demand into the water column, resulting in oxygen deficient dead zones or harmful algae blooms. This inefficient method of pulling a fishing net along the sea bottom behind trawlers removes around 5 to 25% of an area's seabed life on a single run.

Blyss felt she could perhaps shine a light on this inexcusable and immoral behavior. Although this ship was extremely large, it was highly automated. The crew was small and most likely fresh recruits with limited training. She was confident that with some planning and co-ordination, she and the Tribe could pull off a successful sabotage.

With her target chosen and her skills sharpened, Blyss summoned Epyphany and the Tribe for a meeting. Since the last meeting they had agreed amongst themselves to do whatever it took to safeguard their fragile world from human exploitation. They gathered in the pool at the base of the Gold Tower, listening intently as Blyss explained her plan.

"We were very lucky in our first victory, considering the unforeseen nature of the conflict. This time we have a distinct advantage, the element of surprise. They still have no idea what happened last time. Their arrogance works in our favor. Humans have thought so highly of themselves for so long they have lost the power of imagination. The longer we can stay invisible means the longer we stay effective. If everyone is willing, I have a new mission. We will use a strategy similar to our first encounter.

"I have chosen to deal with only one ship, but it is the largest ocean going vessel ever constructed. Though it is large, it has a very small crew. The ship known as the "Silver Finn" is basically a giant, floating robot. The smooth operation of the factory, the actual fishing, and the navigation all depend on computers. As a result of my improved projection skills, I'm confident that I can disrupt some primary programs in their system. In addition, I plan to confuse key members of the crew in hopes of creating further distractions and chaos. All the while I will need you to work in the water as you did before. Since Epyphany won't be wasting energy and her special skills communicating long distance with me, she will be free to assess and act on the results of my work. The down side of my plan is, I can't predict the exact result of my energy projections. The interference will be random, so everyone must be ready to abort the mission and pull back. If we can interrupt their workflow I would consider the mission a success, but if we can disable them and free the catch I would count it as a complete victory.

Blyss, Epyphany, and the Tribe spent the next two days working out the details of the plan. They were excited and confident that they could actually do something to make a difference.

OBSESSION

Within days of the acrimonious split with Sadjah, Thurrow was standing on the bow of his beloved Samudra Hantu. The warm wind caressed him as Samu skimmed along the smooth waters of Puget Sound heading out to the the open sea. He had plotted a leisurely course, with a stop in Hawaii, then perhaps he would swing down to New Zealand, make his way around Australia, spend some time in Bali, then do some exploring in the Indian Ocean. For some reason, he had a strong pull towards the Maldives and the coast of India. He had visited Mumbai in the past and Thurrow had made a few friends in the flourishing film industry there known as Bollywood.

Thurrow's dreams of beautiful islands continued nightly, and so he decided to follow those dreams. The images of three enchanting women consistently haunted those dreams. Moderately unsettling but ultimately pleasant visions, they seemed so real he was always disappointed to wake and find them gone. The most intriguing of the trio was the most alien, a mythical creature, a beautiful and powerful mermaid beyond imagination. As the journey progressed, so did his connection to the dreams. After each busy day in the lab or studio, Thurrow would fall asleep at night hoping to see her.

Though he had been consciously avoiding news of the world, Thurrow would occasionally check in to see if there was any good news. A few weeks into his trip he heard the name Pisces Corp on the broadcast and dropped what he was doing. He remembered Sadjah mentioning some troubles with their fleet, but he had been too involved with their personal drama to pay much attention. Pisces was continuing to experience mysterious interruptions in the communication and navigation systems on some of their vessels. It was costing the company time and money and they had been unable to track the source. There were rumors implicating GORU. Thurrow was shocked when he heard his name mentioned. They were trying to connect his sudden disappearance with an organized plot to sabotage

Pisces. He couldn't believe it! Would Sadjah stoop to this kind of revenge? Was she trying to lure him back at any cost? These were serious allegations even if they were only rumors. The last thing he wanted was to return just to make a case for his innocence, but he was concerned about the credibility of GORU. Thurrow had spent years of hard work doing research and fundraising to ensure that at least one organization was monitoring the health and welfare of Earth's magnificent oceans. Thurrow decided not to take the bait; he would continue on his quest. He hoped he was making the right decision.

The days flew by and Thurrow found himself impatient to reacquaint himself with the Indian Ocean. He would wake from his dreams with a renewed sense of urgency. With each dream he felt closer to some kind of breakthrough. They were starting to feel like memories and he was questioning that feeling a bit less each day. The island in his dream felt comfortably familiar. The creatures seemed like friends, and the mermaid, the sturdy little athletic witch doctor, and the images of the majestic statue all seemed more real than fantasy.

He revised his itinerary to head straight to Indonesia, enjoy a short visit to Bali, then sail on to the Maldives off the coast of India.

In all his years of criss-crossing the globe, Thurrow had never managed to spend any time in Bali. Upon arrival he rented a scooter and spent the first few days visiting the coastal cities. Similar to the island in his dreams, this island was surrounded by coral reefs. The beaches in the south tended to have white sand while those in the north and west were covered in black sand. Bali's highest mountain, known as "mother mountain" was an active volcano where Thurrow spent a couple days hiking and exploring. In the early evenings he relaxed in the natural hot springs at the base of the mountain, amused by a flock of young women vying for his attention.

Thoroughly relaxed from his days on the coast, he headed

inland to discover Ubud. Thurrow instantly fell in love with the vibe. This small bustling town was Bali's cultural centre, renowned for its highly developed arts, and it awoke the artist in him. With all the pressures of research, business, politics, and romance, Thurrow had neglected his creative side. It had been months since he had picked up his guitar and he couldn't remember when he had last designed anything for the pure fun of it. On every street, people of all ages were making things; painters, sculptors, musicians, metalworkers, and dancers honed their artistic skills. It was intoxicating.

Thurrow rented a little bungalow in a family compound near the center of Ubud. His landlords were a small family of artists and musicians. Despite the language barrier, they communicated easily through their mutual love of art and music. The beautiful young woman who served him breakfast every morning spoke enough English to help him find his bearings. Often when she had finished her work she would act as a guide. They visited the homes of other artists, writers, and even an architect. Thurrow was impressed by the simple, elegant homes and the unencumbered lifestyle of the people. Theirs was a life focused on creating, not consuming. Though many made part of their livelihood selling things to tourists, much of their art was just for the joy of creating. Wandering the streets of Ubud, Thurrow found himself tapping his feet to the joyful rhythm of the day.

Bali was a country of friendly and spiritual people. They seemed to have found a pleasant balance of work, play, and worship. Their religion was woven into the pattern of their daily routine. Often an entire village would stop work in the middle of the day and everyone would start painting signs, preparing food, or creating costumes for a celebration. Within hours, the streets would be filled with dancers, musicians, and artists. Parades of smiling people lined the streets and alleys.

Thurrow was tempted to extended his stay further. Although he knew he had never experienced Bali, his visit triggered even more memories. He was starting to become frustrated. Even with the sound of celebrations outside his door, that strange melody still haunted his days. He had to solve this mystery; it was bordering on an unhealthy obsession. Thurrow decided to continue his journey.

On his last night in Bali, the sweet smells of incense and ganja and the sound of competing gamelan ensembles filled the air as Thurrow made his way back to the Samudra Hantu. Bali was so much like his dream, but for the fact that he was beginning to actually hear something calling him toward the Indian Ocean, he could have easily made it his home.

TIME

The relaxing atmosphere of Balinese culture inspired Thurrow to continue to spend a few hours each day in meditation and contemplation. One theme in particular kept returning . . . What is time? You can't touch it or see it. No matter how you measure it, it still flows. What part does it play, relative to coincidence, fate, or choice? He would recall statements such as, "She was the right one but the wrong time" or "I'd love to learn how to play guitar but I haven't the time" or "I will travel someday when I find the time." He would smile to himself and ask, "Where will you look for the time? Did you have it, then misplace it? Did someone hide it from you? How much of it do we have to begin with?" Still talking to himself, he would respond, "Whatever time you might have had, you probably spent it without really thinking about it, and you probably sold it way too cheap. Whatever it might have been worth to you then, now it is gone. You can't buy it back for any price." Time was becoming very precious for Thurrow.

Time was different for Blyss than it was for the world around her. Though she too was unable to buy it back, she had been given what appeared to be a platinum card, a blank check, a bottomless well with infinite buckets of time. Time had been on her side and she had used the years well. But like the rest of humankind, she was not immune to the inconsistencies of time, she could never count on its velocity. One day it might drag, the next it might zoom by so fast she nearly misses the whole day. Of course, there are also those rare moments in which time seems to stand still.

At this particular moment in time . . . many miles apart . . . three hearts began to beat "in time", and in that instance, time began to speed up for Blyss, Epyphany, Thurrow, the Tribe and . . . Sadjah.

Thurrow's weeks on Bali had been more than just a relaxing vacation. They had opened his eyes and his heart. His view of life had been tilted. Peering at the world from this alternate angle, things were more clear; his peripheral view seemed to have widened, he could absorb and retain more information. With this wider understanding he felt closer to the true nature of existence. It was a cleansing of the soul and a spiritual rejuvenation. When Thurrow left Bali, it didn't leave him.

Thurrow approached the Samudra Hantu eager to resume his quest. The moment he stepped on deck he thought he heard something. Thurrow stopped and listened . . . it was his heart . . . it was louder. He smiled, unconcerned. He continued to the control room where he gave the order to depart.

Back on Oojai, the moment had come. There was no more planning to be done, no more discussion and no more waiting. Blyss retired to the Temple Cavern where she lay resting at the foot of the Chrysylyss. The Tribe was gathering in the lagoon and Epyphany was enjoying a few moments of solitary meditation at the Chancel. With her mind and body in harmony she opened her eyes. She took a deep breath and was about to slip into the water when she heard a sound. Epyphany stopped and listened . . . it was her heart . . . pounding in her chest. Not faster, just louder. It felt good! She slid into the surf and joined the tribe as they made their way into the bay. They were ready to challenge the monstrous floating machine.

Sadjah felt like a time-bomb with only seconds left on the clock. Since the day she walked out on Thurrow her life had been in constant turmoil. The board was not at all sympathetic to the news of Thurrow's rejection of their offer. After the glowing recommendation she had given him, they could only think that if he wasn't with them, he must be against them, and he was now considered the enemy. Sadjah could be a very cold-blooded adversary, but in spite of what she had said to Thurrow, she didn't want to make him an enemy. But now . . . in order to maintain her standing in the company, she would be forced sacrifice his reputation.

At first she was unsure how that might be accomplished.

Thurrow had a long list of powerful supporters in his camp. He was known throughout the world of business and politics as incorruptible. But within weeks of his departure there had been news of several more mysterious incidents of sabotage. It was a well known fact that Thurrow and his companies owned many cutting edge patents, some of which were connected to advanced naval technologies. By spinning the news of his uncharacteristic disinterest in joining a generously funded environmental research facility, and connecting the timing of his mysterious disappearance to the news of sabotage, it was easy to cast suspicion without an actual accusation.

Having survived another long day at Pisces, Sadjah was in desperate need of solitude and sleep. She arrived at her penthouse completely spent. Sadjah hadn't taken time for a meal or a snack all day; she knew she should eat. Knowing a hot bath would help, she kicked off her high heels, stepped behind the bar, filled a snifter from the first bottle she found, and dragged herself to the bathroom. Sadjah started the bath water, then leaned heavily against the marble sink. Feeling too weak to even undress, she was tempted to just slide into the bath with her clothes on. She tipped her glass and gulped it down like medicine. Startled by the taste, she threw back her head and began to laugh like a madwoman. Then the laughter turned to sobs and she cried out loud, "CRUZAN! . . . THURROW . . . YOU BASTARD . . . LEAVE ME ALONE!" She threw the glass across the tiled space. This time she took out a beautiful, delicate, and ancient Minoan ceramic vase depicting a giant squid, not unlike the Pisces logo. Shards of glass and pieces of pottery adorned with severed tentacles, were scattered all over the floor. As if in a trance, Sadjah stood and crossed the short distance to the tub. Oblivious to the small shards piercing her feet, she leaned over to turn off the water. In the soothing silence she took a step into the tub, then she heard something. Sadjah stopped and listened. A loud thumping filled her head. Confused, she flopped into the tub and sat up straight. "It's my heart . . . my heart is so loud . . ." She clutched her chest and leaned back.

Sadjah was still trembling with fear when she fell asleep in the steaming hot water, fully clothed.

ON COURSE

Thurrow felt great. The downtime in Bali had affected him in more ways then he could have imagined. It was reaffirming to see a culture mindful of the quality in their lives, successfully balancing productivity and recreation, blurring the lines of work and play. He needed to keep this example in mind, this was a model he would like to emulate.

While Samu managed the details of the journey, Thurrow had time to finally consider his future. He felt that he was nearing some conclusion to the mystery that had plagued him this past year. Whatever the answer, he knew there would be some life-changing choices ahead. It had been a couple days since they left Bali and he was a getting a little restless. At the end of his third productive day in the lab, he decided to spend some time in his recording studio.

It had been a while since Thurrow had booted up his recording program, and it took him a couple of hours to get up to speed. Inspired by the Balinese rhythms, he scanned his extensive sound library for some digital samples. After a few hours of mixing and matching some loops, he had produced a simple hybrid rhythm section with a unique blend of traditional Indonesian instruments and some early-80s funk. Thurrow hit pause and plugged in his guitar when it dawned on him . . . there had been no strange dreams since the first night in Bali, and he couldn't remember the last time the mysterious exotic melody had seeped into his consciousness.

Thurrow managed to recall a version of the intoxicating melody and spent the next few days working up a rough mix of a new composition. He was so into it, he set aside his other work for several more days and just hung out in his music studio adding tracks and tweaking the arrangement. He hadn't had this much fun with his guitar for a long time. Thurrow remembered those early years when his parents couldn't pry the instrument out of his hands. Music was his first love and he felt blessed to have been born with the aptitude and desire. He knew musicians who had made music their profession. For some, it was not such a blessing. It wasn't the music that did them in, it was the music business. From the beginning, Thurrow found music to be like a gateway drug to the thrills and highs of learning. It opened his subconscious mind to the rhythms all around him, in nature and math and science. It enhanced his curiosity, taught him discipline, and supplied him the tools to solve problems. It was the key that unlocked the door to his future and gave him the confidence to walk through it. He was thankful for those stimulating times and right now he felt like that kid again.

It was late, his ears were fried. He had listened intently for so long he had lost objectivity. Thurrow shut down the studio and walked up to the moonlit upper deck. Standing there watching the stars with Samu steadily slicing through the gentle waves, he realized his ears were still ringing. At first he thought it was just the residual effect from all those hours in the studio. Then it got louder. The ringing wasn't just in his ears it was in his head. The sound quickly morphed into an image. He grabbed the rail, suddenly disoriented. Thurrow couldn't decipher the image. It reminded him of an impressionist painting. He closed his eyes and tried to concentrate. He was shaking. That door in his mind was opening and inside lay the answer he'd been searching for. His mind's eye focused on the image. Some part of him knew what he was looking at. It was like watching a magic act wherein what you actually see and what you believe are two different things. A memory flickered . . . he was sitting before a wise woman. She spoke. "If you can suspend disbelief you will be rewarded with a key, then the choice is yours. Will you open the gate to the world of magic that surrounds you?"

With those words came a flood of memories. Those magical days on Oojai, the Cavern, Chrysylyss, Blyss, the Tribe and finally —painfully — the memory of Epyphany.

The sound in his head grew unbearable, but then in an

instant there was silence. The sound had transformed into a message . . . he remembered the language . . . he could hear the tribe . . . they were in trouble. The message lacked any detail but it was definitely a distress signal. Thurrow was faced with a massive physiological and psychological adjustment. It was mind-blowing, but it rang true. He had been in love with a mermaid, not an imaginary creature and not imaginary love. He still had a lot to sort out but there was a crisis at hand.

The Ship

Epyphany and the tribe had been swimming steadily for several days. Thanks to the previous journey, they were all in top shape, fully capable of traveling for hours at a time without a rest. Blyss continued to monitor the situation from the Cavern. Though she was still unable to pinpoint his exact position, Blyss could feel her connection to Thurrow growing stronger and was certain he was closing in on the Tribe.

It wouldn't be long before the Tribe made contact with the Silver Finn. The weather had been in their favor until the fifth day. It started out sunny and mild but as the day progressed the seas began to rise and the wind was starting to pick up speed. Reefer was managing to stay a few miles ahead, but the elements were working against him. Epyphany felt the vibration about the same time Reefer spied the ship. She could feel the alarm in his message . . . "This looks more like an island than a ship . . . I hope Blyss . . ." Now it was Epyphany's turn to be alarmed.

No sooner had she lost contact with Reefer, Epyphany felt Blyss connect. She signaled the Tribe to proceed quickly and cautiously. Just a few miles ahead the Silver Finn was doing business as usual. The ocean was starting to rage and crash against the sheer walls of steel, but the ship stood firm in the water as if it were bolted to the ocean floor. The rising wind carried the clanging metallic sounds of chains and pulleys, of levers and conveyors, of cranes and swinging mechanical arms, all working in harmony to create a sad symphony of destruction.

Still concerned about Reefer, Epyphany empathized with his reaction when she saw the trawler for herself. It was a monster in every way. The frightening red logo, three stories high, staring out through the fog and the mist, sent a chill down her spine. The ship was so big it was creating anomalies in the air pressure as the wind slid along it's massive hull. Small waterspouts were popping up intermittently all around the ship, sometimes leaving the surface and quickly growing into small tornados before they melted into the powerful wind. She hoped Reefer hadn't been scooped up by one those twisters.

Sadjah

Sadjah had taken a couple days to recover from her minor meltdown. She was back at work and almost up to speed. She was strong and she wasn't going let her power slip away without a fight. When Thurrow skipped out, she had the foresight to alert her contacts around the world to monitor their sources for any sign of the Samudra Hantu. He eventually showed up in Bali. At this stage no one had any evidence that would connect him to the Pisces disturbances. Sadjah decided to have him tailed. She knew his ship was well equipped with state-of-the-art technology on board, including surveillance equipment. The men were ordered to be discreet. The ocean team stayed far behind him while they used satellites and high altitude reconnaissance to track his movements. Sadjah received an unconfirmed report that he was headed to India, possibly Mumbai. Although Pisces had some operations in the area, this wasn't highly suspect. Sadjah knew Thurrow had friends in Bollywood. Nevertheless, she imagined how nice it would be if they could get some footage of Thurrow and his ship in close proximity to a Pisces vessel.

INTERSECTION

The powerful blasts of wind were increasing steadily and the rolling seas were starting to affect the yacht's progress. Thurrow was on high alert. "Samu, scan for any vessels in the near distance, then expand your search."

She instantly replied, "There is a very large stationary trawler about five miles off our heading. There is a much smaller vessel traveling at our speed nine miles behind us. I detect a small pod of activity in close proximity to the trawler and a very large bird flying erratically in our direction, quite possibly on a collision course."

"Do you have a visual on the bird?"

The monitor lit up with a blurry image of an impossibly large pelican struggling to stay in the air.

"MY GOD . . . IT'S REEFER! Samu, slow down and extend the lift net."

Watching the monitor, Thurrow focused all his mental energy and tried to tap into his memories of Oojai. He had known the language, now he just needed to project . . . he stared at the screen and concentrated.

"REEFER . . . THIS IS THURROW . . . IF YOU'RE IN TROUBLE . . . LAND IN THE NET"

Thurrow ran topside while Samu did her best to anticipate Reefer's trajectory.

Reefer had been trying to describe the trawler to Epyphany when a blast of air swept him up and hurled him straight toward the monstrosity of the ship. Before he could even try to compensate, another blast came from below and he found himself swirling skyward uncontrollably. The twister spit him out above the trawler when another stream of air put him into a tailspin. He gained control momentarily just in time to avoid smashing into the giant crane used to manage the oversized nets. He was totally disoriented and weakened from the thrashing. He did his best to just glide. Grabbing the next violent thermal, he ceased his struggle and let the wind take him where it would. He had no idea how far off course he was, and he had little strength to navigate.

Then Reefer saw a large streamlined yacht in the the near distance. The wind was carrying him swiftly toward the unusual craft. He heard a familiar voice in his head. Reefer instantly recognized Thurrow's image and life saving message. Using the last of his strength, he steered straight to the boat.

Samu slowed to a near stop and maintained her course. Thankfully the forgiving wind relented for a moment, then SPLASH! Reefer was in the water. Thurrow gave Samu the signal. They raised him up and set him gently on the deck. Thurrow was overjoyed, but before he could enjoy the unexpected reunion, he realized he was still getting a distress signal.

"Sorry, Reefer. No time for pleasantries. I'm getting a strong but confusing signal from the Tribe. Do you know where they are?"

Thurrow could see Reefer was barely able to think straight and told him to relax.

"Samu, full ahead to the trawler." In the excitement he had completely forgotten about the ship on their tail.

Sadjah's crew were having a few problems of their own. Due to the weather, the overhead surveillance was useless. The overcast skies and electrical storm were messing with the satellite transmission and communication was sketchy. Fearing they would lose contact, they decided to take a chance and close in on Thurrow.

Epyphany was very worried about Reefer, but she didn't have much time to act on it. The storm was getting worse and she knew her team was getting nervous. She assumed they would stick to the plan. The rough seas would certainly create a challenge, but they didn't have many options. Without Reefer to scout, she would have to depend on her intuition and psychic powers. She had already started to pick up an uneasy vibe from the crew, and on the positive side, most of the heavy machinery had ceased to operate. The nets were up. Unfortunately, the catch was well into the processing stage. Epyphany hoped Blyss was aware of their circumstances and decided to wait a while for a signal or a sign.

On board the trawler things were still pretty much business-as-usual. The captain had been watching the forecasts and thankfully moved up his timetable in anticipation. As a result, his catch was a bit less than expected, but still a very profitable trip for the Silver Finn's maiden voyage. The fishing operation was locked down and the processing was running smoothly. This storm had his virgin crew a little spooked, but so far the ship had performed admirably.

Blyss could feel the tension. She could not have anticipated the chain of events in play. She wasn't sure what effect an electrical storm would have on her projection abilities, but so far she had been able to manage the barrage of data entering her consciousness. She knew Reefer was safe for now so she could focus on the task at hand. She would have to make her move very soon but she was undecided on the actual goal. Now that the catch was complete, she needed to make some other kind of a broad stroke. Blyss wanted to cause as much financial damage as possible.

Blyss transmitted her new plan.

When Epyphany received the message, she had a short moment of doubt. She hoped Blyss wasn't overestimating her vocal abilities.

The turn of events had left the Tribe with very little to do in the way of physically affecting the productivity of the Silver Finn. The storm was wearing them down, and their energy and morale were low. When Epyphany transmitted the new plan it was like a spark. The whole tribe would be working closely together to pull off this illusion. It was easily as dangerous as their previous encounter with Pisces Corp, but it had an element of magic that appealed to all the inhabitants of Oojai. The weather would be working in their favor, enhancing the subterfuge.

With everything running smoothly and his crew out of harms way, the Captain relaxed and decided to take a break from his duties. He ceased monitoring the security cameras and turned his attention to his favorite pastime. When Blyss chose this ship, she couldn't have guessed the irony of her choice. The Captain was an expert on mermaid lore and his personal library was legendary.

The initial success of the Tribe's participation in the plan hinged almost entirely on Epyphany's enchanting vocal ability. The tribe made their way carefully to the rear of the ship where the daily catch was hoisted from the water and deposited on the loading platform. The waves had calmed down momentarily but the wind was still whipping up curtains of mist and fog. Epyphany made her way to center stage, where if one were standing on the loading platform he would see her beautiful visage bobbing sensually on the rolling sea.

With the rest of the tribe spread out behind her, Epyphany began to sing. Each member of the tribe picked a note and with their strange sonic language harmonized and amplified the effect of Epyphany's song. At first the small delicate parts of the ship began to vibrate, then cables began to hum with sympathetic tones. Soon sheet metal expanded and contracted with the rhythm, until eventually the entire ship vibrated to the music.

It wasn't long before the members of the crew started to slowly make their way to the source of the sound. With hesitant steps and sideways glances their curiosity lead them to the platform. Back in the cabins, others felt the sound before they heard it. They opened doors and searched hallways, winding their way towards the loading platform.

The Captain was still immersed in his studies on the far side of the ship, still unaware that the legends and myths of his dreams were manifesting only 200 yards away.

With most of the crew standing on the platform excited and engaged like awestruck fans at a rock concert, the tribe held their notes while Epyphany continued to mesmerize. Still singing, the tribe started to swim around, criss crossing and splashing in an effort to simulate a large school of fish. The wind began to pick up and the rough sea was beginning to affect the Silver Finn. Epyphany moved closer to the platform. Through the thin veil of fog and swirling mist she rose out of the water, flirting and taunting the young sailors. As she had hoped, one man finally got the idea to try to haul in this mermaid and her crazy choir of fish. The word spread. Caught up in the excitement, the crew fell to their tasks.

The ship was starting to rock. The waves danced and the wind howled. The eerie sound of Oojai's magic choir rose up and was carried away in the wind.

Not far away, Thurrow and Reefer heard the music. An eerie and beautiful song whispered in the wind, guiding them through the storm. Rising above the rumbling, howling storm, it filled their hearts and gave them hope. They couldn't see the trawler through the fog and high seas, but they knew they were very close.

A short distance behind the Samudra Hantu, Sadjah's men heard it too. The effect was not the same. In spite of their training, these hardened, battle-proven mercenaries felt a chill in their hearts and the unfamiliar sensation of fear.

The Captain, immersed in his studies, suddenly looked up from his book. The lights on his control panel were flashing, bells were ringing, buzzers were buzzing, and strange music filled the cabin. He experienced a sensation he had yet to notice on the Silver Finn. His ship was actually listing from side to side.

Sitting perfectly still on top of the Gold Tower, Blyss remained calm. So far there was nothing she could do but monitor the event. She dared not interfere until the others made their choices. In this case her job was to react, and so time slowed down for her as she counted the seconds and waited to make her move.

Epyphany and the Tribe pretended not to notice while the frenzied crew fought the elements trying to manage the complex machinery. In order for her plan to succeed, the timing would have to be perfect. Once the nets were under the water the crew would let them sink then try haul them in quickly in an attempt to scoop up Epyphany and the Tribe.

Machines whirred to life, chains clanked through the pulleys, nets splashed into the water, and the cranes were swinging wildly in the wind. Completely under the spell, the men were oblivious to the hazard they were creating. As soon as the nets hit the water, Irie and Zip swam away to safety. Storm, Dali, and Epyphany continued to maintain the illusion while Magnum dove down to intercept and weaken the net.

The young officer gave the signal and the nets rose quickly. The crew were so intent on their special catch they completely ignored standard procedure. All the precautions of a typical haul were forgotten as the nets came to the surface. First one crane and then another swung out beyond it's center of gravity. One of the chain winches jammed and the net twisted. Stressing the cranes further, the wind caught the twisted net and it billowed like a sail.

Everything happened so fast Epyphany was caught slightly off guard. When she saw the sailor raise his hand she gave the signal to dive. Magnum hadn't quite finished his work but it would have to suffice. He slipped through the weakened net. Storm led the way, planning to break a larger hole in the nets and add a little more tension to the already strained cables. They were all surprised when the first attempt temporarily slowed the rising net but didn't break through. Magnum swam quickly to the rescue, furiously chopping away the thick netting while Storm flipped his powerful tail to swim against the net with all his strength. Dali had managed to slip through a smaller hole, but Epyphany was nowhere in sight.

When Thurrow saw the Silver Finn he wasn't surprised by the size. He had followed the design progress of the super ships and was familiar with their unprecedented scale and capabilities. But he was shocked to see this enormous ship healing dangerously back and forth, lights flashing, and warning alarms blaring. Through the mist he could make out a scene of total chaos on the fishing platform. He and Reefer both picked up the distress vibe from the tribe. He put Samu on emergency alert and they were at the scene in seconds.

Thurrow took over as pilot as they navigated the churning sea into the disaster area. Reefer was in direct contact with the tribe and relayed the news to Thurrow. The tribe was safe but Epyphany was missing. Focusing his mind, Thurrow scanned for any sign of Epyphany. Nothing . . . then he saw her. She was unconscious and tangled in the net swinging dangerously at the end of a broken crane. In the water below lay all manner of twisted steel and cables. The trawler was still swaying and the crane looked like it could break off and tumble into the sea at any second.

The spell was broken and the crew had scattered. Many had been washed overboard and the rest had run to the safety of their cabins.

Thurrow turned to Reefer and asked, "Are you ready to fly?"

Reefer replied, "I think I know what you're thinking. I might be able to carry Epyphany a very short distance, but the weight of the net would be impossible."

"If I can manage to pull up alongside the platform and extend my lift net up and over the wreckage in her direction, I will just need you to quickly guide her down."

"What about her tangled net?"

"I have lasers mounted on board. Samu can lock in on target and simultaneously cut the net above and below. The timing has to be perfect, but it's our only chance. That crane could crash any second."

Thurrow issued his commands to Samu and carefully

steered his yacht through the labyrinth of snapped chains and broken beams. Reefer was ready for flight. The wind and rain would make an already complex task almost impossible, but there was no other choice.

Blyss understood exactly what Thurrow had in mind. She sensed the purity and the strength of his rediscovered love. She turned her attention back to the Captain. Then she waited.

All the pieces were in place. His lift net was as close as he could manage. Reefer would have to fly her down at a steep angle. Samu would track Reefer and blast the nets at the last possible moment. Thurrow need only give the signal. He looked up at Epyphany hanging helplessly, swinging in the wind, her life in his hands. Her eyes opened. Epyphany gazed directly into his eyes and smiled.

He gave the nod to Reefer. Reefer fought the wind and circled swiftly above the crane. Gaining momentum, he then dove straight towards Epyphany. Milliseconds before Reefer made contact, Samu triggered the lasers. The long tangle of net fell away into the wind as Reefer wrapped his large webbed feet around Epyphany. Though she was free of the crane, she was still enclosed in a substantial amount of netting. Instantly Reefer knew the weight was more than he could support. He was able to slow the decent but he couldn't maintain the proper trajectory.

This was one of those moments when time played it's tricks. Thurrow had been optimistic when the co-ordinated effort between Reefer and Samu, appeared to work. Then he realized in horror that they were going to miss the lift net. The scene unfolded in slow motion. He saw Reefer lose his grip. Heard Reefer cry out. Epyphany instantly dropped away, falling straight down towards the deadly shards of steel. Reefer had to glide off to the side to avoid fragments of the wind-blown netting. Then time went from slow to a complete stop. No more than ten feet from a deadly blade of stainless steel sheathing, Epyphany seemed to stop in mid-air. The ocean rose up to meet her and she was suddenly enclosed in a giant sphere of water. Another wave swelled and carried her slowly towards Samu. Epyphany floated gently onto the net as the giant droplet melted into the next wave.

Then time came racing back. The waves were still crashing and random debris was still a threat. Samu maneuvered them to safety while Thurrow winched in his net and lowered Epyphany to the deck. With the help of his research "bots" he got her on the dolly. They rolled her to the interior holding tank and slid her gently into the shallow end. She had passed out sometime during the fall; her breathing was steady but very slow.

Still sitting peacefully on the tower, her body drenched in sweat from exertion, Blyss opened her eyes. She was pleased but she wouldn't relax until they were all back in the safe harbor of Oojai.

Meanwhile the Captain, startled from his studious reverie, had been temporarily immobilized by sensory overload. The noise and the swaying ship served to disorient him briefly. He overcame inertia and ran over to the monitors. He froze in front of the screen, thinking, "I'm having a nightmare. My crew is trying to catch a giant whale, a mermaid, and her dolphin friend." Suddenly the room went black. The only sound was the creak of the straining hull fighting against the turbulent ocean. Between the pitching floor and the absolute darkness, he couldn't find his way out. Then he felt someone or something pick him up and buckle him into his chair. For the next few hours he sat powerless while his ship was assaulted by the elements.

WATER KINGDOM

Samu managed to avoid the dangerous debris and sped away from the Silver Finn, resuming her course to Mumbai. The Tribe gathered around Storm and they made their way to the closest safe harbor. Dali decided to keep tabs on Epyphany, so he did his best to keep up with Samu.

With Epyphany unconscious in the pool, Thurrow performed some tests. She had a large gash on the back of her head where she had been knocked unconscious. Strange to think that getting tangled in the net was actually a lucky break, otherwise she might have drowned. He was able to stitch her up and patch some external wounds, but he would need a large portable scanner to check her for internal injuries. He went back to the control room, where he could monitor the pool while checking on some sources in Mumbai. Thurrow found what he needed at one of Mumbai's biggest tourist attractions. The Water Kingdom was one of the world's largest water parks and aquariums. He knew some scientists there and was able to make arrangements to borrow a scanner. From his reputation and tone they knew well enough not to ask too many questions. After a brief conference with Samu he returned to check Epyphany's wounds. Thurrow was astounded to find they were already showing signs of healing.

When Sadjah's team had finally caught up to the trawler, they were just in time to video Thurrow transferring his strange catch from the lift net to his deck. Due to weather conditions, the footage was blurred and shaky but at the very least it would serve to implicate Thurrow as a key player in the destruction of Pisces property. With no time to preview the clip, they immediately uploaded the video along with an update on their situation. Within minutes they watched Thurrow speed away. They assumed he was headed for his original destination. They waited a short time, then continued their mission.

During the overnight trip the storm passed and the sea

became calm. Thurrow watched the sun rise as Samu cruised just north of Mumbai Harbor to Manori. As they motored into Manori Creek, Thurrow recalled the week he had spent there relaxing at a beach resort with Isha. He had brought her to these beautiful shores to escape the hectic Mumbai scene. Thurrow had fond memories of that short affair. Isha was an up-and-coming Bollywood actress, and though they truly enjoyed each other's company, their lives were on entirely different paths. While vacationing in Manori they spent some time at the Water Kingdom. Though he was not a fan of simulated recreation, Thurrow had to admit the wave pool was impressive. It used a new technology that came very close to simulating a true-to-life surfing experience. The Water Kingdom was also the home of several state-of-the-art aquariums. He had made a point to meet several of the staff researchers and they had stayed in touch.

Right now he was very thankful for the connections and anxious to find out if Epyphany had sustained any further injuries. As soon as they docked, Thurrow confirmed his arrangements, then checked on Epyphany one final time before he left. He had never used the portable scanner and would need to get a couple hours of instruction with the technicians. Thurrow was a little uneasy leaving her alone, but he knew he was just being paranoid.

The Manori Creek was a very popular tourist area. Boat traffic was high and large yachts were a common sight. Sadjah's team had no trouble shadowing Samu and docking nearby. During the night they had received an urgent but somewhat cryptic message directly from Sadjah. Their task was to steal Thurrow's cargo while avoiding any serious injury to him. Without specific details, they were simply instructed to procure equipment that would allow them to safely transfer a very large dolphin to a holding tank on their boat. And to deliver the cargo alive. The emphasis was placed on secrecy. No one was to take any photos and they were sworn to secrecy, with a promise of generous rewards for success and extreme consequences for betrayal.

This was a tall order even for these professionals. They set to work, calling in favors and threatening where necessary. By the time they docked, the equipment was waiting. That morning, while monitoring Thurrow's communications, they discovered where he would be and how long he would be gone. They were prepared to delay him if it came down to that.

As soon as Thurrow was in a taxi and on his way, the men headed for his yacht. They had done a great deal of research into the Samudra Hantu before they left Bali. Having hacked the database of several companies employed in her design and construction, they had gained substantial working knowledge of Samu's systems and layout.

First they scrambled video surveillance and disabled on-board alarms and communication. They were aware of the maze of motion sensors in place, but since the alarms were off, the sensors effectiveness was nullified. In the guise of a research team, they boldly moved all the special equipment directly to Samu's loading platform. The team drew plenty of curiosity but no real suspicion.

Samu instantly recognized the anomalies in her security system. She detected unscheduled activity in several areas. The security cameras and all of the alarms were malfunctioning and she'd been cut off from outside communication. It was unlike Thurrow to leave her out of the loop whenever it involved visitors or deliveries. Whomever the trespassers were, they didn't know who they were messing with. She immediately linked to a satellite feed. Government protocol demanded a minimum waiting period for security-level checks and priority standings. Thurrow was a regular customer, so his clearance wouldn't take too long. Samu had detected a degree of anxiety in Thurrow and assumed that whatever was occurring was related to the guest in the lab tank. She scanned recent audio and visual data from the lab. Samu found she was now home to an unusual aquatic mammal in the dolphin family who was injured and of utmost importance to Thurrow. He had programmed a direct link to the lab that would allow him to monitor Epyphany's condition from his mobile phone, but the intruders had somehow managed to disable that as well. Fortunately, Samu still had direct access to the lab as well as an extensive archive of onboard audio and visual data. She ran several filters at once, enabling her to piece together an adequate picture of the situation. She needed to find a way to communicate with this creature. Samu accessed the most recent audio and searched for anything unusual in the recent weeks. She found several related recordings. There was a mysterious broadcast interruption over a month ago that was similar to Thurrow's latest studio composition. Samu created a loop of these two recordings and transmitted it over the lab speakers. She needed to alert Epyphany.

Barely conscious, Epyphany felt like she was floating in one of the shallow Cavern Temple pools. The familiar soothing sound of the swhorl washed over her and diminished her pain. Then the sound faded into an alien percussive sound punctuated with syncopated rhythms from indescribable instruments. The swhorl melody played on top of the rhythm, but again, it had an unfamiliar tonal quality. It wasn't unpleasant and the total affect was joyful and heartfelt. Though it wasn't from her world, Epyphany felt a strange connection to it.

She was awake now with a disjointed memory of the Silver Finn events. Then it came to her . . . she had seen Thurrow. The rest was a blank. She had no idea how she came to be in this pool but she knew it must have something to do with Thurrow. She sensed danger and her instincts kicked in. As she turned to scan her surroundings, her vision blurred and a dull pain throbbed in her head. She became acutely aware of her injuries and knew she would have to move slowly.

Epyphany sensed the approaching men and their adversarial intentions. With little understanding of her current surroundings, Epyphany was helpless to defend herself. She decided to feign unconsciousness.

Samu didn't have enough information to make any immediate decisions. She understood that Epyphany might be in fragile health and in danger but she didn't want put her life in jeopardy. She would have to wait.

Blyss was concerned. She had lost contact with Epyphany during Thurrow's brave rescue mission. Conjuring the protective sphere of water and manipulating the powerful wave had required her focused attention. Epyphany's head injury was most likely the problem. There wasn't a single moment that Blyss could recall when she had been unable to connect with Epyphany, resulting in a rare feeling of anxiety. She was well aware of Thurrow's good intentions, but his decision to bring her to a highly populated area was questionable. Due to Thurrow's fledgling language skills, Blyss found that her ability to communicate with him was very limited at this distance. Like Samu, she must simply wait.

CLOSE CALL

Sadjah's hired guns approached the door to the lab. Strange music echoed though the short hallway and the men found it suspicious that Thurrow would have intentionally left music playing. They had performed a thermal scan on the ship before boarding, revealing only the expected dolphin in the lab. They entered cautiously. There was no sign of anyone, just a tail fin partly exposed at the end of a small tank.

As they rolled the equipment into the lab, one of the men walked over to the tank. He jumped back and exclaimed, "Whoa . . . you guys have got to see this!"

Epyphany was lying on her side with her back to the men, trying to reign in her survival instinct. Even injured she could be terrifying if provoked.

The other men rushed to the tank.

"That ain't no dolphin!"

"No wonder they said no pictures."

"Turn it over"

Epyphany realized she was outnumbered. She let herself go limp.

"Wow . . . that's one fine lookin' fish."

"Looks like she put up a fight."

"She's gotta be worth a fortune!"

"OK guys, the show is over, we've got work to do."

Realizing her exceptional value, they took special care lifting her from the tank and gently slipped her into the transport tub.

Samu was tempted to lock them in the lab but instantly saw the folly in that plan. The satellite feed had finally linked and she would be able to monitor their movements when they were in the open. While the men slowly rolled Epyphany to the platform, Samu used the feed to relay a message to

Thurrow. She hoped he had booted up his laptop.

With the scanner manual from the aquarium uploaded, Thurrow was about to shut down his Macbook when it started beeping at him.

"That's strange, I'm not expecting any Satellite info."

He opened the feed and logged in, the message alert icon popped up and with one more click he was faced with the alarming message . . .

Thurrow-return-to-ship-immediately-use-extreme-caution-you-may-be-detained-or-followed-Samu

He had only been about an hour into his instruction. Thurrow apologized, asked to borrow his friend's car, and had them pull it around the back. An assistant helped with the scanner, and after it was secure he drove slowly out of the lot. Thurrow checked his mirror constantly and resisted the urge to race back to his yacht.

Samu was monitoring the kidnappers' progress through the feed. She wasn't exactly sure how to proceed, but using GPS and real time satellite video she had locked her lasers on the team. Samu had no specific programming or instructions for this type of scenario but she had access to thousands of defense strategy simulations. Seeking more input, she retrieved the appropriate algorithms from her data base and found the odds were not in favor of a timely intervention by Thurrow. The mercenaries were almost to the boardwalk that lined the channel; soon she would loose the opportunity for a clear shot . . . still no sign of Thurrow.

Epyphany's senses were on high alert. She was ignoring the pain, waiting for that instinctual moment. As they rolled her up the dock, she could hear the water slapping against the large wooden dock supports. There was no way of knowing what lie between her and the water below. She felt the dolly level out. The men stopped briefly at the top to catch their breath. One of them spoke. "I guess we're getting a little soft."

Then she heard a brief electric buzz followed by a groan . . . a loud splash, then someone yelled, "hey!" Then another buzz and a cry of pain as another man thumped against the tank. The other men were yelling to each other as they scattered and ran for cover.

Epyphany sprang out of the tank with all her strength toward the sound of the splash . . . she was in the channel . . . above her more yelling . . . she dove . . . her head was pounding and her breathing was uneven . . . she had to surface.

Gasping for air, she found herself surrounded by boats of every shape and size. They seemed to come at her from every direction. In near panic, she dove again. She saw a tunnel and went for it. Thankfully the tunnel opened into a narrow channel. Charged with adrenaline, Epyphany dove once again.

Confused and disoriented, and still weak from her injuries, Epyphany was trying to stay focused. She had momentarily escaped her captors, but she found herself trapped in one of the worlds largest man-made wave pools. There were people on all sides. She hadn't been discovered yet but she knew it was just a matter of seconds. The waves were pounding her down as she tried to avoid being hit by the excited surfers. The sound of screaming children and heavy metal music filled the air and confused her further. Epyphany dove into a wave and tried to hide inside as it barreled down the length of the pool. Swimming just inside the wall of the wave, Epyphany could see through the thin barrier of water. At the end of the pool people were jumping out of the water screaming and pointing. Before she could figure out what was going on, she felt something touch her tail fin. The next instant she was eye-to-eye with a young surfer. He had been sliding down the tube of rolling water, slicing the glass surface of the wall with one hand when he brushed her smooth fin. His eyes widened and he pitched off his board screeching like a wounded dog. Epyphany needed air; she had to surface. Fortunately the boy's scream was lost in the cacophony and chaos still playing out at the far end. She caught a glimpse of a large dorsal fin breaking the the surface and heading straight toward her. She instantly recognized Dali and burst through the wave to meet him. The path was clear by this time, but the noise had grown intolerable. She grabbed his fin and he guided her out of the pool at top speed. People were lining the pool with their phones and video cameras. Most would only capture churning water and a streak of gray.

Epyphany was weak, and they were not out of danger yet. Sadjah's men were still on the lookout and had been drawn by the noise. In all the confusion, Dali and Epyphany managed to remain undetected as they navigated the chutes and tunnels leading to the deeper waters of the marina.

By now Thurrow was back on the ship quizzing Samu and checking satellite footage. He had underestimated Sadjah's aptitude for revenge. He never imaged she would go to such lengths to track him to the other side of the globe. It had been a mistake to leave Epyphany alone, and he would never forgive himself if this blunder resulted in her capture.

Samu interrupted his thoughts. "Thurrow, Dali is at the platform . . . with Epyphany."

Thurrow grabbed a cargo dolly and raced to the platform. As soon as Epyphany was safe inside the laboratory pool, Thurrow yelled, "Samu let's get out of here! Activate stealth mode!"

"If only I had thought to activate stealth earlier . . . "

The ship sped silently out of the marina and into the bay. Dali followed, swimming away from the dock as fast as he could. Neither stopped until the bright lights of Mumbai were far behind.

THE REWARD

It was the evening of the Silver Finn event, which the crew referred to as "the vision." Sadjah had just shut down her computer. It was late, she was exhausted, and she had a little rum buzz. She jumped when her phone rang. It was the Bali team. At the time she just couldn't believe what she was hearing. She gave them instructions, hung up, then went to the kitchen to make some coffee. Sadjah knew it was going to be a long night.

Several weeks earlier, after receiving news that Thurrow was in Bali, Sadjah had recruited the best surveillance team available, they were embedded on the island within twenty-four hours. The men were instructed to only contact her when they needed an executive decision. They were to follow Thurrow and upload any information, photos, or video to a dedicated server. One of her top-level techies was managing Sadjah's own little Thurrow "cloud."

Sadjah had fallen into the habit of ending her day by sitting alone in her apartment, scanning the daily reports and media while sipping a glass of Thurrow's favorite rum, Cruzan. This daily ritual proved to be a powerful antidote to the pressures of her grueling schedule. Sadjah couldn't deny this strange and admittedly unhealthy obsession had become a form of perverse entertainment as well. She thought, "I have become a high-tech stalker."

Day two, following the Silver Finn incident did not start well for Sadjah.

As a rule, the only screen Sadjah checked before she was in her office was her phone. She would ease into her day by checking the very short list of people with access to her personal number or email. It was the mental analog to an athlete doing a few stretches before the race. She made a conscious choice not to open any news links or listen to any reports until she was officially on the job.

So when she sat down at her desk, still weary from the past two days of managing the trawler fiasco, the first thing she saw was a list of headlines accompanied by blurry images and speculative illustrations.

"It's True! Mermaid invades Water Kingdom!"

"The Mermaid! Believe it! She's the Real Deal!"

"Is it a Hoax? Mermaid Sighting in Famous Water Park!"

At least there was nothing in the news that connected the mermaid sighting with Pisces Corp. So far she had been able to suppress any information about the Silver Finn disaster. The trawler's crew had been sequestered temporarily and the ship had been towed further out to sea. They would repair the Silver Finn far from the curious press.

A week after "the vision" and "the sighting," Sadjah was still mired in a swamp of corporate accusations, incriminations, and firings, as well as increasing pressure to come up with a plan. She had yet to decide what to do with the incriminating video of Thurrow, but at least now she had a bargaining chip. The whole affair was beyond belief and Sadjah was having difficulty processing the mysterious facts of the event.

Her team had arrived at the scene only minutes behind the Samudra Hantu. Observing the extensive damage, they reasoned the ship must have sustained the destruction before Thurrow turned up and there had been no evidence to indicate he was part of any plan. The seas had been brutal but the Silver Finn was designed for much worse. None of her experts could explain the unusual nature of the devastation. The testimony of the surviving crew made no sense whatsoever and although some very strange video footage was salvaged, none of the men, including the Captain, had any clear memory of the events.

The trawler's security cameras had recorded less than a minute of the event before the entire system shutdown. The crashing waves and the swirling mist and fog made it hard to make out any detail. There was no audio, but the video showed the ghostly image of an extremely large and strangely beautiful woman who appeared to be rising out of the waves, singing in front of a dozen or more mesmerized crew members as they stood transfixed on the loading platform. Behind her was an equally unsettling view of a variety of unlikely fish leaping randomly in and out of the waves. This included a glimpse of a monstrous blue whale. If she had't known better Sadjah would have thought she was watching a surreal scene from a low budget sci-fi movie.

The most alarming information was the possibility of the existence of an actual mermaid. Sadjah was still skeptical in spite of her team's first hand knowledge. Her squad of kidnappers had all been individually debriefed. Sadjah had hired sketch artists to work with each member of the team; their stories and descriptions all matched.

The events at the Water Kingdom were equally unclear. Her people had interviewed dozens of witnesses and compiled several hours of video clips, none of which had captured a clear shot of the escape. A young surfer, still somewhat traumatized from the experience, gave a matching description but still she had no factual evidence.

She knew Thurrow had spent a lot of time at sea, alone for weeks, sometimes months at a time. If he had made such a discovery or had been instrumental in some bizarre biological experiment, he had given no hint to her or anyone in his circle. That kind of information would be nearly impossible to keep to one's self. Even for a man like Thurrow.

According to the recent reports, all contact with the Samudra Hantu had since been lost. Thurrow had completely disappeared along with his precious cargo. Sadjah's frustration was close to debilitating, until she could locate Thurrow, the Silver Finn video would be useless. Her life had gone terribly wrong since they had parted and she still missed him incredibly. Sadjah's ultimate goal was to get him back but she was too self involved to realize her own distorted values were to blame. In her mind, the only solution was to bend him to her will. Until she recognized otherwise, she was playing a losing game.

The image of the mermaid haunted her dreams. Some mornings she would awaken still trembling or sometimes crying. In her recurring nightmares she would see Thurrow locked in a lovers embrace with this strange creature, swimming and laughing with talking fish, surrounded by an island paradise, or battling a sea monster with the visage of her own likeness. These restless nights were having a negative impact on Sadjah's productivity and credibility at Pisces. She would have to do something.

With no clear solution, Sadjah decided at the very least she should appear to be pro-active. The board was losing patience. She got her marketing people together and proposed a campaign. She wanted to offer a very large anonymous reward for any information leading to the capture of "The Mermaid." Sadjah knew it would attract the loonies, but she wanted to put pressure on Thurrow. She figured if she could find the mermaid, she would find Thurrow.

Using a composite sketch from the multiple descriptions and a great deal of artistic license, the media department put together an engaging and controversial video. They created a photo-real 3D character that was then animated and composited in a short clip. The video was edited in such a way as to give the impression of actual realtime footage. Fueled by the media attention of the Water Kingdom sightings, Sadjah's video went viral within hours. The ports and islands around the world became hunting grounds for tourists and professionals alike. She had to hire more than a dozen people just to screen the responses and filter through the comments and replies. Rumors slowly leaked that it was Pisces Corp who had offered the reward. As it turned out, this did nothing to harm their reputation and was worth millions in free advertising.

The board was singing her praises. For the first time in many weeks, Sadjah could breathe easy.

HEALING

When Thurrow felt confident they we're out of danger, he told Samu to switch to cruise mode and to keep the stealth program engaged. His yacht was one of the first private ships to incorporate the latest stealth technology. The entire hull was covered with a layer of small metamaterial tiles. Among the remarkable properties of these tiles was the ability to capture or refract light or sound and funnel it around an object, rendering his ship invisible to satellite surveillance, advanced radar and sonar. Thurrow never imagined this wise investment would be used to escape the cold hearted scheme of an ex-lover.

While Epyphany was recovering, Thurrow used the time to process the recent events. He revisited his lost days on Oojai. In retrospect he found it difficult to reconcile his decision to abandon and forget such a spiritual and life altering experience. His heart ached when he thought back to the moment he had turned his back on Epyphany and walked away from the intense bond they had formed. Thurrow was ashamed of the flaw that led him to choose Sadjah's world over the magical world of Oojai. Then he had a minor revelation, ultimately he had made the right choice. Blyss had been right, he and Epyphany were deeply infatuated with no understanding of what a successful union would take. He had chosen to step away from that world, allowing them both time to taste reality, to drink deep from the well of truth, to swallow the harsh medicine of rational thought, and eventually make a decision with a foundation of knowledge and perspective.

In the recent months Thurrow had gained a deeper understanding of his true nature. The rewarding time in Bali opened his eyes to the joy of living creatively, supplying valuable insight into the kind of life he wanted to live. The time apart also allowed Epyphany to gain first hand knowledge about the true nature of the world outside of Oojai. He felt they were ready to face the world together. Blyss and her beautiful music had opened the floodgate, and his desire for Epyphany and the purity of her world proved strong enough to overcome the powerful mind cloud. He had never stopped loving Epyphany.

During the trip back to Oojai, Thurrow and Epyphany spent much of their time getting reacquainted. For several days it was just the two of them and Samu. As Epyphany became stronger her curiosity grew. She would have never imagined the existence of the Samudra Hantu's mind-blowing technology and all her dazzling state-of-the-art equipment. Thurrow was astounded by Epyphany's ability to comprehend. With her unquenchable thirst for knowledge Epyphany kept Thurrow busy with constant questioning. In order to get some work done, he setup a direct link and let Samu field Epyphany's steady stream of questions. Thurrow was equally impressed by Epyphany's power of rejuvenation. Within a few days she was feeling strong enough to spend some time in the ocean. Each day Samu would slow down and Thurrow would lower her into the ocean. It was't long until she was swimming alongside the boat for hours, at full cruising speed. Thurrow insisted she come aboard at night; Epyphany agreed without argument. They both knew it was more about the intimacy of the pool than for medical reasons.

About a week into the journey back to Oojai, the rest of the tribe caught up with them. Samu stopped, allowing Thurrow and Epyphany some time for swimming, relaxing, and catching up with their friends. A short time into their exchange, their casual conference was interrupted when Samu paged Thurrow. "Please come aboard, there is some important information you need to see."

Samu played Sadjah's mermaid video. Thurrow wasn't happy with the news. As much as he admired the technology used to create the video, he was always saddened when people used it for evil. This video was good enough to convince the average person that they were seeing live footage of a real mermaid. Though it didn't look exactly like Epyphany, it was close enough.

Thurrow went back to the platform and summoned the Tribe. He described the situation and shared his thoughts, explaining how every lunatic, tourist, fisherman, and bounty hunter would be on the lookout for Epyphany. He stressed the importance of a hasty return to Oojai. Thurrow was sad to say he would only continue on with them for a couple more days to allow Epyphany to fully recover. He assumed his stealth technology was working but he didn't want to take a chance of leading Sadjah straight to Oojai. He would have to stay away for awhile until he could be sure that Samu was truly undetectable.

This news was a blow to Epyphany. Blyss had warned her that being with Thurrow would not be easy, but she underestimated the lengths to which humans would go for personal gain. Epyphany was disheartened to end their reunion so soon, but she knew Thurrow had her best interests in mind.

When Thurrow escaped from Mumbai with the wounded Epyphany, he had no idea where he was heading. Once they were in the open sea and out of danger he had a long talk with Epyphany. It didn't take them long to reconnect. Thurrow reassured her that, though the mind cloud had been successful, throughout the separation he was continually plagued by a troubling sense of loss. Now he could understand why the very day he reached home port, he experienced a strong desire beckoning him back to sea.

During their extended conversation it became clear to Epyphany that Thurrow never knew the location of Oojai. When Epyphany discovered him, his ship was off course and Blyss had made sure both he and Samu had no record of their route.

The first few days of their return trip, Epyphany, still feeling the effects of her head wounds, was unable to communicate with Blyss. She alone, would have to make the decision whether or not to share the sacred coordinates of Oojai. She decided to wait for her wounds to heal in the hope that Blyss would shoulder that decision. It wasn't that she didn't trust Thurrow; Epyphany was concerned about his safety. She was beginning to understand the enemy and she felt they would stop at nothing in order to locate her and her home. There was no doubt that some humans would kill for that information. The abrupt change in plans saved Epyphany from her decision.

Over the next few days Thurrow spent as much time as possible with Epyphany. He hated the the idea of leaving her again, but he just couldn't take any chances with the secrets of Oojai. When it came time for goodbyes, there were no more words. Dali, Storm, and the others waited at a polite distance. Thurrow held Epyphany. They looked intently into each other's eyes and made a silent promise. Thurrow kissed Epyphany for the first time since their last day on Oojai, seconds turned to minutes as they felt the electricity surge between them. They pulled apart reluctantly and once again they parted. But this time they had worked out a method of communication.

Samu recorded the exact co-ordinates where the two were parting ways. According to Epyphany, Oojai was only a three day swim from that location. When Epyphany got back to Oojai she would have Blyss feed their bearings into the Gold Tower's mystical data bank. They would monitor that location at regular intervals until they figured out a better solution. At the very least Thurrow could navigate near those co-ordinates if he needed to get a message to her. From this distance they were confident that Thurrow could send and receive simplistic thought bundles.

Epyphany couldn't know that Sadjah's relentless search for Thurrow wasn't just about money. Ever since Sadjah had read the reports and seen the original mermaid footage, something had changed in her. As she continued to watch the Pisces reward video, she came to see Epyphany as a real threat to her personal happiness. This creature was coming between her and Thurrow. She had to finally admit to herself that she was jealous. There was also a larger underlying fear she couldn't quite explain. Sadjah thought perhaps it was simply the fear of the unknown . . . where had this mermaid come from? . . . what does her existence mean? . . . is she an intelligent being? . . how is it, of all people, Thurrow makes such a myth-shattering discovery?

POSITIVITY

Thurrow watched Epyphany and the Tribe until they disappeared from view, then continued to stare out over the horizon. He was a man accustomed to being alone. In fact, he normally relished the company of his solitary thoughts. Thurrow enjoyed an active, inquisitive imagination, and so much of the chatter of society seemed more distraction then enrichment. But now he remembered how on Oojai that wasn't the case. It was a place where no time was wasted on artifice, where every creature lived in a world of heightened awareness. In every waking moment there was something to engage the senses or the mind and usually both. It was a sensuous lifestyle where every variation in the environment had a personal impact. There was no need to anesthetize or alter your brain; with such an abundance of beauty and activity to entertain and delight 24/7, there was nothing to escape from. The number one source of human stress and unhappiness was irrelevant. On Oojai no time was wasted thinking about money.

For the first time in a very long time, Thurrow felt lonely. The sudden reconnection and subsequent departure of Epyphany and the rest of the Tribe left a void in his life. At this moment his heart's desire was to order Samu to turn around and follow them back to Oojai.

Thurrow retreated to his music studio. He booted up the system and loaded his latest work in progress. He had named it "Oojai Sunrise." Listening to the rough mix gave him solace. For the next few hours he lost himself in the world of sound and the pictures it conjured in his mind.

Creating music had a healing affect on Thurrow. It brought him closer to the universal spirit. It was a pure language—a language of vibrations, a language that bridged the gap between cultures and races, genders, and even species. He didn't know of a single society that didn't attempt to communicate their joy or sorrow through music. With music as the common language of humankind, he could never comprehend why people couldn't get along. Thurrow had entertained an idealistic fantasy since he was a young man. He imagined a world where suddenly every gun and deadly weapon on the planet was magically replaced with a musical instrument. Where battles would turn into jam sessions. Where marching soldiers would become marching bands. It was an amusing and beautiful mind movie. Even now, it made him smile to think about it. This train of thought put Thurrow in an optimistic mood. Maybe he should try to reach out to his ex-lover. Thurrow thought, perhaps part of his role was to bridge the gap between Oojai and Sadjah's world. Caught up in the momentum of positivity he decided to contact Sadjah.

In addition to the stealth technology that allowed the Samudra Hantu to elude radar, the ship also had the ability to send multi-layered encrypted voice, text, or email messages anonymously. After several hours of consideration, Thurrow came up with a plan. He choose to trust his instincts though he knew, given Sadjah's history, that the odds were not in his favor. He didn't know if he could pull it off, but at the very least he would find out if his encryption program was effective. Thurrow composed a short message and hit "send."

As expected, the mermaid video was creating a lot of response but nothing of substance. Sadjah was temporarily relieved. She really wasn't sure what she would do if she found the mermaid. She wasn't naive; Sadjah fully understood the pressure she would be under from the religious and scientific communities, the government, and the Pisces shareholders.

If a capture was successful and the news leaked, it would be a circus. In spite of her longing for Thurrow and her curiosity about his mermaid, Sadjah would be happier for the time being if the whole issue just faded away. She knew the press and the public had a very short attention span. It wouldn't be long until they moved on, then maybe she could move on as well.

Sadjah was able to extricate herself from an early evening business dinner and arrived home in a pretty good mood. For the last couple of days she had kicked the habit of reviewing the Thurrow reports. There hadn't been any signs of foul play with the fleet since the Silver Finn incident, and she was thankful for the respite. She treated herself to a little after dinner drink and was just settling down with a good book. She knew her friends would laugh if they saw what she was reading. For the third time in ten years, she was making her way through the classic Harry Potter Series. Sadjah wasn't ashamed, but she certainly wouldn't advertise her choice of reading material. She didn't believe in magic, but it was a great antidote for the poisonous world of high finance.

Light electro-latin jazz played softly in the background while Sadjah curled up comfortably on her couch with the sweet raspberry taste of Chambord lingering on her tongue. She was pleasantly anticipating a new episode of adventures at Hogwart's School of Witchcraft when she heard her phone vibrate on the kitchen counter. She had turned off the ringer so she wouldn't be tempted to answer. She decided to check it later. About two pages in, Sadjah found her mind wandering. She laughed at herself as she slowly rose from her cozy couch and said out loud, "Oh well, I yam what I yam."

While she was up, Sadjah freshened her drink, grabbed the phone and returned to the couch. With the drink in one hand she tapped the phone with her thumb. The name and number flashed across the scene and she spilled the drink all over the couch. She hesitated a moment before opening the message. Her peace evaporated, her pulse raced, and an anxious tear ran down her cheek.

She read the short message. "We need to meet. Reply to this number for details but don't waste your time trying to trace it. And please keep this correspondence between us."

Once again Thurrow had managed to blindside Sadjah. She was conflicted. She knew she couldn't ignore the message, there was too much at stake, but she just wanted the whole affair to go away. She longed for the simple days when she could just use a man and enjoy her privileged lifestyle unfettered by emotion and drama. However the recent weeks without Thurrow had been hell. Maybe he was right. Maybe she had it backwards . . . maybe they could work together for change. She thought, "Here I am again with the same old dilemma."

Taking him on his word Sadjah responded truthfully, "Between you and me, what is your plan?"

He instructed Sadjah to find an excuse to disappear for a week or more, as soon as possible, and take a circuitous route to the Maldives. She was to share her plans with no more than one trusted friend, to travel light and to keep a low profile. He would book a room for her and give her further details on arrival.

RENDEZVOUS

At first Sadjah was unsure how to proceed. She trusted Thurrow meant her no harm. After the stress of the last few weeks, the idea of getting away from Pisces sounded very attractive. She didn't know if this was yet another chance to get it right with Thurrow or whether she was just being a fool. At the very least her curiosity about "the vision" and "the sighting" would most likely be satisfied.

There had been a few other occasions in her past when Sadjah had needed to disappear, so she knew what to do. With a little research and a few calls, the plan was set in motion. At Pisces there was no one she needed to report to directly, she need only have her faithful assistant clear the calendar and cover her tracks. There was only one other person Sadjah trusted as much as she trusted Thurrow.

Sadjah hadn't seen or her heard from her father for quite some time. She thought, "What mischief have you been up to, Bill?" She smiled thinking how she used to call him "Mr. Bill" when she was a small girl. These days the press referred to him as "Wild Bill." He had given them plenty of reasons for the nickname. In spite of their disparate business philosophies and their separate social circles, Sadjah loved her father and wanted him to know she was safe. She also knew he would honor her privacy and respect her decisions. He was a hard man to please, but he had never let her down. There would be no need to tell him the facts, so she left him a text saying only that she would be unavailable for a short time.

Sadjah set off for the Maldives. She was actually excited to leave everything behind for a while. She tried to clear her mind and heart of any expectations, though she was unsuccessful in caging the growling anticipation of Thurrow's touch.

A couple days and several private jet transfers later, Sadjah had successfully hopscotched her way across the globe. She booked alternate routes, canceled and improvised her schedule on the fly. She had used false passports and was well disguised. When she landed in the Maldives, she was exhilarated by the charade.

On the last leg of the trip, she notified Thurrow and he promptly returned the information as planned. He told her to await further instructions and to be prepared to leave in a moment's notice. It was dusk when she landed, and on the short taxi ride to her hotel she received a new message. There would be another taxi waiting in the parking lot of the hotel. She was to wait for the first taxi to leave, then take the second taxi to this new location. He gave the address of a small private marina, where there would be a water plane waiting. The pilot would give her the last instructions when they landed. The fun was starting to wear off for Sadjah. She respected his need for secrecy, but she was starting to question her decision as well as Thurrow's mental stability.

She set her fears aside and followed his instructions. After a very short flight, the small plane landed in a quiet bay. In the faint silver light from the waning crescent moon and the distant stars, Sadjah could barely make out the silhouette of the deserted shoreline. The plane taxied up to a long narrow dock, and Sadjah apprehensively stepped down to the pontoon and climbed the ramp. The pilot's only instructions were, "Wait here." Standing alone in the hazy moonlight at the end of a rickety pier, on a tiny isolated island somewhere in the Indian Ocean, Sadjah watched her plane fly away into the darkness.

The next twenty minutes were the longest twenty minutes of her life. Sadjah couldn't remember a time when she felt so vulnerable and so alone. From somewhere below the dock came the sound of waves sloshing and water bubbling. Then suddenly she was trapped in an intense beam of white light. Disoriented, Sadjah gasped and nearly fell off the dock. The blinding glare seemed to be suspended from some sort of pole rising out of the water. As the light rose higher, Sadjah could now see it was attached to a small yellow submarine. The sub popped out of the water, then came to a gurgling halt at the end of the pier.

Sadjah was frozen with fear, then she heard the sweetest sound she had heard in months.

"Been waiting long?"

Sadjah couldn't find her voice.

"I apologize for all the cloak and dagger stuff, but I know you have been hiring some pretty sketchy characters recently."

Sadjah finally caught her breath. "You're right, I suppose my motives and methods have been questionable, but I'm here now and I promise I did my best to shake any possible tails."

"Did you tell anyone where you were going?"

"I just told my dad that I'd be gone for a short time and not to worry."

Thurrow frowned but said nothing. He had never been on good terms with Wild Bill and he didn't trust him. There was no use trying convince Sadjah that her father was not the "misunderstood saint" she thought he was. He decided it was a topic for another day.

"Well, climb aboard. It's small but it's comfy. One more short ride and you can get some rest. We can talk tomorrow."

Sadjah thought she would be claustrophobic underwater in such a tiny space, but when she settled into the passenger seat it felt like it was personally designed to fit her body. She relaxed instantly and let out an audible sigh.

"Comfortable?"

Sadjah felt like she was at a spa. "Is it my imagination or is this seat giving me a massage?"

"Sort of. These are prototypes of my new mood-sensor chair for long distance traveling. I call it the 'Envelope.'"

"Good name."

With a quiet hum, the tiny sub slid beneath the waves. Sadjah closed her eyes and within minutes dozed off. Her first peaceful dream in months was soon interrupted.

Thurrow spoke gently. "We're here."

Thurrow guided his sub into it's cradle and they rose smoothly into the belly of Samu. He helped Sadjah out and they went to the kitchen. They ate a light snack in silence, then Thurrow showed Sadjah to her room.

ANOTHER REUNION

Sadjah slept for 12 hours. All that jetting around the globe had taken it's toll. She finally opened her eyes but was lulled briefly back to sleep by the gentle rocking of the ship. Eventually it was hunger that pulled her back to reality. The smell of something divine found its way to her cabin. Sadjah rose slowly, did a few gentle stretches, then breathing deep, she filled her lungs with the clean ocean air and meandered up the stairs to the main deck. Leaning against the smooth teak railing while the warm breeze tickled her neck, she smiled at the wondrous and vast ocean vista. A perfect blend of deep blue skies, puffy white clouds, and the sparkling emerald sea. Sadjah hadn't felt this rested and peaceful in months. She thought, "This is Thurrow's life. I want to be part of this. Why do I keep pushing this incredible man away?"

"Lost at sea?"

Sadjah jumped. Consumed by her thoughts, she hadn't heard or seen Thurrow setting the breakfast table.

"Didn't mean to startle you . . . hungry?"

She turned and saw Thurrow smiling as he poured a couple of mimosas. She felt like she was truly seeing him for the first time. He was so intensely himself when he was on his ship—composed and confident, washed in an aura of calm and purpose. In this moment, she would gladly cash out, throw away her titles and power, and just sail the world with him.

"Hey . . . are you ok?"

"What? . . .Yes . . . I'm . . . I'm wonder . . fantas . . . sorry, yes I'm fine. All this pure oxygen must have gone to my brain and . . . I'm weak with hunger. Wow! What a spread!"

The table was a masterpiece of color and tantalizing aroma. In the center was an elegant fruit bowl made of blown glass so pure and clear, the assortment of exotic papaya and mangoes seemed to be floating in midair, on either side of the bowl there were steaming silver platters piled high with hot banana pancakes, apple and cheese stratas, Canadian bacon, and scrambled eggs. A tiny vase of delicate flowers was set off to the side of a unique handmade ceramic plate flanked by intricately etched silver cutlery. Sadjah sat down feeling like she was still dreaming. As she sipped her mimosa, she could smell the intoxicating flowers and the fresh Kona coffee brewing.

"You certainly know how to treat a girl."

"Just wanted to show my appreciation for your efforts to join me."

"I didn't know how much I needed this. I hope we can avoid any serious conversation for a little while. I'd like to get to know Captain Thurrow."

"OK, let's try a couple freestyle days. No schedules, no agenda, no pressure. I've got several projects I'm working on, so you can relax and do as you please. My door will be open and my time is yours at your bidding. When you want some company or conversation let me know. All I ask is truth. Deal?"

"Deal."

Thurrow and Sadjah enjoyed their breakfast. Sprinkled with light conversation, some comfortable silence, and occasional laughter, it felt like a fresh start to what could be a true friendship.

Sadjah drifted through her first day back on the Samudra Hantu with a pleasant sense of timelessness. She ate when she was hungry, slept when she was tired, read some more Harry Potter with only a sideways glance from Thurrow, swam in the pool, and exercised in Samu's amazing high-tech gym. At one point she dropped into Thurrow's studio briefly and they made plans for a sunset dinner. Sadjah informed Thurrow that she would work with Samu preparing the menu and meal.

The sun started sinking toward the horizon and the sky filled with gold and green rays of light. The air was still, but for a tiny vibration, like a low voltage current connecting everything to everything. The vast sky, the restful sea and the endless horizon all sewn together by this invisible thread, this electric spirit—Sadjah had never seen or felt anything like it.

Sadjah found herself thinking back to some of the past dinner dates on board. She tried to keep her mind from going down that road but her body seemed to be in the driver's seat. She couldn't remember the last time she had experienced such a perfectly balanced day. No drama, no recriminations, no phones, no news—just being present in each fragment of the day. It was so refreshing. And now she was starting to tingle. She loved the tingle, the tiny ripple of anticipation. Sadjah clung to the fleeting sensation knowing from past experience that it would be interrupted and extinguished or grow into something more. With Thurrow around it usually transformed from a tingle to a throb.

Thurrow

It had been twenty-four hours since Sadjah arrived and Thurrow felt that things had gone quite well so far. After he set his plan in motion, Thurrow had experienced a small case of second thoughts. He knew there were some tough decisions ahead and he suspected the dinner date would be the beginning of the big questions; hers and his. His first hurdle was coming to terms with the undeniable and equally strong attraction to both Sadjah and Epyphany. When he saw Sadjah standing alone on that desolate pier, obviously frightened and powerless, he felt he was seeing the real Sadjah for the first time. He saw the young girl trying to prove herself to a powerful distant father and the rigid young successful woman who would never show her softness. And in that moment, he understood she was just another lonely creature trying to survive in a complicated world. There was so much goodness in Sadjah, if only she could shake off the restrictions and expectations she had placed on her life.

It would be difficult for Thurrow to reconcile the differences between Epyphany and Sadjah. He had no doubts concerning his love for Epyphany, but he had thus far avoided thinking about how they would manage a future together. Right now Sadjah was on his ship, and even knowing the lengths she had gone to track him down, his desire for her had never flagged. Conflicted, Thurrow still hoped there was some way to bridge the gap between the natural, spiritual worlds of Oojai and Bali, and his and Sadjah's world of technology and commerce.

Thurrow set these heavy thoughts aside and focused on the moment at hand. It would take a serious leap of faith, but he needed to share his secrets with another human being. If his plan worked, he and the inhabitants of Oojai could have a powerful and effective ally in Sadjah.

Sadjah

Once the menu was decided, Sadjah left most of the preparation to Samu's capable technology. She had a few hours left before sunset, so she poured herself a glass of wine and climbed the stairs to the observation deck. Sadjah needed to figure out what could be gained from this rendezvous. There were so many questions. A lot had changed since she had last seen Thurrow. The Silver Finn incident and the questionable existence of a real mermaid would certainly make for some very interesting dinner conversation. Thurrow had asked for the truth, so she assumed he was ready to answer all her questions in like fashion. Sadjah realized that the mermaid question was at the top of her list. The concept of a new species was mind-blowing, but she found Thurrow's personal involvement even more important to her. Sadjah forced herself to abandon conjecture. She went back to the simple problem of "what to wear?"

Seeing Thurrow in his natural element and enjoying this short respite from the rat race that was her life, had provided Sadjah with some unexpected insight. Though her desire for Thurrow was still strong, she had lost all interest in manipulating him or using him for her own personal gain. It had become exceedingly clear that his choices, both moral and economic, served him far better than any alternative she could offer.

She would not dress to seduce him. In fact, she decided to keep it completely casual. A light summer dress and sandals, minimal makeup, and no jewelry. Perhaps she could get used to a life of unfettered simplicity.

THE TRUTH

As Thurrow climbed the stairs leading to the upper deck, he heard the sound of steel drums drifting in the warm evening breeze. He smiled and thought "I do enjoy Sadjah's taste in music." When they first met, she entertained him with a surprisingly diverse and extensive collection, and he had been impressed with her knowledge of the singers, songwriters, and the musicians.

He hesitated briefly at the top of the stairs, enchanted by the scene in front of him. Sadjah stood at the rail once again, staring up at the sky with both hands on the rail, backlit by the setting sun, Sadjah's body was a slender sensuous silhouette framed in fiery gold, her thin summer dress glowed as it fluttered gently in the breeze, slowly wrapping itself around her long firm legs and clinging to her narrow waist. Thurrow had hoped that his growing love for Epyphany would provide him a certain immunity to Sadjah's irresistible sensuality. His conflict heightened.

Without turning, Sadjah spoke.

"It's so incredibly beautiful out here. I can see why you get so restless in the city. I think I could get used to this." She sighed. "You may have to force me to leave."

As she turned to face him Thurrow asked, "How long have you known I was standing here?"

Thurrow joined her as she walked over to the food transporter to retrieve their dinner.

"I felt your presence as you climbed the stairs."

They carried the food to the table in silence. Thurrow pulled the bottle of champagne from the ice bucket while Sadjah removed the dishes from the warmers. Before they sat down, he filled the glasses and proposed a toast. Looking straight into her eyes Thurrow said, "Truth and beauty." Sadjah responded, "The beautiful truth."

Their fingers touched briefly as they tapped glasses; the

crystal flutes made a single pure note that hung in the air around them, then slowly faded into the sound of the sea, signaling yet another round of discussions.

In the short silence that followed the toast, Thurrow sensed an uncharacteristic gentleness in Sadjah's bearing. She seemed at peace. He observed her lack of accessories and makeup, this simplicity of style served to accentuate Sadjah's natural beauty.

As they took their seats Thurrow commented, "You seem changed, radiant . . . I take it things have been going well?"

"Quite the contrary. My life has basically been hell since you left."

Thurrow leaned back, surprised at the blunt honesty of her response.

Sadjah continued. "I am changed. You may not believe this, but the change you see and the change that I feel only began the day I got your message. The farther I have traveled from Pisces, the better I have felt. It's as though with each mile traveled I shed a pound from the tons of baggage I've been carrying since I started working there. Then, the moment I settled into your comfy little yellow sub, a small seed of contentment started to grow inside of me.

"I see change in you as well and I feel you are part of something that I need. At first I thought it was just the undeniable physical attraction we share. But it is more than that. By now I'm sure you're aware of the lengths to which I've gone just to keep my eye on you. I'm not proud of it, but I guess in some strange way it succeeded in bringing us here, to this moment . . . our dinner is getting cold . . . should I continue?"

Thurrow leaned closer as she spoke. "We can eat and talk. Go on."

"There are so many questions I need to ask, but this past day on your ship observing you, your quiet strength and boundless energy, has answered the most important one for me. I ask you now to confirm what I feel must be true. Are you in love with that mysterious and miraculous creature?"

Thurrow almost choked on his salad. He sat up straight, took a drink of water, set the glass down slowly, then looking directly at Sadjah he began his story.

The hours passed as Thurrow related his complex tale. They nibbled at their meal. Sadjah would ask the occasional question, but mostly Thurrow spoke and Sadjah listened. They got up and walked around the ship, and visited the studio to listen to "Oojai Sunrise." All the while Thurrow did his best to convey, not only the facts, but also the spirit of his connection to Oojai, the Tribe, and most importantly, Epyphany. Attempting to convey his excitement and uncertainty about his future with Epyphany, he tried to be as honest as possible while remaining mindful of Sadjah's feelings toward him. Listening to himself, Thurrow wondered how all this must sound. He had experienced these events in fragments, with time to process, and still there were moments when he couldn't believe it. His respect for Sadjah grew as she remained calm and curious, accepting his strange story as the truth.

The sun had long set and the moon was high. They stood on the bow, shoulder to shoulder, watching the whitecaps sparkle in the moonlight. Thurrow had finally run out of words and Sadjah had run out of questions.

Sadjah had never felt closer to anyone than she did at that moment. If she had doubts about her love for Thurrow before, she had absolutely no doubts now. But it was a different kind of love. It was the kind of love that asked for nothing in return.

They walked in silence, heading below deck where they decided to have a nightcap and listen to some quiet music. Sadjah settled on the couch while Thurrow retrieved two glasses and what had become a mutual favorite—aged Cruzan rum.

Sadjah took a sip and tilted her glass toward Thurrow. "So

much has happened since I trapped you with this drink at the fundraiser."

Thurrow remained standing. Let us toast . . . "To the Cruzan."

Sadjah put her drink down, rose, took a sip from Thurrow's drink, set that down, then took his hand in hers and said. "Wanna dance?" . . .

Sadjah opened her eyes and immediately had a small panic attack, it took her a few seconds to remember where she was and how she got there. Even then she thought she might still be dreaming. The moonlight was streaming through the porthole, filling the room with a silver haze. She heard the waves slapping against the hull and felt a slight vibration. Samu was cruising swiftly through the night fog. Sadjah wondered where they were heading.

She turned her head slowly, scanning the room until her eyes rested on Thurrow. He was sitting naked at a small desk not far from the foot of the bed, his face washed in the blue light of his laptop. Their eyes met. He smiled and said, "Would you like to meet Epyphany?"

Sadjah sat up, looking like a ghostly angel, her smooth white skin shimmering in the moonlight. She paused, then pointing at the computer, smiled back and asked, "Is that thing permanently attached?" Without waiting for an answer she slid beneath the sheet, gazed into the moonlight for a moment then answered . . . "Yes."

THE MESSAGE

After parting ways with Thurrow, Epyphany and the tribe made good time on their return trip to Oojai. The welcome sight of Tigress Baku poking up through the clouds washed away all the stress from their recent adventures. As they swam into the peaceful bay, they found Blyss, Yew, and Cheeks waiting for them at the Chancel. It was so good to be home.

Over the next several days they met casually in the Cavern Temple and related their experiences to Blyss. There was no talk of future plans. Blyss knew they would need some time to recover, and she had yet to formulate the next move. The adventure had been extremely draining on her as well.

Epyphany did her best to put Thurrow out of her thoughts. She tried to keep a positive outlook concerning their future. The experience with the Silver Finn and the kidnappers had made it undeniably clear that she and Thurrow could never find peace together in the present state of the world beyond Oojai. She found it difficult to imagine a time when their differences would be accepted. Humans were still fighting each other over something so trivial as skin color; how would they ever approve of interspecies relationships?

With the recent past thoroughly discussed and the immediate future still in question, Epyphany committed herself to enjoying the moments of her days. She spent many peaceful hours resting and meditating at the Chancel. Neither happy nor sad, she dedicated herself to mindfulness. The many wonders of Oojai became magnified. Her awareness was such that she became enthralled with the minutiae. Shrinking her world down to the finer points, she discovered beauty in the minute details before her. As she compressed the outer world her inner world expanded. Epyphany felt a sense of potency she had never known. Swimming at the foot of the Gold Tower she came to enjoy a strengthened connection, an enhanced bond similar to the link Blyss had made with the Tower. Her real world experience and her time of introspection had given her a renewed sense of confidence. Epyphany felt prepared for whatever future Blyss might envision. There were so many questions unanswered, yet she was filled with a quiet patience. The answers lay in simply living the moments.

On one of her morning excursions Epyphany found herself at the site of Dali's underwater masterpiece. She dove down to visit the impressive statue of Chrysylyss. The forces of nature had rearranged some of Dali's well placed elements, but overall the work was intact. Epyphany marveled at the effect of the flickering rays of light and the gentle movement of sea life. She lost track of time as she floated in front of the image, mesmerized. Her reverie ended abruptly when she heard a voice. She swam closer to the Chrysylyss, trying to find the source. She heard it again. "Remember this, I'm still with you, we are One." She knew it wasn't Blyss. The sound was vaguely familiar. A voice from her dreams, but she wasn't dreaming. If it weren't for the gentle sweetness in the voice, Epyphany would have been alarmed. She rose to the surface feeling a wonderful lightness. Epyphany hadn't realized how alone she had been feeling. She had reason to believe there was not now, nor had there ever been, another creature such as herself on this planet. Hearing that voice somehow eased her singular burden.

Just as Epyphany arrived back at the Chancel she heard another voice in her head. It was a bit confusing at first but she recognized Thurrow's voice immediately. The thought bundle was somewhat fragmented but the images slowly started to form into a coherent picture. Epyphany did her best to make sense of the message. There was an awkward subtext that confused Epyphany. She would have to relay it to Blyss and perhaps between the two of them they could figure it out.

Blyss smiled knowingly when Epyphany relayed Thurrow's message. Epyphany asked. "Should I accept his invitation? Should I meet the woman responsible for the failed kidnapping, the reward on my head, the selfish manipulation of Thurrow? The person whose company is raping of our precious ocean?"

Blyss replied. "Follow your heart. Do you trust Thurrow?"

Epyphany knew she would go. She would have to trust that Thurrow knew what he was doing. She was experiencing an odd feeling though. It fit the descriptions she had come across in some of the novels and poems she had scanned. Jealousy. Such a negative, counterproductive human emotion. It wasn't pleasant, so she decided to discard it and move on.

Thurrow had given no instructions in his message. Blyss trusted Thurrow but she didn't trust Sadjah, and so recommended Epyphany choose a traveling companion. Sadjah choose Storm, he would slow her down a little, but Thurrow didn't give the impression of urgency. When Dali found out about the trip and Epyphany's choice he was hurt and upset. He couldn't help but wonder why, so he confronted her. Epyphany tried to explain that she needed solitude and security, and that Storm was a creature of few words who would not be in the least slighted by her silence. She explained that Storm's presence would help her feel less vulnerable and that she could rest on his back if the need arose. Dali said he understood.

The following day Epyphany sent a message back to Thurrow telling him she would meet him at their chosen coordinates in three or four days.

Upon receiving Epyphany's message Thurrow informed Sadjah, then he set to work on a new improvement he had recently designed for the Samudra Hantu. He worked with Samu an the laboratory robots night and day for three days refining and building an automated transport system that would allow Epyphany to enter and exit the ship's pool at will.

Meanwhile Sadjah took advantage of her solitary time to rethink her future with Pisces and to map out an outline for redefining her career and lifestyle. She hadn't had this much fun in a long time. She loved creating strategies, and with this newfound freedom she was encouraged to see the positive, profitable possibilities unfold.

Sadjah was only moderately apprehensive about meeting Epyphany. Thurrow had painted a very detailed picture of this beautiful intelligent creature, and Sadjah was intrigued.

GETTING AQUAINTED

When Epyphany was within a day's traveling distance from Samu she started sending messages to Thurrow. As she drew near, they began to carry on regular conversations without too much trouble. In the beginning Thurrow had to pace himself due to the concentration levels required, but in time he found that he could actually multi-task during their communication.

By the time she reached the Samudra Hantu, Epyphany had already been briefed on the functions of Thurrow's new system. Samu need only activate the system, allowing Epyphany to simply swim through the series of mini locks and propel herself through the final tube that opened into the large pool on the main deck.

Thurrow informed Sadjah that Epyphany would be joining them later that morning and asked her to meet him at the pool. He wasn't sure of his decision, but he felt Sadjah should meet Epyphany alone. The idea was to let them experience their first impressions unencumbered by his presence. He remembered his first encounter with Epyphany, the magic and mystery of being in the presence of a uniquely intelligent and beautiful creature, and he wanted to give Sadjah the same life-changing opportunity.

Sitting in the control room, he monitored his new system as Epyphany approached. He let Epyphany know that Sadjah would be at the pool to greet her and that he would join them shortly thereafter. Thurrow felt the charge of anticipation. A pleasant sensory ediness enhanced his perception, similar to the electric vibe he felt when he was in his creative zone. It was the most unlikely situation a man could find himself in. The two most important souls in his life, meeting for the first time to help him make decisions that could directly affect the course of the future for an entire planet. The air around him shimmered, he could discern an audible shift in Samu's power source. Time seemed to stop. His heart beat louder. Epyphany was in the pool.

Epyphany

With the ship in sight, Epyphany sensed a change in the atmosphere. The breeze faded, and the surface of the sea became mirror calm. Storm stopped to let her approach Samu alone. Epyphany swam under the ship, and as she entered the lock she felt her heart beating louder. It made her feel stronger . . .

Sadjah

When Thurrow said he would meet her at the pool, Sadjah knew she would be facing Epyphany alone. She was glad. There was no way to prepare for a moment like this, so Sadjah had embraced the opportunity without prejudice. She had fought the temptation to question Thurrow further or to try to imagine what she might say or what Epyphany would sound like. Her mind was blank. Suddenly her heart beat louder . . . this time she was not afraid . . . she felt connected.

Sadjah turned toward the pool. The water stirred, then in the strange shimmering light she saw Epyphany rise slowly and swim quietly toward her. Sadjah rose and walked to the side of the pool. Kneeling down, she held out both hands as Epyphany reached up and wrapped her long fingers around Sadjah's wrists. Sadjah returned the grasp and in that moment there passed between them a true understanding. A wordless bond was forged.

Sadjah immediately felt as though she had been released from the last vestige of greed, insecurity, jealousy . . . all the chains she had locked around her heart were dissolved in an instant. They relaxed their grip and for the next few hours, Sadjah sat by the pool sharing stories with Epyphany as if they were old friends.

During the next several days, the three of them grew closer. Thurrow's decision was reaffirmed daily by the easy nature of their time together. As they slowly formulated a plan to deal with monitoring and protecting the ocean's resources, it became obvious how strong the bond had grown between Sadjah and Epyphany. It was as though they were long-lost sisters. Their world experience had been so different, yet somehow they had come to relate on an almost spiritual plane. With Epyphany's vast knowledge of the ocean, Sadjah's insight into the complexities of geo-politics and the inner workings of corporate finance, and Thurrow's knowledge of current technology, they started to believe that they could actually affect a change. They met every day to work out the details of possible strategies while Epyphany kept Blyss in the loop with daily thought bundles. After the meetings they often went for swims together. Epyphany introduced Sadjah to Storm, and a couple of times the trio ventured out for the afternoon with Sadjah riding on Storm's back.

One day when Thurrow had stayed on board to do some research, Samu picked up a lone blip on the sonar. It didn't appear to be a threat, but Thurrow wasn't taking any chances. He immediately lowered the sub and headed out for a closer look. As he got closer, he followed a hunch and sent out a thought bundle: "Hey Dali, are you lost?"

That afternoon when Sadjah and Epyphany returned, they were surprised to find a large, friendly dolphin waiting in the pool. Sadjah was enthralled. The world of Oojai was beginning to seem real to Sadjah. She dreamed of a journey there; she longed to experience Epyphany's world.

The day Epyphany left Oojai with Storm, Dali found it difficult to hold himself back. After only one day he just couldn't stand it. He missed her, but more than that he was afraid for her. He didn't care if she got upset, he just had to be at her side if something went wrong. When he reached Samu he planned to maintain a watchful distance. Unprepared for his immediate discovery, Dali wasn't sure how he would be received, but Thurrow welcomed him aboard and Epyphany seemed genuinely pleased to see him. Then there was Sadjah . . . Dali had never considered humans attractive, in fact, he really had never considered them at all until Thurrow floated into their world. But Sadjah was a striking specimen of femininity and she seemed so attentive. He wished they could communicate.

Samu soon located a small island nearby, so the group decided to check it out. With Thurrow clinging to Epyphany's shoulders and Sadjah holding onto Dali's dorsal fin, the four of them flew across the waves. Now they could really cover some distance. The tiny island was a perfect habitat. They set up a small outpost that fulfilled all the needs of their diverse little tribe. There was a deep channel leading into a small cove with a beach and shade trees. A freshwater spring trickled over the rocks, creating a pleasant little stream that attracted a small population of island critters. Both Samu and Storm were able to navigate the channel, allowing Samu to anchor near shore. It became their petite paradise.

The days were full and Thurrow was encouraged by the progress they were making. He was thoroughly enjoying this unlikely collaboration and had been avoiding thoughts of the day when they must go their separate ways. He knew the time was drawing near when they would have to choose a course of action and set that plan in motion.

AMBUSH

Thurrow, Epyphany and Sadjah had been working from their island post for about a week. It was another beautiful morning and the meeting had been fruitful. The trio was getting down to the finer points of the strategy. Using the statistics, graphs, and charts that Thurrow had assembled, Sadjah was convinced that she could persuade a majority of the Pisces board that if they were willing to take a longer view, it was possible to "feed the world" without destroying the ocean. If they didn't see it her way, she was prepared to pull out, take the good people with her, and start her own company.

Thurrow had been studying the problem for a long time. He kept an optimistic view at the meetings, but he knew that whatever they accomplished would only buy them a little time. All his diagnostic software analyses pointed to the same conclusion. The tipping point had been reached. The ocean was warming at an alarming rate, storms would increase in severity, the polar caps would disappear, and an extreme rise in sea levels was inevitable. The only question in his mind was how soon? He figured there was no point in demoralizing the group with doomsday prophecies, so he emphasized his hope for innovation. Action was the only way forward no matter what the future may bring. He suggested they spend at least half their time and money on adaptation.

After the meeting, Thurrow left the group and motored out to Samu, where he planned to spend the rest of the day working in his lab. Epyphany, Sadjah, and Dali lingered at the shore for a while then decided to take a short swim around the Island.

It was one of those days in the lab when time had no meaning. Thurrow was lost in his work; he forgot lunch, he didn't hear the trio's good natured taunting on their way to the channel, and he didn't look up to see the sky darkening on the horizon. He was so lost to his work that he was totally confused when he simultaneously received a distress signal from Epyphany, a surveillance alarm, and a storm warning from Samu. He had no idea what time it was and the dark sky served to confuse him further.

Thurrow came to his senses and yelled, "Samu, prioritize intelligence."

Samu replied, "I currently have scrambled sonar images of activity in the channel and archived images of Epyphany, Sadjah, and Dali heading in that direction just moments ago. There is an indication of potential tornado touchdown any time between now and . . . "

"SAMU!" Thurrow lost audio from Samu. The ship was shaking and water was flying straight up in vertical sheets outside the porthole. The door to the lab flew open and Thurrow's feet flew out from under him. He found himself floating horizontally, clinging to the console with all his strength. Everything that wasn't bolted down was flying into the hallway.

Then it was over. Panting, Thurrow fell to the floor. He felt like all the air had been sucked from his lungs. The sky cleared and rays of sunlight fell across the room. When he caught his breath, he spoke in a raspy whisper. "Samu . . . Samu . . . damages?

The console flickered to life and Thurrow sighed in relief at the sound of Samu's soothing voice. " A few main circuits were blown but the backup system has taken over. There is no damage to the hull or power grid, just some minor cosmetic damage. There is no further activity in the channel but I'm getting a pingback that looks like a mined laser net has been placed at the mouth of the channel. I have a full damage report ready upon request."

"Any sign of Epyphany, Sadjah, or Dali?" Thurrow was getting a very weak distress signal.

"I'm picking up some very slow movement on the surface of the bay just this side of the channel."

"Prepare the Sub."

Thurrow stopped his mind from imagining the worst. He needed to gather information first.

On his way to the channel Thurrow found Dali swimming very slowly toward the ship. He appeared to be wounded, but Dali assured Thurrow he could make it back to Samu on his own. After instructing Samu to ready the lock and to take extra care in transferring Dali to the pool, Thurrow dove carefully into the channel. The sub was well equipped for exploration and Thurrow probed the rock walls for any clues that might explain the mysterious event. He was hopeful that Dali could fill him in, but he was looking for any helpful details. At the mouth of the channel, Samu's analysis proved correct. Whoever had set the trap, made no effort to disguise it. Multiple beams of light intersected and danced in random patterns blocking the underwater entrance and at least a dozen small mines floated silently between the beams of light. Thurrow had no way of knowing if the lasers were armed triggers or harmless decoys.

Thurrow was familiar with the design. Though it looked imposing, it was relatively easy to defuse. Whoever set this trap wasn't trying to kill him. They meant only to slow him down. He couldn't hold back the sinking feeling any longer . . . someone had captured Epyphany and Sadjah.

Upon returning to his ship Thurrow asked Samu, "How's the patient?"

"He'll be alright physically but his mental state is weak."

Thurrow sat next to the pool and gently probed Dali's mind with questions.

There had been a surfaced submarine waiting around the bend in the channel. When they saw it, they turned back, only to find a net had been dropped and about a dozen divers on sea-scooters were approaching them with stun guns. Dali supposed Epyphany hadn't sensed it because they had all been distracted trying to simulate the Sea World tricks Sadjah had told them about. Dali had been swimming in figure eights with Sadjah riding on his back while

Epyphany dove in and out the water doing midair somersaults over Sadjah's head. In spite of Thurrow's insistence that no one could have anticipated the treachery, Dali was feeling responsible.

It happened very quickly. Epyphany dove and managed to disable several divers, but in spite of her incredible strength she was soon overwhelmed and rendered unconscious by multiple shocks. In the next moment the sky darkened, the wind started whipping up the waves, then a diver came up under Dali and stunned him while Sadjah was still on his back. When he awoke he was laying on an outcrop of the stone wall that formed the sides of the channel. Everyone was gone. Thurrow didn't want to press Dali too hard, but he continued to gently question him for the slightest fragments of memory. Dali finally remembered one small but important detail. There had been a small round figure standing on the sub wearing a bright multicolored shirt. He may have had a mustache and Dali thought he heard him yell Sadjah's name.

Thurrow was stunned . . . "Wild Bill! How did he find them? . . . Sadjah?" She had been so convincing when she said she wasn't followed! He had totally believed her! She might have been able to con him, but surely Epyphany's intuition would have picked up any hint of deception. Although he knew he should give Sadjah the benefit of doubt, Thurrow couldn't help feeling suspicious.

Samu conducted a thorough search using every technology available and came up with nothing. Whoever they were, they had managed to disappear completely

Thurrow let Dali rest and wandered listlessly down to his studio. He kept hoping for a signal from Epyphany or Blyss, but nothing came. He played his guitar for awhile, but not even music could give him solace. He hung up his guitar and went up to the lounge and poured himself a drink. He almost fell off his stool when his phone buzzed. Thurrow looked at the number in disbelief. It was a text message from Sadjah's phone. "Don't worry, Epyphany will be safe with us as well. She'll be our other big-little secret for now. I'll be in touch."

Thurrow was confused by the words, "as well" and "other." He wondered aloud, "What could she possibly mean by that? Anyway, she need not worry about me leaking the story." There was only one person Thurrow could tell, and he was sure Blyss already knew.

THE CHASE

While Thurrow sat pondering the strange message from Sadjah, a thought suddenly occurred to him. "Where was Storm though all the madness? He must have been on the other side of the channel. Perhaps he got a glimpse of the enemy submarine."

Thurrow took a moment to collect his thoughts, then he formulated some questions and sent them out to Storm. About a minute later he received a weak and very brief transmission from Storm.

"Sub in hearing range . . . following."

Thurrow's heart lightened. He was incredibly thankful for Epyphany's wise choice of a traveling companion.

Thurrow snapped out of his malaise. He went back to the tiny island one last time and dismantled the temporary outpost, then returned to Samu to prepare for an immediate departure. It took him a couple of hours of work in the lab and another two hours working underwater in the mini-sub, but he successfully disarmed the mines and added them to his arsenal. After confirming Dali's slow but steady recovery at the pool, he instructed Samu to set a course for the Maldives. His only hope was to stay within close range of Storm and try not to lose track of the captors. All the while, Thurrow struggled to believe that Sadjah was just a pawn in her father's evil game.

He was still baffled about Wild Bill's method for tracking him down. Thurrow was starting to put a general picture together. He reasoned that since Samu had not detected the presence of a submarine outside the bay, W.B. was most likely using the same stealth technology he had installed on the Samudra Hantu. He assumed the team of divers were extremely well trained and capable of laying the mines in minutes. The strange coincidental timing of the freak storm was troubling but it certainly worked in W.B.'s favor as well. Thurrow also realized that he had lowered his guard and failed to program Samu for any extra security measures. The fact that Storm remained undetected and immune to the new stealth technology was a stroke of luck. W.B. would never suspect such an unusual adversary. Storm's invisibility would serve Thurrow well, provided he was able to keep up with the sub.

Samu was practically flying as she exited the channel and headed toward the Maldives. Still unable to communicate with Epyphany, Thurrow tried not to imagine the worst. He turned his thoughts to the problem at hand. Precious time had been lost wallowing in self recriminations and dismantling the mines. Now Thurrow was concerned with losing his connection to Storm. His hope began to fade when the initial weak signal was lost completely. It appeared the first guess had been wrong. Thurrow instructed Samu to initiate satellite surveillance, and using some very sophisticated programs he had developed for his marine research orbital scanning system, he began a progressive scan. He knew it was the "needle-in-the-haystack" scenario, but he was out of ideas . . . the screen flashed . . . he was in luck . . . Samu picked up activity far from the Maldives, a large vessel several hundred miles from them and a considerable distance from any registered shipping lanes. Then it dawned on him . . . the Silver Finn . . . Pisces must have kept it at sea to avoid the media. Thurrow was pretty sure he had found the sub's destination. He changed his heading toward the trawler and within minutes the connection to Storm was renewed.

Storm was growing tired and the sub was gaining distance on him, he signaled his concern to Thurrow. By this time it was obvious that W.B. was headed straight to the Silver Finn, so he told Storm to slow down and rest. While Samu cruised at top speed toward their destination, Thurrow had time to review the past couple of weeks. Things with Sadjah and Epyphany had turned out better than he could have anticipated, the three of them had made incredible progress as a team both personally and strategically. As he considered the situation, he was still on the fence in his judgement of Sadjah. Her change of heart was quite sudden and unexpected but it had affirmed an underlying belief he held from the beginning of their relationship. Thurrow always felt there was a deeper side to Sadjah, he had glimpsed moments of compassion and understanding. All the things she told him recently made sense . . . or was he underestimating her acting ability? She said all the things he wanted to hear. Had she changed her strategy having failed to bribe him into her world? There was no use theorizing further. Until proven otherwise he would trust his instinct.

Thurrow had no plan. He was out of communication with everyone but Storm and had some doubt about the reliability of Samu's stealth status. W.B. had found them, but he suspected the successful ambush had something to do with tracking Sadjah, not Samu. Lacking any reasonable alternative, he would have to trust the stealth system. Thurrow decided to navigate within a safe distance from the Silver Finn and monitor surface activity. If the the sub docked it might be possible to gain some information from his satellite connection.

ON BOARD

Even with her eyes wide open, the darkness consumed her. The tank was barely large enough to accommodate her long, lean body. Her tail fin was cramped and folded and her elbows were pressed tightly against the walls. The top lip of the tank curled in so low her head was forced forward, chin pressed against her chest. Epyphany fought her animal instinct and summoned the will to remain calm. Her body and mind were hyper-alert, sensitive to even the smallest changes in vibrations, temperature, and smell. Adrenalin cursed through her veins and though she lie perfectly still, she was like a time bomb only seconds away from exploding in the face of the next unsuspecting antagonist.

She remembered swimming at top speed, trying to outmaneuver the armed divers and overwhelm the men on sea scooters. Her highly evolved observation skills had taken in the entire scene in a single instant. The submarine, the net, the mercenaries above and below the water, and most importantly, the small round man wearing a wide white hat and a multicolored shirt, with a drink in his hand and a smile on his face, standing like a privileged spectator at a private arena.

Now she lay immobile in this cramped tank, captured prey at the mercy of greedy, heartless humans. Epyphany focused her keen awareness. Using her minds eye, much like a thermal scanner, she mapped the positions of the sailors and captain. She picked up on the tension; this was not a happy crew. Then she felt the unmistakable presence of Sadjah. The bond they had made in the recent weeks was genuine. Epyphany had no reason to believe Sadjah had anything to do with their predicament. She could feel Sadjah's anxiety, discomfort, and confusion.

Epyphany tried to send out messages to Blyss, Thurrow, Storm, and Dali, but she was blocked by a strange interference. Something was distorting and disabling her thought bundle. She remembered Thurrow's explanation of

Samu's stealth design and reasoned the submarine might be equipped with the same meta-materials. If those exterior tiles were only scrambling her outgoing messages it explained why she could still use her powers within the confines of the sub. Epyphany had never been in such a claustrophobic circumstance, she felt unfamiliar feelings start to surface . . . fear, dread, and worst of all, helplessness.

Wild Bill's sub was reasonably large, designed for a crew of 16 or so, but it wasn't designed to provide for a very large mermaid. On W.B.'s last-minute orders, his engineer hastily improvised a water tank for Epyphany. Unfortunately they had underestimated her size. There was no time to remedy the error so they decided the accommodations would have to suffice for the remainder of the trip. Wild Bill wasn't intentionally cruel by nature, but he lacked sympathy for anyone he perceived as weak. He couldn't be more wrong in his judgement of Epyphany.

Sadjah

It was the pain that woke her up. She must have been out cold for quite awhile. Sadjah's shoulder was throbbing and her right leg from the knee down was completely numb. She had been unconscious on her back with one arm stretched above her head, hand cuffed to the steel frame that held her bunk to the wall. Her right leg was dangling over the hard edge of the thin stiff mattress, cutting off the circulation at her knee. She moaned, then once fully awake, slowly maneuvered her leg onto the bed. The pain of pins and needles made her cry out loud as the blood rushed back into her calf and foot.

Sadjah lay there trying to piece together the events that had brought her here. She recalled riding on Dali's back having more fun then she could remember since her childhood. Then came the sudden realization they were being ambushed and herded like dolphins in a trawler's net. She heard a familiar voice calling out her name and just as she turned to see her father waving from the deck of a submarine, she felt a burning electric shock. Sadjah had no idea how much time had passed, but from the pain caused by her unfortunate position on the bunk she knew it must be several hours since she lost consciousness.

Sadjah's mind suddenly filled with questions. "What has happened to Epyphany and Dali? How did W.B. find them? Does Thurrow have any idea they've been captured? How could W.B. do this to his own daughter? Why? Why? Why?"

She took several deep breaths, a technique Sadjah often used before an important presentation to the board. It always served to quiet her mind and focus her thoughts. This time she had to take several more breaths to coax her heart rate back to normal. If her father could resort to such drastic tactics, it must be extremely important to him. Perhaps he is being blackmailed, or more likely, blinded by his feelings of entitlement, he has lost all sense of consequences. Sadjah was forced to reconsider everything she had ever assumed or believed or felt about him. It was almost too much to process.

Sadjah could not deny she had "father issues." All her memories seemed to have shadows attached. She had no real memory of her mother, only second hand information from stories overheard at parties or Wild Bill's drunken ramblings. When she questioned her father, his vague answer was simply that her mother's name was Christine and she had left him soon after Sadjah's birth. She was raised by a series of nannies or temporary "girlfriends." When she did see her father he was more like the fun uncle who brings presents and tells stories. As she grew older and showed signs of extremely high intelligence and the awkward blossoming beauty of a pre-teen, he started to take a more serious interest in her rearing. Thinking back, she realized there were very few choices in which he was not instrumental in guiding her to his way of thinking. Her education and career path were laid out at an early age. She really wasn't bitter about his role, but up until this moment, she had never really questioned it. W.B. had always made her feel like she was making the decisions, and as she came to understand what would make him happy, the little girl in her loved to make him smile.

Sadjah advanced rapidly through her education, taking high school courses in middle school and college courses in prep school. Early on she came to understand that knowledge was power. Sadjah devoted herself to summer courses throughout her teens and completed her masters degree in business at the age of eighteen. As a result of her advanced education she was more comfortable in the adult world and had very few friends her own age. Sadjah was sexually and intellectually precocious. She learned the power of her beauty at a very young age and few men could resist her. After her astounding academic achievements she immersed herself in the world of high finance. With access to the hallways and boardrooms of the movers and shakers, Sadjah started to hear stories about her dad's questionable business ethics. There would be half joking references to his "pirate" days and his "swashbuckling" ways. He seemed like such an unlikely pirate she never took the stories seriously. She exceeded her father's expectations. Sadjah made international headlines, and with her meteoric rise up the corporate ladder, became the famous "wunderkind" of the infamous Wild Bill.

It was only now that she realized the probable source of the sweet deals that fell into her lap on a fast track to a successful closing. She recognized that her father's connections were helpful in the beginning, but with each success he began to distance himself from her and she was thankful. Her confidence grew and she began to feel totally independent from her father and his business philosophy.

Now here she was, some kind of pawn in one of his unscrupulous schemes. She had trusted him and he had used her. As she lay helpless, chained to the bed, her anger rose and her suspicions grew. Sadjah reminded herself that this was like any other high stakes business deal. She needed to relax and use all her skills to uncover and undermine his ignoble plan.

So much had changed so quickly for Sadjah. She had glimpsed an alternative world; she was finally part of something good. Epyphany and Thurrow chose to include her and trusted her beyond reason. An option she could have never imagined had been laid at her feet and she wasn't going to let him destroy that future. Sadjah was beginning to see her father for what he was and she would not let herself become another victim of the scandalous Wild Bill.

With that in mind, Sadjah relaxed. She felt the tension evaporate as she welcomed the refreshing karma of true and positive intention. At that moment she heard a voice. It was Epyphany. She waited . . . she heard it again . . . it seemed to be getting closer. How could that be? Sadjah knew they were on a submarine and assumed W.B. had Epyphany locked away somewhere on board, so how could the voice get closer? Sadjah lay back again and opened her mind, this time she knew Epyphany's voice was in her head. She heard these words: "Sadjah, I know you are here somewhere. I hope you aren't injured. If you can hear me, just empty your mind . . . I will ask you two simple questions. I want you to take your time, think my name, then answer consecutively in your mind, yes or no . . . do you hear me? Are you alright?"

Sadjah took a deep breath, exhaled, then thought . . . "Epyphany . . . Yes . . . Yes." Sadjah could feel Epyphany's delight. With Epyphany locked in her cramped wet coffin and Sadjah chained uncomfortably to her bed, they spent the next few hours conspiring to win their freedom.

Dubya-B

"Mission accomplished!" W.B. raised his drink in a toast to the captain of the sub. Although several men were seriously wounded when Epyphany tried to protect her friends, Wild Bill considered the ambush a complete success.

Weeks earlier when Sadjah paid him a short visit to let him know about her little "vacation," W.B. already knew what she was planning. He was overjoyed that all his years of manipulation and subterfuge were finally paying off. He had imagined this day since he first met Sadjah's mother over twenty years ago. There wasn't anything Sadjah had ever done, in her entire life, that W.B. didn't know about. In the earliest years the nannies reported to him daily. When she grew older and more independent he monitored her every move through phone tapping, video surveillance, private body guards, and paid spies. Sadjah never knew that at least half of her "friends" had been on his payroll. Then when the technology became available, his dental specialist implanted a very expensive, advanced micro bugging device in one of her perfect molars. From that day forward WB knew where she was at all times and the intimate details of her life, including her half of every conversation she entertained. If it were possible, he would have monitored her brain.

And now he had all three of his prized possessions. It wasn't about money or fame for him anymore. He held more of the earth's wealth than anyone on the planet could imagine. Wild Bill considered himself the ultimate collector. The only difference was the masterpieces he collected were not created by mortal men.

With the unsuspecting help of Sadjah's young, brilliant mind, W.B.'s worldwide interests were hidden in hundreds of shelter companies. He was the "man behind the curtain" and less than a handful of people on the planet had even the foggiest idea to the extent of his power.

THE RETREAT

Many years ago, before Wild Bill got his nickname, he was in the ocean "salvage" business. He was a self-taught sailor, and as a young man he hooked up with several other entrepreneurial young men who roamed the world searching the shallow reefs for sunken treasure. They didn't let regulations impede their explorations and cared little for bookkeeping. There were rumors speculating that some of the "sunken" treasure was still in the holds of floating ships when they "discovered" it.

However suspect their methods may have been, they were very successful. The young team got rich quickly. The number of original members dwindled as Wild Bill slowly thinned out the management until he was captain of the entire operation. The wealth grew and WB bought more ships. He diversified into fishing and cruise lines, attracted investors, and slipped slowly out of the spotlight. Wild Bill eventually claimed to be retired and successfully cultivated the image of a harmless and laughable aging playboy.

Early in his successful years while exploring the islands and criss-crossing the vast blue ocean, WB happened upon a small mountain of uncharted rock poking up out of the sea. From a distance it had the surreal appearance of a solemn stone glacier floating alone in the middle of the Indian Ocean. He was instantly captivated by the desolate peacefulness of the scene. Sailing closer, he was further intrigued by an unusual combination of sounds. He heard the expected crashing of waves on rock. He listened to the rustling of wind through the short, sparse stand of trees waving from the peak, their roots like spindly claws clinging with all their might to the barren landscape. But there was something else, a mysterious low frequency whistling echo drew him closer. As he navigated toward the sound, WB was suddenly caught in an undertow, which, without his time honed skill as a sailor, would have sent his crew and ship hurtling toward violent and complete destruction upon the ragged rocks that lined the base of the natural fortress. In that instant he fell in love with this harsh chunk of unlikely real-estate. It challenged him.

Wild Bill continued around the island, carefully circumventing the towering cliffs until he found the source of the sound. He saw a narrow black shadow stretching from the top the mountain to the roiling surf, it was as though the sheer stone wall had been ripped cleanly open. Upon closer inspection it turned out to be a tapered opening, leading into a dark channel. The singular sound was generated by the howling wind, it's echo carried through the channel and up the vertical crevice like a giant whistle blowing inside a cavernous chimney. The resulting sound was enchanting. WB anchored at a safe distance and lowered a powerful skiff.

Once inside the channel he was awestruck. The walls were so high and sheer they blocked the daylight in such a way as to create a shadowless eerie twilight. It had an intoxicating affect on Wild Bill. As he continued to explore, he was surprised to see the channel widen at the waterline where perpetual tides had worn two opposing cavern ceilings, creating a giant astrodome where an equally oversized, overhead tunnel siphoned light from the reluctant sky. With the engines cut he closed his eyes and drifted silently, letting the sound and solitude seep into his soul. Floating alone in this dark mystical setting he felt an icy-hot chill run up his spine. There was power here . . . he felt destined to live here. This would be the center of the universe he had yet to create, an impenetrable retreat from the chattering clamorous world. From this secret citadel he would rule his ocean kingdom. The young pirate smiled at his own inflated ego, knowing he was getting a bit carried away. Then a thought entered his mind . . . almost a premonition: "This ocean castle will need a very special queen."

The years passed and Wild Bill's riches grew. With nearly unlimited funds, he succeeded in constructing the world's most advanced, self-sufficient, highly fortified, luxurious, architectural achievement ever attempted. His designers had managed to maintain the illusion of an uninhabited, nondescript, uninviting chunk of rock and his engineers attained unprecedented immunity from surveillance. No less miraculous was the fact that he accomplished this while maintaining complete secrecy. From time to time, rumors of The Retreat would surface, but WB would laugh them off or distract attention with a well rehearsed social scandal that would remind everyone he was just another billionaire buffoon.

The Retreat was a marvel of technical ingenuity that rivaled or surpassed kingdoms and castles, past and present. WB had to laugh when his contemporaries mentioned Thurrow's accomplishments. In fact, Thurrow had unknowingly contributed to some of the designs included in The Retreat's long list of high tech features. Though he never knew it, Thurrow had accepted grants from several companies and non-profits that were shell corporations or money laundering schemes, all dangling in the ubiquitous web of the Wild Bill empire.

SHADOW MEMORIES

Blyss was hopeful. It had been quite a surprise when Epyphany came to her with the strange invitation from Thurrow. She smiled to herself thinking "I have spent many, many years on this planet, I have sharpened my skills and developed my insight beyond expectation, and still I have yet to successfully navigate the maze of human logic and emotion."

Throughout Epyphany's journey and her subsequent meeting with Sadjah, Blyss maintained steady contact. Thurrow's instinct had proven true and Blyss couldn't have been more pleased with the trio's progress. She was impressed with the information Epyphany relayed and encouraged by the pure and positive vibe between Sadjah and Epyphany, palpable in Epyphany's enthusiastic descriptions of their interactions. Blyss looked forward to meeting Sadjah one day soon . . .

As Blyss pondered the information, she felt like she was missing something. Though she was not immune to the "shadow memories," it was unusual for Blyss to be plagued by uncertainty. There was some event in her past, or something she had seen, that was hiding from her mind's eye. It tiptoed behind her in her dreams, whispering below earshot, like a singular mysterious mumbling in a crowded room, and it eluded her like a familiar faceless voice. Frustrated, she felt as if she was trying to decipher the fading words of an ancient manuscript. The uncertainty continued to trouble her but most of the time she managed to let it go. Epyphany, Thurrow, and Sadjah were getting close to a viable plan and Blyss approved of the general outline.

The day of the ambush, Blyss rose from a restless night's sleep. The shadows from her dreams still haunted her in the sparkling light of the Oojai sunrise. As if in a trance, Blyss made her way to the Cavern Temple and knelt in front of the Chrysylyss. She was jolted out of her trance by the echo as she involuntarily slammed both palms on the damp cavern floor. Blyss flew to her feet, her head tilted back at an unnaturally sharp angle and she stared up into the welcoming arms of the Chrysylyss. Her mouth was open wide in surprise as tears ran down her cheeks dripping gently on her tongue. The salty taste of life and love and sorrow washed away the shadows as the whispering voice spoke softly but crystal clear in her mind. She could't believe she had forgotten the sound; the cheerful sound of the young girl's voice that had brought meaning to her dreary eternal days of preparation. Blyss was transported . . . that first day in the the bright sun with the laughing waves, the singing winds, and the diamond glittering sand, Blyss had approached the girl silently, capturing her in shadow. Unafraid, the youth looked up, squinting and shading her large bright eyes with a strong yet delicate hand. Blyss recalled those first three words that had made her laugh out loud.

"You a witch?"

Now, standing in front of the towering statue, Blyss heard a similar voice speak three words again . . . but she didn't laugh. It was the sadly forgotten voice of Chrysylyss . . . "I am here."

Still somewhat dazed and trying to make sense of her sudden revelation, Blyss received the second jolt of her day. Epyphany was trying to contact her. There was a lot of interference. The thought bundle was a confused jumble of distress and images. While under attack, Epyphany was making an effort to simultaneously transmit images and defend herself and her friends. In an instant the connection went dead. Blyss tried to contact Dali . . . nothing. Then she tried Storm. He managed a short burst of info before she lost contact with him as well. From what she could glean from Storm, it appeared that Sadjah and Epyphany had been captured and Storm was trying to follow a submarine.

Blyss sailed to the top of the Gold Tower, took her meditative position, let her mind dissolve into the the soothing vibrations of the tower and focused on Thurrow. Time melted away for Blyss but hours passed before the hazy images began to sharpen until she felt the unsettling jolt of connection. Blyss was plugged into Thurrow, not actually communicating but linked to his consciousness in such a way as to share his sensory perception. She couldn't exactly see what his eyes were seeing—her input was directly from his brain's interpretation of the scene and it took intense concentration on her part to make sense of the information. Blyss recognized thoughts of the Silver Finn and wondered what had happened that could possibly inspire Thurrow to return there.

THE SILVER FINN REVISTED

The Silver Finn loomed large on his radar so Thurrow ordered Samu to slow down. Using the satellite feed and a highly sophisticated telescope of his own design, Thurrow planned to monitor the rendezvous from a safe distance. Samu slowed to a stop, and while waiting for WB's sub to appear, Thurrow tried to make sense of the ambush.

It had been over a decade since Thurrow could recall hearing any news connecting Wild Bill with Pisces. Long before Sadjah popped into the limelight, WB had all but disappeared from the Wall Street rumor mill. If there was any news of him these past few years, it was in the form of an embarrassing photo of his mustached face and toothy grin in the gossip column, making a fool of himself with some naive young starlet by his side.

Thurrow could understand how WB's sense of entitlement would be enough to compel him to possess the world's first known mermaid, but why kidnap his own daughter? He kept coming back to that cryptic message: "Don't worry, Epyphany will be safe with us as well. She'll be our other big-little secret." Thurrow reasoned that if Sadjah was just a pawn he would then have to assume WB was using her phone. Then it dawned on him, "Of course . . . the phone was bugged! But if that was the case, when would WB have managed that? Perhaps her phone has been bugged for quite some time."

Thurrow's thoughts were interrupted when Samu spoke. "We have a siting." Thurrow checked the video feed, which showed activity at the Silver Finn's loading dock. He quickly walked over to his powerful telescope and peered in. The freshly raised nets were still dripping and there was a clear view of the surfaced submarine floating below. A few men were milling around on deck, but no sign of the precious cargo.

Thurrow watched patiently, and after several minutes he was relieved to see Sadjah step out onto the deck. She seemed to be limping slightly. Thurrow straightened up and let go of the telescope, his mind jumped to conclusions, his fists clenched, and he could feel his heart race. He quelled his anger, made some adjustments on the scope, then leaned back in and focused his attention. There were two large men standing close on either side of Sadjah. Right behind her, Wild Bill made his way slowly through the hatch, dressed in a gaudy and somewhat comical version of a captain's uniform, topped with his trademark ranchero hat.

A ramp was lowered. Sadjah walked awkwardly behind the first guard from the sub to the loading dock, followed by WB and the other goon. Epyphany was somewhere on that sub. As hard as he tried, Thurrow had no success sending her a message. He figured she might be unconscious and hoped he might have better luck later.

Thurrow's impulse was to put Samu into hyper-drive and race to the rescue, but he kept his emotions in check. There was little he could do until he found some way to communicate with Sadjah or Epyphany.

COLLABORATION

The ramp was a little shaky. Still stiff from her confinement, Sadjah had to concentrate to keep from falling as she made her way carefully from the submarine to the loading dock. WB wasn't taking any chances and his guards were well trained. There wasn't much she could do even if she could outsmart her escorts; she was on a trawler out in the middle of the Indian Ocean. Sadjah knew she would have to stick to the plan she and Epyphany had come up with.

Since they lacked any hard facts relating to their predicament, the plan was loose and designed for improvisation. The success of the strategy depended heavily on Sadjah's dramatic skills. The first order of business was to convince Wild Bill that Sadjah was still his darling, obedient daughter. She would be acting, but she would use the truth of her emotions wherever possible. The first act in this high stakes drama would be the easiest. The outrage she felt was real and she would unleash it and reign it in as needed. She and Epyphany agreed that the initial goal was to gain as much insight as possible into WB's intentions. They needed to know what motivated him, and with that knowledge perhaps they could slowly ease him into a sense of false security. Sadjah knew their one big advantage was his megalomanic ego.

Initially she gave Wild Bill the silent treatment. When he made the effort to speak to her she simply stared at him in defiance then looked away. She wasn't sure, but Sadjah thought she saw him flinch. It was reassuring.

During the short distance from the ramp to the first of many flights of stairs her body loosened up and Sadjah began to feel almost normal. WB signaled the guards to give him some room and he stepped up beside her. When they reached the first step of the stairway, Sadjah feigned a stumble. WB instantly grabbed her arm to stabilize her. She thanked him with a cold smile. He tried once more to engage her and this time she let him speak.

Playing his part in the charade WB took a contrite tone and said, "I'm so sorry that I've had to put you through this ordeal and I hope you will try to understand that it was crucial that I make you appear to be my prisoner. I need you to convince the mermaid that you are on her side. Things will go so much smoother if she thinks you are her friend."

Of course WB knew all about their friendship but he couldn't let Sadjah know he'd been privy to at least one side of all her conversations with Epyphany. Although the implant was an admirable surveillance tool, it was one of the first of it's kind and lacked the ability to clearly record both sides of her conversations.

Sadjah smiled to herself, warming to the role she had taken on. She and Epyphany had completely forgotten that not a single person aboard would imagine the symbiotic relationship between them. And although some of the submarine crew had witnessed Epyphany's incredible strength, none of them would have a clue to her superior intelligence. Sadjah was confident that she and Epyphany would find a way out.

Summoning some righteous indignation sprinkled with a dash of smoldering rage, Sadjah spoke through clenched teeth and a forced smile. "I could have been killed by your clumsy goons! Did you think of that? What if that dolphin had thrown me? I could have drowned! How did you find me? What have you . . . How long . . . Why do . . . Oooooh . . . don't even answer. I can't talk to you now." With that Sadjah hurried up the stairs leaving her sputtering father behind.

One of the goons yelled. "You okay, boss?" Wild Bill just waved his hand motioning them to stay back as he struggled to catch up.

WB was out of breath and sweating profusely when he finally caught up with his daughter on a landing high above the loading dock. Sadjah was blown-away by the size of the ship. From where she stood the submarine bobbed like a toy under the flapping nets.

Her next words to WB were practically honey coated. She assumed a concerned demeanor. "Are you alright? Do you need to sit down?" Then she said, "What about that poor creature? I saw her in that cramped tank. If I'm to act as her friend then you must give her a reasonable pool to swim in immediately."

WB smiled thinking, "if I hadn't pushed her into finance she would be a famous actress by now." Being the man he was, he found himself feeling somewhat prideful of Sadjah's skill in this game of cat-and-mouse. He said, "Why, of course. Brilliant idea." He pulled out his phone and issued the orders, then turned back to Sadjah. "I put my men on it and they will have something ready in a day or so. You can deliver the news after you settle in." Sadjah maintained her daughterly concern and answered, "But Daddy, if you want me to prove my friendship, we mustn't let her suffer a moment longer than necessary. Why don't you put more men on it and I'll go tell her right now. Doesn't this boat have an elevator? Get one of those goons to bring me back to the sub." Before he could respond, Sadjah headed back down the stairs. WB stood with his mouth open for a minute then he got back on the phone and did what he was told.

CONTEMPLATION

There was nothing in Epyphany's experience to compare with the ill treatment she was suffering under the orders of Wild Bill. Epyphany realized how life on Oojai, nurtured and protected by Blyss and the Tribe, had done little to prepare her for the harsh realities of living among humans. In Epyphany's world there was no greed or malice. The members of the Tribe weren't immune to minor conflicts but they all understood that their survival depended on working as a team. The ocean could be a brutal environment but it was not mean-spirited. The planet was designed with a balanced food chain and the existence of each individual species depended on that balance. Epyphany couldn't understand why humans had chosen to ignore the rules and put the entire ecosystem at risk. Through her recent collaboration with Thurrow and Sadjah, Epyphany had learned much about the sad and disturbing realities of life beyond Oojai. She understood that though he may be one of the worst offenders, WB was not alone in his plundering of the ocean's riches. She couldn't grasp how so many intelligent beings could be so greedy and shortsighted that they would knowingly undermine the safety and future of their own species.

The first day on the sub was the worst day of Epyphany's life. She had faced life threatening danger before, but in each situation she had been unrestrained and fully capable of defending herself. She also recognized that no matter how dire those circumstances had been, she could always count on her connection to Blyss and the Tribe. However, during the ambush Epyphany was completely overwhelmed by her captors. Swimming and surviving in the ocean, her confidence was her biggest asset, but lying in the ill-fitting tank she felt powerless and demoralized. Worst of all, she felt irrelevant.

If it weren't for Sadjah, Epyphany knew she would have never survived that first day. When she awoke in the cramped tank in the belly of the submarine, it was all she could do to reign in the panic. If a crew member had threatened her at that point, she would have surely lost control and made a fruitless attempt to escape. After she and Sadjah connected and formulated the outline of their plan, Epyphany was able to accept her temporary circumstances and face the isolation. On Oojai she cherished her moments of solitude, in confinement she decided to use the time similarly and contemplate the course of her life . . .

She thought back to the day she found Thurrow . . . how she'd woken with a premonition, an unsettling feeling that her life was about to change. Even as she lay wounded in the tank with no hint of her fate, she felt no regrets over her decision to rescue him. Thurrow had changed her life. Thurrow had opened her eyes to a world that needed her. Thurrow had introduced her to Sadjah. Thurrow had shown her the pain and joy that goes with living and loving with all your heart. He was responsible for an intellectual, emotional, and spiritual growth that life on Oojai could never have supplied.

She thought about Sadjah . . . the moment they met and clasped hands the electricity had surged between them, welding their hearts and their futures together. She experienced a bond of love no less strong than her love for Thurrow but distinctly different. Epyphany couldn't say why, but her connection to Sadjah provided a comfort beyond the romantic love she felt for Thurrow or the familial love she felt towards Blyss. She admired Sadjah's strength and intelligence. Impressed by her ability to navigate the complex and treacherous world of high finance, she saw Sadjah as an equal. Epyphany knew Thurrow still loved Sadjah and that Sadjah was still very much in love with him. But for reasons she couldn't explain she knew their love was not a threat. Most humans struggled constantly to define and confine their love. It seemed there was something in their DNA that made them long for exclusivity. In love, in business, and in lifestyle, it often appeared as if their whole existence was wrapped up in a never-ending competition for ownership. They weighed their relationships down with promises that ran against their human nature, then reinforced their delusions with self deception. Epyphany could admit to an initial inkling of jealousy when she first heard of Sadjah, but she chocked it up to her deficient human genes and discarded the emotion as counterproductive.

The days spent working with Sadjah and Thurrow on the little island outpost were some of the happiest and most informative moments of her life. During those productive and playful days, she and Sadjah spent many hours sharing the vastly different experiences of their lives. Sadjah admitted regret in giving into the worst of human nature. Given her upbringing, it was no wonder her values were skewed to an extreme sense of entitlement. Her father, her peers, and her schooling constantly reinforced a self perception of being exceptional and beyond reproach. She confessed that without the example of stubborn, unflinching honesty and the high standards set by Thurrow, she might never have achieved the complete and successful re-evaluation of her purpose in life. Sadjah knew Thurrow wasn't fully convinced of her conversion, but time would buy that proof.

Epyphany thought about Blyss and the Tribe . . . she missed them and she missed the peaceful Oojai vibe. There was so much news to share. With people like WB on the planet she wondered what would become of places like Oojai. There was no doubt in her mind concerning both the documented and predicted rising sea levels. The strange thing she realized, ever since Thurrow and Sadjah had brought the issue to her attention, was that Oojai had remained unaffected. Thurrow quoted one prediction that mentioned there would be a few areas around the globe where the land is rising due to plate tectonics. In those regions, the oceanic plate is descending below the continental plate pushing up the coastline and negating the threat of rising tides. It was a reasonable explanation in general, but in the case of Oojai Epyphany suspected it was more likely related to the mystifying powers of the Gold Tower.

She thought about the Cavern Temple . . . there was such magic there, such contrast—the simmering omnipotence of the Gold Tower and the tranquil, spiritual presence of the Chrysylyss . . . lying in the stagnant water lost in thought, Epyphany forgot her pain and her loneliness . . . exhausted, she drifted into a deep sleep and she dreamed . . .

The Dream

 She was a child and the sparkling world was reflected in her large, shining, laughing eyes. Epyphany's young, strong body propelled her, head first, through the pounding surf. With Dali only inches from her side, they pierced a towering wave, exploded through the crest, flipped, crossed in mid air, slid down the next swell, and rode the following wave until it receded into the warm pools of the lagoon.

Blyss was waiting for them and signaled Epyphany to meet her in the Cavern. Dali got the message, gently splashed Epyphany with his tail flukes, and headed back to the bay.

Once in the Cavern Temple, Epyphany suddenly felt disoriented. The water and the air were abnormally cool and she began to tremble from the chill. She swam swiftly around the pool calling out for Blyss but there was no answer. A thick fog rose from the chilly water, concealing the Gold Tower. Epyphany quickly lost her bearings. Then she heard a voice whisper, "Epyphany, I am here."

Epyphany whispered back, "Blyss, is that you? Where are you?"

She squinted through the fog. Seeing a faint lavender glow on the far side of the cavern, she swam slowly toward it. Her body continued to tremble and her heart pounded loudly in her chest, she could barely take a breath. A single confusing thought flowed into Epyphany's mind, "Mother?"

The fog thinned and the light grew brighter as she approached. She stopped at the edge of the pool . . . her body was shaking as she looked up at the glowing

Chrysylyss. This time the words filled the cavern "YES, I AM HERE."

"Epyphany wake up! I'm here, it's alright, it's Sadjah, I'm right here."

When Sadjah entered the hold and saw Epyphany crammed inside the make shift tank shivering and shaking, lost in fitful sleep, she almost burst into tears. A weaker creature would have never survived such cruelty. At the sound of Sadjah's voice Epyphany opened her eyes and smiled. She had been unable to move her arms and hands enough to even splash herself, her exposed skin was dry and flaking, Epyphany's lips were cracked and her mouth was so parched she could barely speak.

Sadjah's anger grew, she didn't know if she would be able to control herself the next time she saw her father. She poured some fresh water gently into Epyphany's mouth, scooped up more water using both hands and ladled it over the tortured skin. Sadjah helped Epyphany move her scraped elbows away from the rough metal tank. The skin was raw and bleeding, almost worn to the bone in places. While she worked to relieve her friend's pain, Sadjah related the recent interaction with her father. Epyphany managed a rasping chuckle when she heard how Sadjah had manipulated the enemy so easily.

In order to save Epyphany the pain of speaking, they continued to use their silent thought conversation. While doing so, it occurred to Sadjah that WB probably hadn't the slightest idea of Epyphany's ability to speak, much less comprehend. They agreed to maintain the mental link as their exclusive means of communication and keep the secret of Epyphany's intelligence and powers as one more weapon in their growing arsenal.

When Sadjah left she assured Epyphany the new accommodations would be ready soon.

THE AQUARIUM

His first impulse was to transport his new prize to the Retreat. Then WB reconsidered, imagining the look on the faces of his esteemed colleagues as they viewed his incredible acquisition. He knew any public knowledge of the mermaid would start a feeding frenzy of both greedy promoters and ambitious scientists, but typical of his egocentric logic, Wild Bill put glory before common sense. He reigned in his overzealous plan and decided to invite only a very select few, each of which would be required to take an oath of secrecy punishable by financial ruin or worse.

Wild Bill owned multiple holdings in the port of Fremantle Australia, one of which was a substantial stake in one of the world's largest aquariums, the Aboriginal Sea. His quirky brain started to hum with ideas. Though he was consistently far more fanciful than practical, WB was often able to accomplish what less imaginative and less wealthy men could not. The more he considered the idea the more he liked it. While the men on the Silver Finn fashioned more suitable accommodations for the mermaid, WB contacted his people at the aquarium informing them to prepare a very large and private tank "immediately if not sooner."

Even after all his years of affluent privilege, WB was still surprised how quickly things can be accomplished when money is no object. Within hours he received good news from the Aboriginal Sea. They were just a few months from opening the Harbor Wing but funding had dried up. Ninety-five percent of the work was done, they just needed money to stock it with native flora and fauna and put the finishing touches on the viewing area. With a large infusion of cash the new tank and viewing area could be ready for his private use within a couple weeks if necessary. By the end of the conversation they agreed that ten days was indeed possible. WB was elated. He couldn't wait to tell Sadjah his plan. He thought, "Now she should be happy. Her new aquatic friend will have the biggest and best tank money can buy."

Sadjah

On her way back from the sub to her cabin she decided to check the progress on Epyphany's new tank. Sadjah began to think about the ambush. Now that so much had changed in her heart and mind, she needed to reevaluate everything in her past dealings with her father. She wondered how he managed to trace her to the Samudra Hantu. Though she had been entirely truthful with Thurrow recounting her long and winding journey from Seattle to their rendezvous, she could understand how he might now find her story suspect. Sadjah just couldn't make sense of it herself. Her strategy was foolproof. If someone had been following her they would have found it impossible to stay on her trail.

Some of Thurrow's enthusiastic conversations concerning high tech innovation must have stuck in her subconscious. She found herself thinking about surveillance technology and the variety of devices she'd grown up with. From her earliest childhood memories to the driveway make-out sessions, she could now recall the ubiquitous cameras. It saddened her to think about the staged and recorded events in her life . . . she decided to do some research on high-tech bugging devices.

Sadjah met her father at the ship's maintenance facility and after reaffirming progress on the new tank they proceeded to his office. WB was bubbling over with excitement as he told her of his plans for the mermaid and the aquarium.

Sadjah's initial reaction was one of horror. Thinking about Epyphany caged in an aquarium, no matter how large, was appalling. She hid her thoughts from her father and pretended to enjoy his enthusiasm for the project. While WB babbled on about the people he would impress and the envy he would stir, Sadjah began to see the positive side. As a young girl she and a classmate had visited the Aboriginal Sea, so she had a general idea of the layout. It was located at the very edge of the harbor with efficient access to both the Swan River and the open sea. WB's egomaniacal grandstanding would undoubtedly afford at least a couple of opportunities for escape.

Sadjah snapped out of her reverie when she heard Thurrow's name. She interrupted WB. "What was that about Thurrow?"

"I said, wouldn't it be nice to invite your boyfriend? He could see that his secret discovery was safe and well provided for."

Sadjah had to bite her tongue. She used all the self control she could muster just to keep from slapping her father hard across the face.

"You need to know that he is not my boyfriend anymore and I doubt he'll be very amenable to dealing with you on any level. You invaded his research area and stole his subject. Why do you think he would even consider it?"

"Well, to my mind, I have two of his favorite females in my possession. I don't want you to take this as a threat, but it would be easy to convince him that both you and the mermaid are my hostages."

"Why do you even want to see him?"

"I need his brain. Thurrow has turned down every opportunity I've given him. He won't work with me no matter how much money I've offered . . . but now I have something he wants. I need you to convince him that it's in his best interest."

Once again Sadjah realized that things were playing right into her plan. She softened her tone. "I'm sure he thinks I had something to do with the kidnapping, he would never believe a man would kidnap his own daughter."

"He doesn't think too highly of me, I don't doubt he would consider me capable of such a thing. Anyway, I have the mermaid, and if he wants to be involved with the research he'll probably overlook most anything. I'm sure you still hold some power over him." WB added in a condescending tone,

"I hear you are very skilled when it comes to manipulating the opposite sex."

What little respect she had left for her father evaporated. Sadjah ignored the implication and asked, "How do you propose I convince Thurrow?"

"I'm sure you'll think of something, you're a trained negotiator." WB returned her phone. "I'm sure he'll answer your calls."

"I'll think about it." Sadjah grabbed her phone angrily. "I need to use your office to get in touch with Pisces. I've got a lot of work to catch up on. Can I have some privacy."

"Be my guest." WB turned and left the room with a satisfied grin.

Sadjah looked at her phone and remembered, "This could be bugged, I don't want to give WB any more info than he already has." She sat down at the desk, logged into her secure account and began researching surveillance technology.

An hour later Sadjah leaned back and sighed out loud. She couldn't believe the options available to spy on people. The devices had been miniaturized beyond belief. She continued her research until she stumbled upon an article relating to one such device that had been successfully implanted in a human. Sadjah clicked a link and an illustration appeared. Blood drained from her face and she turned ghostly white as a cold shiver ran up her spine. It was a satirical cartoon from a popular men's magazine depicting a woman anesthetized, lying back in a dentist chair with her mouth wide open. The dentist held up his oversized tweezers holding a very tiny pellet-sized device. He was addressing a man opposite the chair who watched the procedure with a big grin on his face. The caption read "You'll never have to worry who she's with again!"

Sadjah gasped when she read it. A memory flashed . . . she was about fourteen, her father was at her side at the dentist office. Thinking back she couldn't remember why he would be in the office with her. She had perfect teeth and she remembered distinctly how the dentist always remarked, "You're my best patient, I never have to do anything more than a cleaning."

If it wasn't for the recent events, Sadjah would have never imagined her father capable of such a despicable invasion of her privacy. When she thought of the implications she was mortified . . . every moment . . . every word . . . all these years! Sadjah decided she would have to take a chance on the phone. She sent Thurrow a short message.

THE CALL

Thurrow was monitoring activity on the Silver Finn through the telescope when his phone buzzed. It was a short text message. "I have my phone back. Can you do a remote scan of this phone to check for bugs? E is safe."

Thurrow didn't realize how stressed he was until he felt the tension flow out of his shoulders and neck. Knowing Epyphany was safe was a great relief, but he still didn't know what to think about Sadjah's role in the kidnapping. He decided there was nothing to lose by doing the remote scan, and if he was really communicating with Sadjah there were a lot of questions he needed answered.

The phone was clean. Thurrow was left with the nagging question: "How did WB find them?" He returned a message. "Phone safe - I'm nearby - bring me up to date."

Sadjah was surprised and comforted to know Thurrow had somehow located them. She explained the situation and after several minutes of texting, he was fully briefed and understood the basic outline of her escape plan. Then she surprised him with an odd request. She informed him of her suspicion about her father, then gave Thurrow all the information she could remember about her trip to her dentist as well as her recent research findings. She asked him if he knew someone who could hack her dentist's computer records. Until she knew for sure, Sadjah dared not speak any words of importance aloud.

Thurrow told her he would do his best and get back to her. He didn't feel the need to let Sadjah know, but he was confident Samu could have the information in short order. One half hour later, Sadjah's suspicion was confirmed. Thurrow wasn't quite as surprised as Sadjah, but the news reaffirmed there was no end to the devious means WB would employ to fulfill his misguided vision. Wild Bill was not a man to trifle with.

In the process of lifting the dental records, Samu took it upon herself to find out the specifics of the implant and the means to disable it. It was surprisingly simple. Sadjah need only, find a thin piece of aluminum foil, place it over the designated tooth and bite down hard several times. The early models used the area at the top of the molar as part of the antenna. The small current generated by the foil was significant enough to short out the delicate electronics in the transmitter.

Sadjah received the news with mixed emotions. She was elated to find such a simple solution and looked forward to her renewed private life, but the confirmation of her own father's shameless intrusion on her life saddened her deeply. Sadjah quickly found a member of the crew with foil wrapped chewing gum, asked for a piece then hurried off to her cabin to endure the short unpleasant experience of chewing tinfoil. She had no reason to doubt Samu but there was no way to confirm if the implant was completely deactivated. Sadjah guessed that WB was beyond showing any consternation openly, but she resolved to stay alert to any unusual questioning.

Wild Bill was enjoying his adventure and very pleased with the way things were going. Then his phone lit up. It was the chief investigator from his full time surveillance team. The man was nervous and stuttering, he finally found the words and blurted out, "The implant is dead." WB's jaw dropped, he couldn't believe what he was hearing. He blasted his man with questions until it finally sunk in. They didn't know how or why but the implant was useless. Sadjah was untethered.

Both Sadjah and WB were informed that the tank was ready for installation. Sadjah alerted Epyphany to the welcome change in circumstances and urged Epyphany to use her heightened empathy to detect any subtle mood swings in Wild Bill.

When she met WB at the sub, the men were bringing the pieces on board. She didn't know if it was her imagination but she thought he was acting a little suspicious. Sadjah decided to press him a bit.

"Everything ship shape on the Silver Finn? You seem a little stressed."

"Very perceptive of you. As a matter of fact, I've just been informed that we've lost contact with one of our important sources of information."

Sadjah hid her surprise. She knew he was testing her but in the process he had showed his hand. She replied innocently, "Will this affect your aquarium plans?" At the thought of the Aboriginal Sea, he brightened. "No, thankfully that will go forward as planned."

The designers for Epyphany's new tank did an admirable job working around the limitations of the allotted space. The new design had enough room for Epyphany to be fully submerged and to adjust her position freely. It also had a cyclical exchange system to allow fresh seawater into the tank at regular intervals. Sadjah insisted on some medical attention for Epyphany while the new tank was being assembled in a different compartment. Under Sadjah's supervision, the men were very gentle as they transferred Epyphany to her improved confinement.

THE ABORIGINAL SEA

WB's relationship with Sadjah was civil but he felt he was losing influence with her. She quizzed him about his interest in the Silver Finn and expressed her surprise at his involvement with the operation. She admitted she'd been under the impression he and Pisces were no longer connected. WB quickly sidestepped her questions and changed the subject. Each day seemed to confirm that many conversations with her father, past and present, although sprinkled with truth, were mostly based on fiction.

During the layover Sadjah was pretty much free to roam as she pleased. At least she was free in name. Since WB insisted she win the confidence of his mermaid, Sadjah had full access to Epyphany, allowing them plenty of time to discuss the various escape possibilities the Aboriginal Sea might afford. As an added precaution, their serious discussions took place on the silent Oojai wavelength.

WB gave Sadjah very little information about his long-term plans. A couple of times she overheard him drop the word "retreat" in conversations with the submarine captain. She was familiar with rumors about WB's secret island, but until now she hadn't given them much attention. With her newfound insight into her father's true nature, Sadjah suspected that such a place was likely to exist.

Doing her best to make good use of her time on the ship, Sadjah spent her days researching details about Fremantle and the Aboriginal Sea. On her visit to the aquarium as a teenager she hadn't paid much attention to details, but revisiting the memory triggered childhood moments of awe. Sadjah relived those wide-eyed feelings again. She recalled jaw-dropping scenes uncluttered by knowledge and experience, feelings of spiritual awakening that made her want to fall to her knees and raise her head to the heavens, and the overwhelming desire to be emerged in that watery, sensuous world. She remembered standing under the of the massive wall of glass, mesmerized by the beauty and majesty of the creatures floating, seemingly flying, through an alien world where color and light played tricks on the eye, where swift-moving shadows flew into shimmering shafts of undulating luminosity, revealing the horrific dead black eye of a shark, or the outrageous translucent rainbow of gossamer fins. Sadjah could almost feel the strain in her neck from the hours she had spent sitting on the floor with her head titled back as the multiple varieties of fish competed for her attention.

As she learned more about Fremantle, Sadjah began to look forward to the visit. It was a charming little port city that was reported to have maintained much of its historical architectural integrity. There was a river running through the town emptying into Fremantle Harbor, which was surrounded by several estuaries filled with a diverse population of birds and aquatic life. She was intrigued by the indigenous black swan, a very large and beautiful bird that made its home along the banks of the Swan River. Sadjah realized this alluring little port might serve her purpose quite well.

She was delighted to find the architectural plans for the Harbor Wing of the aquarium, along with the blueprints of the original construction. Much of the information made little sense to her, so Sadjah forwarded all the links to Thurrow with the hope that he could come up with a viable plan.

Using Sadjah's information as a starting point, Thurrow handed off the investigation to Samu. After a short while he had more information than he anticipated. Lacking any factual information about WB's sub and its capabilities, he did his best to put together a few different scenarios and fed them to Samu in an effort to narrow down the possibilities of what a successful strategy might look like. He needed to rescue both Sadjah and Epyphany safely and efficiently. Though he gained some valuable insight, Thurrow was disappointed with the results of the analysis. Samu simply didn't have enough specifics about WB's submarine or the timing. There was no way of knowing how many people would be involved or what type equipment would be used for the transfer. The weather would also be a big factor as Thurrow knew firsthand from the recent ambush.

He hated to admit it to himself but it seemed a safe rescue was highly unlikely at this time. Samu recommended he bide his time and just observe the transfer, reminding him that it was only Epyphany's immediate freedom at stake, not her life. Thurrow bristled at the thought of WB treating Epyphany like a trophy and parading her in front of his cronies like a show horse.

The upside of all the research and strategizing was the wealth of knowledge he had gained about Epyphany's new habitat. She would certainly have plenty of space. The new tank was one of three of the largest tanks in the world. It would hold a staggering 7,500 tons of water, approximately two million gallons, roughly equivalent to three olympic-sized pools, and featured a two foot thick acrylic panel 30 feet high and 100 feet long. The press release promised a diverse aquatic population including whales, sharks, electric eels, sting rays, seahorses, giant crabs, and a variety of fish of all sizes. Thurrow paused as he tried to imagine what the press would say if they knew it was to become the temporary home of a real mermaid. Thurrow had no idea if the tank would house anything other than Epyphany while WB held it for his private use, but he suspected she would have some company. He also had no clue how long she would be held captive for the pleasure of Wild Bill and his guests.

After a week aboard the Silver Finn, WB was growing restless. Rumors of a captured mermaid started to spread among the crew and a few survivors of the "vision" started comparing mermaid nightmares. Word of this reached Wild Bill, so he decided they had better prepare for departure soon. The daily communication with the aquarium team at Perth served to increase his impatience, and his excitement was growing as the project neared completion.

With Epyphany settled safely into her new accommodations, WB ordered his men to prepare for departure. Thurrow noted the renewed activity on the sub and Sadjah confirmed the pending departure with a short text. Since he knew their destination he wouldn't need Storm to tail them; in fact, he decided not to tail them at all. He instructed Samu to chart a course for Fremantle. Thurrow planned to get there ahead of WB and observe preparations.

MESSAGE RECIEVED

Before departure, Thurrow sent a text message to Sadjah. "Any communication with Blyss?" She replied, "Epyphany thinks the sub is using a similar stealth system to Samu's and it's blocking her signal." Frustrated, Thurrow tried to think of a way to get through to Blyss, then he remembered Storm. Perhaps he could boost his range by merging a message with Dali and Storm.

Throughout the days of monitoring the events on the Silver Finn, Thurrow made a point to check in with Dali regularly. Dali was fully recovered physically and had been venturing into the ocean a couple times a day. As a result of some helpful counseling and conversation with Thurrow, he had also reconciled the facts of the ambush and come to terms with the realities that were beyond his control. Dali was ready to help.

Thurrow summoned Dali and Storm and shared his plan. They decided it would be worth a try. Floating just below the surface, Storm and Dali swam in close to Samu and waited as Thurrow lowered himself into the water. Thurrow dove down between Storm's monstrous head and Dali. He placed one hand next to Storm's large penetrating eye and with the other he held Dali's dorsal fin. Thurrow figured it couldn't hurt to be physically as well as psychically connected. The message was brief by design. They closed their eyes simultaneously, concentrated their mental focus on Blyss and sent the message: "All safe. Hope to rescue Epyphany and Sadjah in Fremantle."

When they could no longer hold the thought they drifted apart, then Thurrow swam swiftly to the surface gasping for air and holding his head. He wasn't injured, but the strain resulted in a unique and disorienting sense of detachment.

He felt like he needed to literally pull himself back together. After a few minutes Thurrow recovered his equilibrium and climbed back on board as Dali swam back through the locks and into the pool. Storm would stay behind and keep tabs on

WB's progress. Thurrow gave the signal and Samu quickly accelerated on a full speed heading, straight to Fremantle.

There was no way Thurrow could know how quickly WB's submarine would get to Fremantle, but he had complete faith in the Samudra Hantu's ability to precede the sub's arrival by a day or two.

Message Received

A ghostly stillness permeated the Cavern Temple. The remaining members of the tribe were swimming in the bay awaiting news of Epyphany. Blyss sat quietly meditating on "patience" at the foot of the Golden Tower. Her fruitless efforts to communicate with Epyphany were disconcerting at the very least. Though she had never taken their extraordinary connection for granted, she would have never anticipated her reaction to this extended separation. Blyss felt uncharacteristically anxious and incomplete.

Suddenly her meditation was interrupted by a brief but informative thought bundle. Blyss immediately bounced the good news to the rest of the Tribe, then relaxed a few moments before trying to analyze the message. It was surely sent from a great distance and she was quite sure that Thurrow couldn't manage that distance on his own. She assumed therefore that "all" included Dali and Storm.

Blyss climbed the Tower and prepared to respond to Thurrow's message. She knew it was too far for an actual conversation but she wanted to confirm the success of the communication. By using the Tower to enhance the connection, there was a chance she could re-establish a more stable link. Blyss thought it possible that each successful coupling would heighten Thurrow's ability, and if she could break though to his consciousness there was a distinct possibility of a more permanent link.

BLACK CIRCLES

The ocean was calm as Samu sliced through the gently rolling waves. For the first time in more than a week Thurrow could enjoy a little down time. After a short nap he rose and headed to his lab. Rested and recharged, he decided to focus his energy on reviewing previous climate research. The freak storm that occurred during the ambush remained a troubling mystery. Life on the open sea is by nature a world of constantly surprising weather events, but the timing, intensity and brevity of that particular storm had no precedent in Thurrow's experience.

Samu kept a continuous archive of international weather events. Thurrow enhanced the program with a filtering system that could aggregate the extreme events as well as small or unusual atmospheric anomalies. If a traditionally dry region experienced unprecedented rainfall or an unusually long drought, if tornadoes showed up in unlikely areas, or if the frequency and strength of weather systems rose above average anywhere in the world, Samu could quickly collate, categorize, and analyze the data.

He accessed the archive and cross referenced the co-ordinates of the small island outpost with the weather data and the date. Initially he found nothing, but when he narrowed it down to the exact time and magnified the short series of satellite photos, there was a visual indication that only served to confuse him further. At first he thought it was a round black cloud hovering over the island, but on closer examination he realized it was much too symmetrical and much too dense. It appeared to be solid black. Then it occurred to him . . . the satellite wasn't registering a black object, it had recorded a complete absence of visual data. Whatever the cause, it successfully obscured that small island from view, momentarily absorbing or dissolving luminosity itself.

Thurrow had to sit back for a moment, relax his mind and body, steady his breathing and quiet his emotions. He was a scientist after all and now was not the time for wild conjecture. Throughout his academic training and the following years of research, the use of the scientific method had served him well. It had become such an instinctive toolset he was surprised at his own emotional response to this new discovery. He smiled to himself and thought, "At least I haven't become a complete analytical nerd."

So he tried to line up the facts in order to make some sense of the information.

*The satellite registered the momentary absence of light.

*Light is electromagnetic radiation whose wavelength falls within the range to which human vision, and likewise the powerful space camera, respond.

*Light consists of energy quanta called photons that behave partly like waves and partly like particles.

Thurrow knew from his recent studies that solar storms were on the increase and large solar flares and the resulting electro-magnetic fallout were responsible for periodic communication interruptions and satellite malfunctions. He also knew that traditionally the earth's atmosphere protected us from the adverse effects of these events. But . . . it was a proven fact that in recent years large holes have been appearing in the upper layers that once protected us. He felt sure that the storm he witnessed had something to do with a powerful magnetic field. He found it suspect that the event would happen at the precise moment of WB's attack. Then his blood ran cold. What if Wild Bill had developed an electromagnetic weapon with which he could manipulate the weather? It was a horrifying thought. Continuing down that dark tunnel of inquiry he wondered if such a weapon would also exacerbate the already growing problem of the diminished ozone layer.

Thurrow thought back to the bizarre event and tried to rewind time in slow motion . . . the water was flying up out of the sea, not raining down! Not swirling like a water spout, but actually raining up! Whether natural or man-made it was an alarming anomaly. He decided to see if it was a unique phenomenon.

With the photo series as a reference, Thurrow entered the new data into Samu's database. His goal was to see if the archives held any evidence of similar black circles. While he waited for the results, Thurrow spoke to Samu. "Initiate a new scan and filter for the top ten extremes." Sitting in front of three large monitors, Thurrow was shocked to see all three screens light up with high level alerts. The pictures were alarming. Within the past couple months several areas of the planet were exhibiting startling transformations. The most frighting was the very recent evidence of an unprecedented increase in ice melting on both polar caps and Greenland.

There must be hundreds of scientists who are aware of these facts. Thurrow wondered who might have the power to suppress that kind of information. It was too easy to blame WB for every negative occurrence on the planet, but the ambush was proof that WB had never really abandoned his legendary legacy of acquisition. Thurrow realized he would have to initiate a serious fact-finding mission. Questions streamed through his mind . . . what had WB been up to in the last ten years since he stepped off the world stage of high finance? Where did he spend most of his time? How much was he worth? Who were the people in his inner circle?

If Thurrow could find a few names perhaps he might stumble onto the trail. The one thing he knew for sure was WB had some major interest in the Aboriginal Sea. He made a mental note to assign Samu yet another new data mining project.

Samu directed Thurrow's attention to the refreshed monitor images on two of the screens. On one screen was a graph charting the location, chronological order, and duration of the "black circle" effect. On the other was a slowly rotating 3D replica of Earth, which revealed an ever increasing number of dots. The first appearance was nearly five years ago; the last was on the day of the ambush. There must have been well over fifty dots speckling the earth's surface. Many were seemingly in the remote areas of the ocean, but some were on dry land with several in densely populated areas. On a whim, Thurrow had Samu superimpose an overlay of the registered shipping lanes on the speckled globe. The map confirmed his worst suspicion. At least thirty percent of the dots lay directly over shipping routes. Thurrow hesitated, afraid of what else he might find. With a sense of sad anticipation he then instructed Samu to add another category to the graph. He wanted to see the date and location of all reported incidents related to the interruption or disruption of shipping, recreational, and research vessels. The screen refreshed again and Thurrow felt his body sag from the weight of his heavy heart. There was no doubt, the black circle was not an act of nature.

THE TRANSFER

Soon after Thurrow left for Fremantle, WB informed Sadjah that they would be leaving within a day. Turning on her charm, Sadjah succeeded in convincing her father that though she couldn't agree with his tactics, she understood his impulse to share the mermaid discovery with the world. She forgave him and reassured him of her enthusiasm for his aquarium project. Sadjah praised WB for the great lengths he was going to in providing such a spacious habitat for his mermaid, and she took the opportunity to thank him for his faith in her own abilities, telling him it was an honor to be in charge of the welfare of such a unique and beautiful creature. WB, still unaware of Sadjah's and Epyphany's telepathic connection, set aside his suspicions and soaked it up without question, responding with a promise to tell the aquarium officials to give Sadjah 24/7 access to his mermaid. While she was on a roll, Sadjah made one more request. "Would it be possible for the men to outfit the mermaid quarters with a bunk for me?"

WB was somewhat surprised but couldn't see any harm in it, and so replied, "If you think it would be helpful for her transition, why not? Yes . . . certainly . . . good idea, child." He knew there was nothing to lose since the room was already monitored around the clock.

Early the next morning, after one final inspection of the sub's improvements, WB gave the order to proceed to Fremantle. Sadjah retired to her new quarters and notified Thurrow.

Epyphany had never experienced such consuming loneliness. Though she was doing her best to keep her spirits up, every hour she spent immobilized in the holding tank served to demoralize her further, pushing her closer to a debilitating depression. Epyphany's heavy heart lightened when she learned Sadjah was going to be bunking in her room. Sadjah was well aware of Epyphany's fragile mental state so when she informed Epyphany of their destination, she did her best to emphasize the temporary nature of the situation and tried to stay upbeat as she described the cutting edge facility. However they both knew a cage was still a cage, no matter how large or luxurious.

Over the course of the journey to the Aboriginal Sea, Sadjah barely ventured out of the cabin. She succeeded in distracting Epyphany from thoughts of further captivity by sharing ideas and expanding on their plan of action once they reunited with Thurrow. Thinking of the future helped to improve both of their moods. The fact that Thurrow was pivotal in their shared imaginings seemed to be an accepted, unspoken truth. Neither questioned the other's love for Thurrow. Epyphany related more stories of life on Oojai, and with the passing hours their bond became even stronger. Equally deprived of childhood girlfriends, they found solace and strength in their new found friendship. The two schemers also managed to find humor in imagining alternate scenarios in which Epyphany might use her strength and powers to frighten WB to death. The dark humor also helped Sadjah deal with the love-hate relationship she had recently developed for her father.

Near the end of the short journey they were pleasantly surprised to receive some good news from Thurrow. He had arrived in Fremantle a full two days ahead of them and was having unexpectedly good luck gathering a small trusted team of potential co-conspirators. Not surprisingly, it turned out WB had succeeded in making more enemies than friends in the close-knit marine biologist community. Though his money was welcome, his management skills left much to be desired. Ever since his directive to take over the the largest tank in the facility, many other important projects were put on hold or altogether scrapped. All the secrecy around WB's new private wing only served to frustrate and infuriate the administrators. It didn't take much coaxing to get them to relate inside information.

Thurrow made a tactical decision to make his presence known. His appearance in Fremantle might put Wild Bill on guard but Thurrow figured WB would still be gloating and high on the success of his ambush and likely to underestimate Thurrow's reprisal.

Thurrow's reputation as a world class inventor, author, and research scientist opened a lot of doors in Fremantle. With no inkling of Thurrow's and WB's contentious relationship, the aquarium's director instructed his staff to answer any questions their distinguished guest might have. Thurrow got in touch with the crew responsible for populating and maintaining the complex eco-system. He learned the procedures by which the diverse species were transferred between tanks, as well as the means of off loading larger sea mammals from the various delivery vessels. Armed with this detailed information, Thurrow knew there was still little he could do until he was able to observe WB's defense strategy. He was sure that WB would be fully aware of his presence by the time the sub arrived with his precious cargo and would spare no cost on security.

Special Delivery

It was no accident that WB chose to deliver his treasure under the cover of night. Samu picked up the sub's trail as soon as it surfaced in the bay, where it made its way carefully into the mouth of the Swan River.

There was no moon, but the night sky was clear and the stars were exceptionally bright. Thurrow was dressed in black, holding a pair of military issue night vision goggles and standing in the shadows on the second story landing of a busy warehouse across the the river from the aquarium's loading dock. His small team of trusted disciples were stationed with concealed video cameras at strategic locations outside and within the Aboriginal Sea. Thurrow planned on documenting every detail of WB's operation and he wasn't leaving anything to chance.

Samu notified Thurrow of the sub's approach and he pulled the goggles over his eyes. The dark night was transformed into a bright alien green world where Thurrow could make out the facial expressions of the small crew standing on the sub's deck nearly a quarter of a mile away. He spied WB as he joined the crew, looking like a demented leprechaun, laughing and joking with his first mate as they plowed through the frothy emerald river. A thin smile transformed Thurrow's serious expression as he thought to himself, "Enjoy Epyphany's company while you can, my greedy friend. You have no idea what you are dealing with."

Two long box trailers pulled up perpendicular to the dock and parked parallel to each other, leaving about a ten-foot corridor between the dock and the loading platform. A large forklift rolled out of the aquarium warehouse and trundled down the ramp balancing a long stainless steel tank. Water sloshed over the side as it turned sharply between the trucks and made it's way down the dock.

Thurrow was glad he had enlisted the video team. With the trucks in place he would be lucky to get even a brief glimpse of Epyphany's transfer. A stretch limo rolled slowly down the alley between the warehouse and the aquarium, then parked near the loading ramp. Two very large men got out and stood waiting near the car. Thurrow was happy to receive a message from one of his team assuring him of a perfect view down the makeshift passageway.

Activity on the sub increased. WB climbed to the top of the bridge to oversee the operation, then a large hatch opened on the side of the bridge tower from which Sadjah and two more bodyguards emerged. Several of the crew went back down the hatch. Ten minutes passed, then finally all eyes were on the deck. More crew members stepped out of the large opening onto the deck and formed a double line back-to-back. Thurrow could sense the tension on board the sub. It was obvious that only a handful of crew members had any clue what their precious cargo was. Everyone stopped talking and the line quickly parted, making room for the four strong men carrying a very large litter. This custom design had extended sides and looked more like an oversized coffin with open ends. Thurrow only caught a quick peek of Epyphany's tail fluke. If anyone else was observing this transfer they would assume it was just a large dolphin.

The men moved hastily down the gang plank and lowered the litter into the tank until Epyphany, still strapped in, was fully submerged and suspended in such a way as to allow her face to remain above water. The suspension straps were secured and the forklift carefully backed its way between the trucks. Meanwhile, WB, Sadjah, and the four guards were picked up by the limo and taxied around to the entrance of the new wing.

Thurrow left his lookout and motored across the river to rendezvous with the outdoor contingent of his team. During his brief boat ride, a hint of doubt concerning his hastily assembled team crept into his consciousness. He decided he should reevaluate his assistants as soon as possible. Before he docked his skiff he sent Samu the list with a directive to do a full background check on each participant. While reviewing the list one name jumped out at him, Warrain . . . he remembered now. He had met the young man briefly a couple years ago at one of his lectures. Thurrow recalled a pleasant, intelligent, informed and enthusiastic conversation. He pulled up to the dock and made a mental note to evaluate Warrain's dossier first. He could use a trusted assistant with the ever increasing responsibilities that had been stacking up recently.

He met the men, and as he collected the cameras he reminded them of the importance of secrecy. If even the slightest hint of this transfer were to leak, their jobs and their futures would be in jeopardy. Thurrow assured them that they would be generously compensated for their assistance and any further information they could supply him.

Now Thurrow was ready for the next phase of the bold plan that he, Sadjah, and Epyphany had agreed upon. Walking straight to the main entrance of the Aboriginal Sea, he took the short flight of steps two at a time. He smiled and made a mental note to give his team a bonus as the unguarded double glass doors slid open. Without hesitation, he entered the vast lobby of the aquarium. Thurrow stopped, looked up, then slowly scanning the space, inhaled involuntarily. The breath caught in his chest and he almost forgot to exhale. "They have spent a lot of money since I was here last." If it weren't for the important mission he was on, he could have stood in that one spot for an hour and still not taken in all there was to see. The cavernous space was dimly lit by simulated moonlight filtering through the water and glass that arched overhead. It was beautiful and frightening at the same time. Overwhelmed by the tons of water above, he felt like the weight of the entire ocean could crush him in an in instant . . . his instinct was screaming for him to flee this place, but the rational part of his mind was ecstatic with both the sensory delight and the awe and respect for the artists and engineers responsible for this masterpiece.

Thurrow snapped out of his reverie and continued to explore the underwater passage. Knocking lightly on the thick door at the end of tunnel, Thurrow was surprised when a large, dark-skinned face poked through the door, grinning ear to ear.

Thurrow exclaimed, "Well, what do you know! Hi Warren . . . I was just thinking about you."

Caught completely off guard, the young man stammered and stuttered for a moment, then held out a beefy hand and said in a thick Australian accent, "It's Warrain, sir. Good to see you again. Follow me."

CONFRONTATION

Thurrow quietly followed Warrain down several dark hallways, marveling at how such a large man could be so light on his feet. Suddenly he was given the signal to stop. They could hear voices at the next turn. Creeping slowly forward, Warrain peeked around the corner. Two of WB's massive thugs were guarding the employee's entrance to the viewing area of the Harbor Wing. One of the men was talking on his phone while the other was texting on his. Before Thurrow had a chance to speak, Warrain quickly moved towards the guards flashing some kind of badge. The men looked up, putting their phones away as they reached into their jackets. The next instant they were on the floor out cold. Thurrow just stood there with his mouth open. He walked slowly toward the door still trying to make sense of what he'd seen. "Wow! Watford! Where did you learn that?"

"Warrain, sir . . . my grandfather was the tribe shaman and my dad was a martial arts instructor. I earned my black belt by the time I was twelve." Thurrow's curiosity was piqued. He looked forward to reading Samu's report on this enigmatic young man.

Smiling, Thurrow asked, "So Watson, do you have any intelligence to share before I step though this door?"

Warrain hesitated a moment, then returning the smile, relaxed a bit and answered, "As of five minutes ago WB's team was preparing to load the specimen into the tank under heavy guard. Although we have extensive video of the procedure up to this point, no one on the team has been able to get a direct shot of the actual fish. Wild Bill is reported to be in the viewing area alone with . . . S . . Sa . . Sad . . ."

"Sadjah? How do you know who that is?"

Warrain tensed up again. "Well, she's very famous, or I should say, infamous, in the oceanographic community. As one of the senior officers of Pisces, she is often quoted on the company's questionable fishing policies. Also, I have an acquaintance who is researching an article on her." Warrain's voice trailed off as he realized he may have said too much. Then without thinking he blurted out, "She's a stunning woman!"

Thurrow laughed. He could see that Warrain was quite smitten. "Right you are on all points." Thurrow was glad to hear that none of his team had captured any footage of Epyphany. He was extremely frustrated with WB's ill conceived decision to bring her to such a highly attended public setting. Thurrow knew he wouldn't relax until Epyphany was swimming safely in the secluded lagoons of Oojai.

Warrain asked, "Would you like me to go in with you?"

Thurrow answered, "No, but you can stay right here and text me in five minutes. If I don't answer, call for backup and enter. I don't anticipate any violence."

Thurrow had a good feeling about Warrain, but he wasn't ready to share any information about his complex relationship with Sadjah and Epyphany.

Thurrow opened the door as quietly as possible and slipped unnoticed into the shadows of the large viewing area. The room was as impressive as the lobby. This large wing was designed with private events in mind. Guests would have to drive through a gated entrance to the VIP parking area. A wide set of marble steps lead up to a spacious veranda overlooking the harbor. The atrium was a marvel of transparency with it's beautiful view of the sea through the unobstructed glass exterior wall and an equally intriguing view into the viewing area through an interior glass wall. Viewed from the outside, the effect was that of a human terrarium within an aquarium.

He suspected that each area of the Aboriginal Sea held it's own unique visual statement. Though the lights were low Thurrow's attention was immediately drawn to the immense statue forming the interior entrance. Some very talented sculptor had created an incredibly lifelike model of the mythological Kraken. It turned out that this rendering of the legendary giant squid was not far from the reality. Using sophisticated deep sea recording equipment, creatures measuring as much thirty-five feet had been documented in recent years. Thurrow had studied some of the footage, and by the looks of this exquisite representation, so had the sculptor.

The artist used imagination and some artistic license to create a spectacular effect. Bathed in deep purple light, the visitor entered and walked under the mantle of the squid where the eight undulating arms formed a maze-like tunnel of tentacled columns. At the end of this short tunnel the two long feeding tentacles curled down within a foot of the floor then curved back up and out forming a beautiful asymmetrical arch. Enthralled, the visitors' eyes would naturally follow the seductive shapes upward where they would find themselves staring into the gigantic single eye of the fantastic creature towering over them. The designers of this project were certainly given an enviable amount of artistic freedom. It was no wonder they had run out of money before WB came along to bail them out.

Thurrow made his way slowly along the wall in order to get a better view of Epyphany's new home. The monumental tank was flanked by two short rows of tall glass columns nearly twelve feet in diameter. Two of these impressive cylinder aquariums contained large specimens of jellyfish floating eerily in the muted white light generated by the integrated LED ports. The others held only gently swaying plant life, but Thurrow assumed these free standing tanks would be alive with exotic specimen when the first visitors arrived. At the foot of the main tank, standing about halfway between the two rows of columns, Thurrow saw WB and Sadjah talking quietly. There was no sign of WB's ubiquitous bodyguards. Thurrow walked out of the shadows and approached the pair. Counting on the element of surprise, he had chosen not to prepare a speech. His primary goal was to just throw WB off guard. He simply said, "Hello, Bill."

WB was so engaged in conversation with his daughter he hadn't seen Thurrow approach. He jumped at the sound of Thurrow's words. It took him a full minute to collect himself. Thurrow took that moment to make eye contact with Sadjah. Lord how he had missed those eyes!

Although WB planned to eventually invite Thurrow to a private showing, he hadn't considered that Thurrow might take the initiative to tail him. Just as WB was about to respond, the trio was interrupted by activity in the tank.

They heard a splash and gazing up into a swirling cloud of air bubbles they witnessed what no human had ever seen or imagined possible. A scene as beautiful as it was sad, they watched the first real mermaid swimming in captivity.

At first Epyphany was totally disoriented. She let herself rise to the top of the tank and for a few moments she just floated motionless. After weeks in confinement her strength had diminished and her flexibility was somewhat impaired. However, Epyphany was a creature of the sea and it didn't take long for instinct to kick in. She swam a few circles on the surface then with a powerful thrust of her tail she dove straight down. Epyphany continued to explore the tank, gaining speed as she gained confidence. Moving swiftly through water was part of her identity, she could feel her brain spark, feel her muscles stretch. Though she was in captivity she let the joy of movement fill her consciousness and she temporarily forgot the past few weeks of misery.

The moment she slowed down to rest, Epyphany realized she was being watched. She surfaced briefly then dove down to bottom of the smooth transparent wall that kept her and several thousand tons of water from crashing down on her spectators. Swimming to the space in front of her friends and her captor, she put her hands against the glass. Thurrow and Sadjah stepped forward, each placing a hand opposite Epyphany's large hands. She closed her eyes and spoke to them in their silent language, "Don't worry, I'll be alright for now. Just do what you have to do." Thurrow looked at Sadjah and they both turned around to face her father.

They were shocked . . . Wild Bill was on his knees . . . weeping!

"She's so alien . . . so uniquely beautiful . . . incredible . . . magnificent."

Thurrow suddenly realized that WB had never seen Epyphany in her natural habitat. All she had been to him was another rare acquisition. He doubted if WB had even visited her after the capture.

WB spoke softly to himself, "What have I done?"

By the look on her face, Sadjah seemed just as baffled by Wild Bill's second statement as Thurrow was.

Thurrow spoke angrily. "What do you mean by that? I'll tell you what you've done. You've caged a very special creature. Far more special than you can imagine. You've tried to lay claim to the most miraculous being this planet has yet to produce, possibly the most important step in human evolution since the beginning of sentient life on earth. You may think I'm enraged because you stole her from me. You are blind! She has never belonged to me or anyone else, she belongs to the sea. You have robbed her of her home as sure as you and your greedy stockholders are robbing all the ocean species of their home. While you plunder the sea for profits you are stealing the future from all children. You are deaf! Deaf to every word that doesn't serve your singular and shallow purpose and deaf to those who speak the truth. You have lied successfully for so long you've come to worship a god of deceit."

Thurrow was interrupted by his vibrating phone. He replied to the text from Warrain, then seconds before he switched it off he noticed the screen distort. He turned his attention back to the wretched man before him.

WB had stopped crying, rising to his feet he walked hesitantly to the glass. He couldn't take his eyes off her. The captor was captivated. Epyphany stared back at him and pressed her face close to the glass. She opened her mouth wide, glaring at the little man in a silent scream with her arms raised high, and her palms open to the heavens. WB became distressed and confused. Was she pleading . . . accusing . . . offering herself?

WB turned away, the sweat rolling off his brow, visibly shaken. Epyphany closed her mouth, winked at Thurrow and Sadjah and gently rose up the wall.

After several moments WB's heart rate retuned to normal. He wiped his brow and a sly grin replaced his concerned expression.

Thurrow noticed the grin and said, "What are you grinning about? Did you hear a word I said?

"What? Were you speaking to me? So rude of me. You see, I was quite entranced with this fine discovery of yours. She is so strangely enchanting. I had a brief moment of regret, but not to worry, I've come to my senses. She is even more spectacular than I imagined. A lot of people would pay a lot of money just to stand in the same room with her. Perhaps you'll consider working with me now? Do think she could be trained? I'm willing to share the glory of her discovery with you. "

Thurrow had to step back before he did something he would regret. Sadjah stayed close to the tank looking up at Epyphany and wondering what their next move might be.

Thurrow managed to stay rational in spite of an intense desire to strangle WB right then and there. He addressed WB in a cold quiet tone, "Do you have any idea how quickly this place will be overrun if even a hint of her existence is leaked?"

WB laughed. "You consistently underestimate me, my good man. You got lucky with your timely arrival, but within the hour this place will be secure beyond your comprehension. The only reason you're still standing here is the simple fact that the distortion field override cameras had not yet been activated. Try taking a picture right now.

Thurrow pulled out his phone and engaged the camera. No matter where he pointed it all he saw was a fuzzy rainbow of color.

"Try recording some audio." WB didn't try to mask his smug tone.

Thurrow played back the track and was rewarded with a single tone of white noise. He thought to himself, "At least WB might keep her safe for a while."

"I don't know how you overcame my guards, but by now every hallway and entrance to this room will be equipped with full surveillance and no less than three men on each door as well as a roaming patrol 24/7. You and Sadjah will no doubt want to catch up, so you are both free to go. Thurrow . . . you'll be getting a special invitation soon. Now it's time for you to leave, I need time to contemplate the future." As they walked under the giant penetrating eye of the Kraken, WB added a final lascivious word. "Hope you two have as much fun as I'm going to have with my mermaid."

Sadjah dug her nails into Thurrow's arm just to keep him moving through the entrance. "Ignore him. He's just pushing your buttons. You know he's no match for Epyphany."

AMBIGUOUS CONFESSION

Seeing Sadjah restrain Thurrow made WB smile. He wasn't used to being rebuked so even the smallest feint gave him pleasure. The moment Thurrow and Sadjah were out of sight, WB was on the phone ordering his guards to bring him some scotch. Within minutes he met them at the rear entrance, took the tray, closed the door, pulled one of the viewing couches closer to the tank then made himself comfortable.

As he picked up the bottle of scotch he addressed the tank. He couldn't see Epyphany but he knew she was watching him from the shadows.

"Well Epyphany . . . alone at last . . . yes . . . I know your name. You'd be surprised at how much I know. I'm not exactly sure how smart you are but I do know Sadjah and Thurrow are quite impressed with your abilities. I'm looking forward to finding out for myself. Right now we're going to celebrate your induction into the civilized world. I think the first thing you should know is . . . how to enjoy a fine glass of single malt scotch."

Epyphany couldn't believe what she was hearing. "Who is this foolish man?" A chill ran up her spine as a question ran through her mind. "Is he insane?" She knew one thing about insanity, it could be dangerously unpredictable.

"So my precious, before we sip the golden nectar, the first thing we do is place one or perhaps two ice cubes in a whiskey glass and gently pour two fingers of this fine blend slowly over the ice." He looked up at the tank and said, "of course I know you're in there and I'm betting you are a curious creature. How else could Thurrow have trapped you in his net? If you can hear me come closer sweet siren and learn."

She could hear WB just fine. Between her enhanced ability and the natural sonic conductivity of water, the thick wall of glass barely muted WB's words. Epyphany was indeed curious. She also figured she might as well play it his way and let him think he was manipulating her. So she swam slowly into the beams of soft diffused light.

"Ah! There you are! So you can hear me. Wonderful! Let us proceed. Now you see the ice is melting, adding just the right amount of water, unlocking the aromas and flavors while keeping the beverage enjoyably cold. Now, do we drink? No. Not yet. Watch me closely now." WB held the glass in one hand and placed the other hand over the glass, covering it with his palm. He swirled the scotch in the glass. The ice made a pleasant sound, reminding Epyphany of the faraway chimes she had hung near her Chancel. Showing off a bit, WB accidentally spilled some of the precious liquid. He looked up, smiling like a moonstruck teenager on a first date and said, "oops! terrible waste!"

"Now the reward." He held the glass to his nose and took a long whiff, losing himself temporarily in the sweet cloud of merciful, fragrant fumes. He raised the glass to Epyphany as she drew near the front of the tank.

"Here's to you Epyphany. To our future! One day you will thank me!"

With that said, WB emptied the contents down his throat.

He sunk back into the couch, took a deep breath, then looking at the empty glass , exclaimed, "Yes! Yes! Yes! . . . my apologies, sipping is the preferred method . . . but I needed that!"

WB poured himself another and said, "what a shame you can't join me. Maybe sometime soon, after we get . . you know . . better acquainted. You'll find I'm not such a bad sort." He took consecutive sips from his drink as the first shot started to relax his tongue. "You know . . . people have no idea how much pressure goes along with being one of the richest men on the planet. It's not easy meeting all those demands and expectations. So you see Epyph, I just allow them to believe I'm only "kinda" rich and I play the bumbling buffoon. They would be frightened out of their skins if they knew how much I'm worth." At that WB hiccuped, then laughed, which caused him to hiccup again until he couldn't stop hiccuping.

Epyphany thought " he doesn't have to play the buffoon, he's a natural."

WB recovered and trying to hide his embarrassment continued his rambling monologue. "I don't have many real friends. My peers can't be trusted, actually I don't feel I can trust anyone, not even my own daughter! I must admit that I have also made my share of enemies pursuing my passion. Yes . . . passion . . . what is life without passion? Oh I'm sure you have no idea what I'm babbling on about but even a simple minded creature like yourself must know a kind of passion. . . in fact I'm pretty sure we share at least one or two passionate interests . . . the mighty ocean! I love the ocean! The sea has brought me untold witches . .hic-hic . . riches. You must have seen so much that I will never see, boundless treasures beneath the rolling waves." With shining eyes WB took another gulp of scotch, lost in time, he gazed into the distance for several moments."

Epyphany took the opportunity to surface, thinking "how long is this drunken sailor going to regale me with his mindless chatter?" She heard him start again and swam slowly down in hopes of hearing something of value.

Wild Bill was slurring his words now. "Oh to be that young pirate again. What a pair we could have made if I had found you then. A pirate and his merrrrrmaid. Well . . yes . . yes indeed . . you'd be surprised to know how close I came to finding you . . . but I found her instead. She was out of her head of course and how could anyone expect me to believe the crazy things she was saying? Hysterical she was, a regular madwoman, and tall, such a long legged beauty . . . had all I could do to pull her up and into my ship. Enough! Enough! You are here and my queen . . . I . . mi . . mi . . . I mith . . . I miss my queen . . . so alone . . . she waits . . . and, and . . . alright now! . . things are going to be fine. . . believe-

me-my-fishy-friend you'll be so . . so . . . st . . st . . stunned .
. . . downright . . . . miraculous . . .

His words tapered off into random mumbles, WB teetered
over on his side and passed out.

Epyphany didn't know what to think but she found his bizarre
monologue curiously troubling.

INQUIRIES

Once Sadjah succeeded in calming Thurrow down, he thanked her for keeping him in check. "I don't know how you manage to conceal your contempt for that man," said Thurrow. "I suppose your management skills must kick into auto-pilot by now. Anyway, it's nice to finally be alone with you. There's not much we can do for Epyphany right now . . . want to take a ride?"

Sadjah nodded and Thurrow walked her over to his car.

"Nice ride! I see you weren't kidding when you said you were going stay in WB's face while you're here. You certainly won't be hard to track in this. What is it?"

Thurrow smiled down at the flashy two-seater. "A good friend here in Fremantle loaned it to me. He's out on tour for a month or so. It's a 2012 Tesla. That was the year they started to get the whole electric car thing right. You think it's too much?"

"No. I think it's you."

They hopped in and Thurrow said, "Buckle up, this thing flies!"

The second Sadjah was secure, Thurrow nailed it. Without leaving a trace of rubber and with only a negligible whir, as promised they practically flew out of the parking lot. They drove over the bridge crossing the Swan River and out onto the winding estuary roads. The top was down and the sun was coming up. With the warm air swirling through her hair, Sadjah could hear the sound of the marsh creatures waking up to a gorgeous day. Safely hugging the road, the silent roadster zipped around a ninety degree turn and surprised a flock of birds. The silhouette of black swans against the early morning light, gracefully rising into the sky, was breathtaking. Sadjah was transformed.

Looking over at Thurrow, his face aglow with boyish pleasure, Sadjah felt that familiar longing. She hadn't thought about sex for days and she sighed out loud. Thurrow glanced her way with a sly smile and said, "I think I know what that sigh means . . ."

Sadjah took his hand from the wheel and placed it on her thigh. Thurrow instinctively slowed the car as he moved his hand gently under her short skirt.

"I'd better not crash my friend's Tesla. He'd never forgive me."

Sadjah smiled and let her head relax against the headrest. Tilting her head seductively, she spoke in a breathy whisper, "I have faith in your multitasking skills."

Sadjah unbuttoned her blouse and let the warm air caress her breasts while Thurrow slid his fingers between her legs and said, "My, my. . . I didn't expect Fremantle to be so warm and damp."

When the couple returned to the Samudra Hantu they were famished. Sadjah offered to make a quick breakfast.

While they gulped down a substantial helping of French toast and fresh fruit, they discussed their options for dealing with WB. Sadjah was still in the dark as to what her father may be planning to do with Epyphany in the long term. She relayed WB's off-hand remarks about some kind of retreat. She admitted to having no idea what WB might be referring to.

At the word "retreat" Thurrow looked up from his food. "That rings a bell. Several years ago he tried to induce me to work on a "hush-hush" project of his. It was something about updating security at his retreat. So many rich dudes like to throw the word "retreat" around I didn't pay much attention. He might have said "The Retreat," I don't remember, but it's worth having Samu do some high-tech snooping.

Thurrow excused himself and headed down to his studio. He gave Samu her assignment, then decided he needed a little distraction while he waited for some answers. There were so many issues to consider: Epyphany's safety, the pending rescue operation, his feelings for Sadjah and Epyphany, WB's next move, and most importantly, how each small decision might impact the larger questions threatening the safety and welfare of the myriad inhabitants of the planet.

Sitting at the recording console, he clicked his folder of original music and selected the latest mix of Oojai Sunrise. It had been a while since he'd listened to the work-in-progress. Even as a rough mix, the song could bring him back to those peaceful days on Oojai. It never failed to sooth his troubled mind. He placed the headphones over his ears and was about to speak the "play" command when he heard and felt that strange but familiar vibration. This time it wasn't an actual "bundle." There didn't seem to be any specific message attached, but it left no doubt in Thurrow's mind that he was linked to Blyss. The tether was fragile but it still gave him comfort to know she was there. There was nothing in the vibe that signaled an emergency so he assumed it was simply Blyss affirming their connection. He leaned back in his chair, relaxed his mind and tried to focus his thoughts. He simply opened his mind and pictured the events from the past several days. When he was finished he had no idea if Blyss would receive or respond but he was left with a pleasant sense of her presence.

Meanwhile, Sadjah had completed her own connection with Epyphany, who informed her of WB's tedious drunken monologue and confirmed that she was not in any danger. Sadjah didn't find it necessary to relate the details of her morning cruise with Thurrow, but it wasn't out of any sense of guilt. She and Epyphany chose not to burden the trio's special relationship with the weight of inadequate rules and definitions. They had come to terms with Thurrow's place in their lives.

THUD!

Standing like a helpless bystander on the fringe of his own dream, some part of WB's consciousness was being held hostage by his own untethered imagination. He was aware, but he just couldn't manage to wake himself up.

It started out as a very pleasant dream in which Epyphany was swimming lazily in his humongous pool. He was on the far side of the pool in the shade of a towering stone facade. The deep blue sky was clear and the sound of a woman's rich, soulful voice was drifting up, mixed with the soothing vibrations of the gently crashing waves below. Epyphany started to do laps around the pool. On each lap she would turn and smile when she passed. WB couldn't take his eyes off her. She started picking up speed and he began to feel dizzy. As the tempo increased, his mind began to play tricks on him. Each time she passed, her head seemed to morph into a different creature. At first they were recognizable species—a dolphin, a pelican, a manatee—but they quickly became strange combinations of turtles and birds and alligators. The sky grew dark and when WB looked up, a small black dot was rushing toward him, growing larger by the second. The wind raged and the singing became a loud and dissonant choir. He was suddenly falling up, surrounded by screaming voices, ringing bells and frightening, unearthly sea monsters, all rising toward the descending black dot. In an instant he was suspended in thin air, looking into the monstrous black eye of the giant Kraken.

WB fell off the couch with a dull thud and rolled on his back, awoken by the sound of his phone alarm. When he opened his eyes he was staring up at the monstrous black eye of the giant Kraken. Disoriented for a moment, he hoped he was still dreaming. He lay there stricken with fear until he realized it was just a reflection of the giant sculpture in a wall of glass. His temples were throbbing as though his head was strapped to a thundering kick drum. When his eyes finally focused, the next thing he saw was an empty bottle of scotch. He looked back up at the tank and everything came rushing back . . . or almost everything. "Epyphany . . . she is here, she is mine! " He recalled some fragments of his one sided conversation. "I hope I didn't say too much . . . god . . . what did I say?"

All night his men had been trying to figure out what to do. The only instructions he had given were to not disturb him unless it was an emergency, to absolutely stay out, and to guard the room from any further intruders. When they finally received a message from WB they were exhausted from worry, but relieved.

Riding back to his suite, WB rationalized his actions and told himself, "She probably has no idea what anything means at this point. Even if she were brighter than a dolphin by a factor of ten, she couldn't possibly have any frame of reference."

After a light breakfast and a couple Bloody Mary's, WB was feeling a little better. He had so much to do. Thinking of his newfound treasure, his excitement was revived. He spent the remainder of his day firming up his plan and compiling a short but impressive list of VIPs. Any doubts about his security measures were overshadowed by visions of glory and gold. Epyphany was a rare treasure and WB, greedy by nature, spent a good deal of thought trying to figure out how to best capitalize on her uniqueness.

There was so much he didn't know about her. It finally dawned on him that Thurrow was right about one thing—he was taking a chance housing her in a public facility. But it was a temporary solution that would serve his immediate purpose; he would take her away promptly after the "exposition." Once he had her settled in at the Retreat he could fly in specialists, take his time, and learn everything he needed to know.

WB hadn't counted on Thurrow finding him so soon but he felt confident that his secret was safe. Thurrow wouldn't risk exposing Epyphany to danger for the sake of revenge. He decided to stay with his original plan and put Thurrow on the guest list. WB snickered and thought, "It will keep things interesting."

Within a few short days WB had pulled together the legal formalities and set his plan in motion.

THE BIG TANK

Though Epyphany never stopped longing for the open sea, after the confines of the submarine, she was finding her new accommodations quite satisfactory. With only the occasional intrusion of the overanxious tank maintenance staff, she had plenty of time to exercise and rehabilitate.

The tank designers had done an excellent job with the interior. It was populated with indigenous salt water plants, and through the tasteful use of actual coral-encrusted rock harvested from the ocean, it achieved an authentic sense of reality. The rock was teeming with a variety of micro and macroscopic marine life. In the aquarium design world it was known as "live rock." While providing shelter for the inhabitants, the live rock, covered with multiple colors of coralline algae, served as both a biological filter and the major decorative element of the aquarium. In this case it was integrated with synthetic materials and used to build a magnificent aquascape of caves, arches, and overhangs. Using LED lighting components made of hundreds of very small bulbs and controlled by a micro-computer, the system cycled through a simulation of the natural variations of daybreak, sunset, and moonlight, including the phases of the moon. Adding to the realism, the tank had been stocked with some of the smaller species of marine life prior to Epyphany's arrival.

After the stress of the transfer and the strange evening listening to WB's drunken ramblings, Epyphany was suddenly overcome with weariness. She curled up on a small outcrop near the surface and slept through an entire cycle of artificial light.

When she awoke from a dreamless sleep, Epyphany had no idea how long she had slept but she figured it must have been quite a while because she was starving. She smiled when she saw the tray of food lying on the rock nearby. Her captors obviously had no idea what a mermaid diet might consist of. There was a variety of samples to choose from; a fresh vegetable salad with dressing on the side, some bread with a shallow plate of olive oil, a stack of lunch meat, a lovely plate of sushi, and finally, an opened can of tuna fish. Epyphany was familiar with the concept of canned food but she still found "fish in a can" depressing.

She started with the most interesting. Like the rest of her senses, Epyphany's palate was highly developed and likely as sophisticated as the most cultured gourmet. She also had the advantage of a digestive system that was evolved to digest just about any nutritional substance available. Epyphany was an omnivore accustomed to living in a habitat stocked with an abundance of nourishing options and flavors beyond human imagination. Though raw fish was her mainstay she had never seen it prepared like the samples in front of her. She pierced a small rice roll with one long sharp talon the same way she might skewer a small fish, and popped it into her mouth. Epyphany was pleasantly surprised by the flavor, and just like any human counterpart sitting at her favorite fancy sushi restaurant might react, she tilted her head slightly, smiled and let out a little sigh of pleasure. After so many days of immobility, discomfort and depression, Epyphany had grown accustomed to her diminished appetite and had ignored her body's need for nourishment. Now her instinct for survival kicked in, and she devoured the plate of fish in record time and continued to make her way through the remaining offerings until she was completely satiated.

She slipped into the water and let herself sink slowly down. Her tail touched the bottom and she swam slowly to the surface, gently inhaled, then repeated the meditative cycle several times. Once her meditation was complete, Epyphany swam over to the outcrop and pulled herself up. The rest, food, and exercise had served her well. She felt good. It was time to focus on her escape.

Epyphany's thoughts drifted, and as she let each notion pass she attained profound clarity. She felt a comforting cloak of serenity enfold her and she became aware of a gentle whispering voice in her mind. Epyphany smiled, barely conscious of place and time. Then it slowly dawned on her, Blyss had found her.

The link strengthened, and for the first time in weeks Epyphany experienced real hope. Though her faith in Thurrow's and Sadjah's abilities never faltered, she had always assumed that Blyss would also be there to back them up. After the ambush and the isolation, Epyphany's confidence was shaken. Blyss was the only other being on the planet who understood her. She was not only a teacher and spiritual guide, Blyss was a trusted friend.

Epyphany managed to control her excitement, and regaining her tranquil state, began to absorb the meaning and intension of each well-chosen word in the transmission.

Even though Blyss was using the Gold Tower to boost her range of communication, it was a strain nonetheless. She had used up a great deal of energy in an earlier link to Thurrow and she needed to be mindful of the extent of her abilities. There still wasn't much she could physically influence from such a great distance and she tried to use her resources efficiently.

Blyss warned Epyphany to refrain from any direct confrontations with her captors and reminded her of the powerful weapons they had at their disposal. She reinforced the need for Epyphany to trust her partners and to defer to their judgement when it came to dealing with other humans. She also relayed some of Thurrow's information and reassured Epyphany they were doing their best to figure out where WB might be taking her when he made his next move.

Epyphany started to feel the link weaken, so she used the remaining seconds to ask Blyss to give her love to the tribe and to tell them she missed her island family.

Then Blyss was gone.

THE INVITATION

During Epyphany's first few days at the Aboriginal Sea, Sadja was able to make regular visits. Within a couple days Epyphany appeared to be totally and miraculously recovered from the painful submarine experience. As the weekend drew near, Sadja overheard WB refer to an unveiling that was to take place sometime on Sunday. She had tried to coax some information out of him but he was maintaining an unusually high degree of secrecy. Then on Friday, Thurrow received an envelope by courier. He sent Sadjah a text and they met for lunch to open it together. They ordered their lunch and Thurrow handed Sadjah the envelope. She used one long, sharp fingernail as a letter opener and tipped the envelope toward Thurrow. A tiny, silver thumb-drive fell on table. He opened his laptop and inserted the drive. The computer automatically scanned the drive for malware before the screen flashed this message:

The honor of your presence is requested in the Harbor Wing of the Aboriginal Sea two days henceforth at 1:00 am. You have been chosen as one of twenty to attend this high-security event, a once-in-a-lifetime chance to view firsthand what is perhaps the most extraordinary discovery in all written history. Clicking the link below will take you to a secure server with details and RSVP options.

WARNING: Should you decide to attend, you will be subject to physical and electronic searches, including body scans. All your private security personnel must remain off premises. All audio,video, and communication devices will be automatically disabled.

ATTENTION: Once you click the link you will have fifteen minutes to RSVP. After such time the site will be unavailable and the drive will erase and eject automatically.

"Choose well; you will not regret it."

signed, WB.

Sadjah spoke first. "Looks like I'm not invited. Do you trust him?"

Thurrow shook his head as he answered. "I have never trusted him, but I need to be there . . . you and I need to come up with some kind of contingency plan."

When he clicked the link he was faced with a short list of demands to which the guest would have to agree in order to attend the exhibition, the central theme being that the guest must not share any knowledge of the event with a single soul until such time as WB decides to make his discovery public, with no guarantee as to when that might be. Also, it ensured the guest was aware that they may have to take their secret to the grave, else face grave consequences. All of which was reinforced by the following injunction:

"If you choose to click yes it will be considered your electronic signature, signifying a legally binding agreement between the promoter of this event and yourself. If after the exhibit you should decide not to honor the agreement, there will be no guarantee for the safety of your reputation, yourself, your family, or your property. This is a threat."

Thurrow read it again slowly then handed the laptop to Sadjah. She read it through and handed it back with a questioning smile. "You've got five minutes left!"

Thurrow moved the cursor over "agree" and clicked.

The screen momentarily flashed, "PREPARE TO BE AMAZED," then went black. The drive ejected.

As he rebooted the laptop, Thurrow looked at Sadjah and said, "We have a lot of work to do in the next 48 hours!" He made a few calls while they wolfed down their lunch, and they quickly returned to the Samudra Hantu, where they would spend most of the next two days working out the details of a dangerous and daring new plan.

OPERATION SPLASH! PART ONE

The invitation was an unexpected opportunity, but two days seemed an impossibly short time to put together their plan. WB had complicated things further when immediately after sending out the invitations he forbade Sadjah from visiting Epyphany. Thurrow needed someone on the inside who could be trusted implicitly. With no time to review the full security report on Warrain, he spoke to Samu. "List education, interests, skills, and current attachments, subject: Warrain." Thurrow smiled to himself thinking, "The kid has a good sense of humor. I don't even know why I started messin' with his name."

Samu responded, "male, Aboriginal heritage, age 28, martial arts, math wiz, percussionist, computer geek, skilled hacker, video editor, Master's degree in both marine biology and environmental sciences, worked on and around boats since childhood, scrimshaw artist, plus a myriad of lesser interests. Currently single, regular communication with a slightly older female living in Seattle, name: Ondina."

Thurrow was impressed but found the Seattle connection curious. "Samu, brief stats for Ondina." Thurrow remembered Warrain mentioning the Facebook friend.

"Age 32, Mexican heritage, single, degree in journalism, minor in creative writing, self-taught illustrator, currently freelance writer for several publications, mostly women's magazines, relocated to Seattle eight years ago."

"What is the status of her relationship with Warrain?"

"It appears to be a budding Facebook romance. They met through a Facebook group focused on mermaids and marine environmental issues called 'Mersophical' and have been messaging and sharing increasingly for over a year. They have never met in person."

"Mermaid and marine environmental group?"

"Affirmative. The members are mostly environmentalists with a well informed 'devotion to the ocean' and a shared interest in mermaid lore, related science fiction and fantasy. The name 'Mersophical' is derived from 'mermaid - philosophical.'"

That was enough to convince Thurrow, so he decided to rely on his instincts and take a chance. Warrain clearly had more than enough qualifications for the job. Thurrow contacted Warrain to set up an interview.

When Warrain got the call he was in the middle of a lively Facebook discussion with Ondina and several other Mersophical members. He signed off without an explanation and took the call. He was surprised to hear from Thurrow and intrigued by the urgency of the secret meeting.

With Sadjah ashore working out some details, Thurrow instructed Samu to take a quick spin around the bay and anchor a reasonable distance from shore. From there, Thurrow was able to leave his ship in the mini-sub without fear of being detected. The meeting took place a couple of miles from the Aboriginal Sea, on a secluded dock where the two men were able to hold the interview in complete privacy.

Warrain reached the pier a few minutes before Thurrow's arrival, giving him a few minutes to ponder the situation. He had been following Thurrow's career since early high school. In fact, it had been one of Thurrow's first documentaries that had inspired him to study marine biology and research. Growing up around the beautiful and diverse aquatic flora and fauna of Fremantle's harbor, Warrain gained a deep spiritual connection to the sea and its inhabitants at a very early age. He was a naturally curious person who had inherited a superior intellect from a long line of Aboriginal shamans and respected elders. Raised in a culture whose tradition and fundamental philosophy was to never worry, he was influenced by his ancestors' practice of Daddiri, "the deep listening and quiet stillness of the soul," also referred to as "The Dreamtime," the belief that all paths will be made clear to them in time.

So when the sub appeared Warrain felt no apprehension,

only an excited anticipation to find out what path his life may be taking. He wasn't disappointed. With the clock ticking Thurrow wasted no time getting to the point. First he exacted a pledge of secrecy to all the information he was about to impart. For some reason, Thurrow had no qualms about trusting Warrain. He thought, "There's something about this kid, something beyond purity or innocence, he seems to embody the essence of truthfulness."

When the short conversation was finished, Warrain had agreed to act as liaison, assistant, first mate, and general all-around sidekick. While Thurrow gave his new associate the abridged history of Epyphany and the world of Oojai, and clued him in on the pending rescue mission, Warrain had to use every ounce of self discipline to contain his excitement. He didn't doubt a single word, but even his sharp mind was taxed to it's limit trying to process the awesomeness of it all. The entire situation was truly beyond his fertile imagination.

At the end of the briefing Thurrow said, "I'm sure you're brain is swirling with questions, and I'll answer as many as I can in time, but right now I need to know that you understand the magnitude of your decision to participate in this dangerous operation. What we plan to do is so far outside the law there is a good chance you will never be able to return to a normal life. I'm hopeful that we can do this without implicating you or killing anyone, but there is no guarantee."

Warrain agreed willingly. His only second thought related to Ondina. They had made no promises to one another, but she was the first woman he had known who inspired a true empathetic connection. He had a feeling she would understand. Ondina was a journalist, and she would often say, "I just have to follow the story." Warrain knew he had to follow this story and hoped that one day he could share it with Ondina.

When Thurrow returned to his ship he checked in with Sadjah, confirming Warrain's participation and firming up their timetable. Thurrow then used Samu's computer to brush up on his physics, crunch some numbers, analyze the data, and run a simulation. He was pleasantly surprised to see the possibility of success landed in the seventieth percentile. No matter how he tweaked it, Samu never gave him any better odds.

Thurrow decided to take little break. He hadn't slept for twenty-four hours, but he was still wired. His brain functions were reaching the point of diminishing returns and he really needed to chill. On the way to the upper deck he grabbed his stash. Leaning on the rail and staring blankly out over the bay, Thurrow filled his pipe, took a deep hit and held it. Then something in the shadows caught his eye and he gagged uncontrollably, blowing out a cloud of smoke. He quickly slid closer to the wall opposite the rail and hit the light switch. Thurrow couldn't believe it.

Reefer! Thurrow had to chuckle. Reefer was perched in the corner of the deck fast asleep on his feet. Thurrow flicked the light switch several times and Reefer slowly opened his eyes. He knew it was his imagination, but Thurrow could have sworn Reefer was wearing a silly grin. The thoughts ran swiftly between them and Thurrow soon learned the nature of this unexpected visit.

When Blyss received the brief message from Thurrow, Dali, and Storm, she had dispatched Reefer to Fremantle. When he reached his destination, Reefer found Storm waiting in the bay just outside Fremantle Harbor. He rested there for a day. Flying only at night for fear of discovery, Reefer cruised the harbor looking for an opportunity to land on Samu. When he saw her anchored in the harbor that evening, he seized the moment, only to find Thurrow gone, so he waited. Happy to gain another trusted ally, Thurrow brought Reefer up to speed on the current operation and enlisted his help for aerial reconnaissance.

Things were pulling together and Thurrow was starting to think the plan might actually work. Once again the element of surprise was crucial. WB would never expect them to try a rescue at such a well guarded event.

Warrain's first task was to hack into the Aboriginal Sea's surveillance system without alerting anyone to his presence. Part of the plan necessitated Sadjah gaining access to the Harbor Wing without being seen or recorded. Once inside the room, her first task would be to brief Epyphany. Much of the success of the operation depended on Epyphany's extraordinary voice, her strength, and her desire for freedom. Thurrow and Sadjah agreed that the decision to continue the mission was entirely up to Epyphany. If she wanted to take her chances with WB they would understand.

Sadjah's second assignment was to supply Epyphany with two small sonic concentrators and the crucial instructions for their placement. Thurrow was ninety-five percent sure that his hastily improvised shields would allow the devices to function, in spite of WB's electronic jamming measures.

The following night Sadjah found her way around to the back of the tank, climbed the stairs and met Epyphany on the maintenance platform. Before handing off the devices, Sadjah knelt down and held out her hands to Epyphany in the same manner as the day they met weeks ago on the Samudra Hantu. Epyphany grasped Sadjah's arms, and locked in their singular embrace, they looked each other straight in the eyes, wordlessly exchanging the fear and love they felt for one another. After a few moments they released their grip and Sadjah handed Epyphany the devices.

Epyphany swam to the back of the tank while Sadjah transmitted the instructions. The devices needed to be carefully hidden but still able to send each of their unobstructed triangulated beams to a specific point on the interior of the tank wall. After a few minutes of experimentation, they were both satisfied with the placement. Sadjah then relayed several more technical questions and instructions. Epyphany had no trouble grasping the details of her role in Thurrow's ingenious plan. As always, she was impressed with Thurrow's knowledge and the innovation required to attempt such a scheme.

OPERATION SPASH! PART TWO

The Event

By midnight on Sunday, Wild Bill was starting to relax. The scotch helped. He stood back and admired the beautifully designed curtain hanging in front of Epyphany's aquarium. WB's shameless homage to himself depicted an artful rendering of King Neptune in his own likeness sitting on a throne of gold, surrounded by a bevy of exotic mermaids. WB raised his glass to no one in particular and proclaimed, "This is my night . . . here's to my greatest achievement."

The caterers were busy putting the finishing touches on the late night gourmet buffet and stocking the bar from an impressive list of fine wine and spirits, including several rare bottles of 1907 Heidsieck champagne from his private stock. The members of the string quartet were warming up on the enclosed stage. The musicians would be seen and heard by the guests, but they were positioned off to the left of the tank and restricted to the stage. With no clear sightline to the tank they would be left to wonder at its contents.

WB's elite security force had been briefed and their numbers were reinforced with a backup patrol to handle the perimeter of the entire complex. The center of the viewing area was tastefully retrofitted with a raised platform of plush auditorium seating. Two tall cylindrical tanks stood off to the left and right side of the room, each set on a four-wheel-drive motorized dolly, ready to be moved into position in front of Epyphany's tank. These rolling aquariums would house the professional aquatic performers WB had handpicked. Costumed in convincing mermaid attire, the four gorgeous, athletic swimmers were scheduled to perform a short synchronized underwater routine just before the unveiling.

He couldn't think of anything he had overlooked. There was nothing left to do but wait for the first guests to arrive. WB caught the eye of the young, attractive bartender. Losing no time, she supplied him with yet another scotch.

Arrival

Like clockwork, the limos started arriving at 1:00 am. The waiting line of cars grew longer as each guest was subject to WB's high-security procedure: a driver pulled up to the entrance and two large men stepped out of the car, met by two of WB's equally large security guards. Then all four of the men opened their jackets, displaying their weapons to establish that no foul play from either party would be tolerated. The rear door was opened and WB's men escorted the guest through a portable rapid-scanning system capable of detecting organic and inorganic threats, metallic and non-metallic objects, concealed liquids, ceramics, plastic explosives, narcotics, contraband, and currency. WB wasn't taking any chances. The jet-setting guests were familiar with the procedure, and in keeping with the agreement, no one among them had anything to hide.

Warrain's expertise was proving invaluable. He had successfully hacked into WB's security system and patched a link to Thurrow's phone. Parked a short distance away, Thurrow was able to watch the amusing parade from his car. The line moved quickly, and as it drew near the end, Thurrow pulled up to the entrance in the Tesla . . . with no bodyguards. When he joined the guests inside, Thurrow scanned the crowd and was surprised to see some familiar faces. He never imagined WB to be connected to such a diverse and powerful network of world leaders and celebrities. WB had been partially right, Thurrow had definitely underestimated his influence.

Keeping to himself, Thurrow took on the role of observer. Looking around at the wide assortment of men, he wondered at the common denominator that brought them to this event. They would not be unfamiliar with WB's questionable reputation, so they obviously knew him on some level far deeper than the tabloid headlines. Perhaps some of them were in his debt and found it useful to humor him. Or maybe they had profited from one of WB's sly business maneuvers. It was hard to believe that many or any of them were real friends. Thurrow didn't imagine WB would be an easy friend to have. His charm was so shallow and, according to Sadjah, he seldom had anything good to say about the accomplishments of others.

Most of the guests were WB's age or older, with only a handful under forty. Thurrow recognized several guests: a twenty-something movie star, a researcher who had testified on Pisces behalf some years ago, a couple of middle-level diplomats, and one unapologizing third-world dictator. There were nearly as many countries represented as there were guests.

Water Dance

The group had been drinking, eating, and mingling for a almost an hour when the lights dimmed and the string quartet ended their last piece. A sensual female voice filled the room, softly requesting that the gentlemen take their seats. It occurred to Thurrow that the men seemed a shade more altered then what a short cocktail hour would induce. He was thankful for not having sampled the refreshments. Settled into the comfort of the luxurious accommodations, Thurrow felt the low frequency pulse of a subwoofer pushing out a subtle trance-inducing beat. In the darkened room, he could make out the silhouettes of the large columns as they rolled smoothly in front of the curtain. Suddenly two tight beams of white light lit up the empty tanks in sync with the introduction of a faint syncopated latin guitar rhythm. A moment passed, then right on cue, a cymbal crashed as two objects fell out of the dark, splashing separately into each tank. The light changed to deep blue, turning the splash to sapphire droplets. The scene repeated— but this time, green light . . . splash/crash. . . a shower of emerald drops.

At each crash the group jumped collectively. When the light turned to a warm amber, the audience let out a simultaneous sigh. Each tank held two gorgeous mermaids floating perfectly still, face to face in perfect symmetry. On closer inspection, Thurrow realized the couples consisted of one convincingly costumed mermaid and one woman clad in a diaphanous ribbon of blood red cloth; the delicate fabric wrapped around the waist, clinging to hips and thighs and floating up and around her partner's long tail. At times they appeared to merge and flow as one, passing through each other like ocean spirits. The effect was hauntingly sexual. As the remarkable water dance continued, these gorgeous half-naked women moved ever so gracefully through a delicate series of slow motion routines.

The music gained intensity as the dancers became increasingly intimate. Weightless, time-stopping perfection! Thurrow now understood why WB made this a "men only" event. He was not immune to the erotic spectacle, but the primal symbiotic reaction of the rest of the men confirmed his suspicion that the they had been given a small dose of some type psychotropic drug. Wild Bill wasn't taking any chances; he wanted to give these guys an extraordinary experience. The more he thought about it, he reckoned WB wanted to loosen the men up for some kind of investment proposal.

After about five minutes into the performance, Thurrow began to wonder when the swimmers would surface for air, but they continued the dance. He double checked the time and started to question his own mental state. Thurrow knew all about the record-setting events in which people with unusually large lung capacity, filling their lungs with pure oxygen and remaining completely motionless, could hold their breath for over 20 minutes. But these women were performing strenuous feats of muscle control and motion. He was also familiar with the progress being made in artificial underwater breathing research. He had read about several alternatives that included pills, liquids, or electronic implants that were capable of improving the human body's ability to utilize oxygen efficiency by a factor of ten, but he was unaware of any documented success. WB was full of surprises.

The Toast

After nearly thirty minutes, the mesmerizing performance came to an end. Thoroughly impressed, the group of men were unrestrained in their cheering and applause as the tanks and their enchanting performers rolled swiftly away. It took a little while to calm the rowdy group, but WB finally managed to get them to quiet down. "If I could have your attention gentlemen . . . first, I just want to thank you for your trust. I'm so happy you enjoyed the magnificent performance. You'll have a chance to meet the lovely ladies a little later. But now . . . we approach the moment you have been waiting for. You will soon see I am a man of my word. What I am about to show you has been the subject of legend and lore in every language and culture throughout the centuries, and served as the inspiration for some of the world's finest works of art, from poetry and prose, paintings and sculpture, to music and theatre. But I dare say all those valiant attempts to render the dreams of imagination are pale in comparison to the reality. Tonight you have the privilege to behold the artist's muse in the flesh.

While WB spoke, the champagne was poured and served until each guest held their glass, politely waiting for WB to finish. The staff exited the room until only the four sequestered musicians, WB, and his guests remained.

"I'd like to propose a toast."

"Here's to curiosity, the mother of discovery."

"Here, here."

"Here's to wealth, the seed of discovery."

"Here, here."

"Here's to courage, the path to discovery."

"Here, here."

"Here's to the most important discovery of modern times!"

"Here, here!"

Curious to see the expression on their faces, WB continued to face his guests. The quartet began to play as the curtain behind him dropped slowly, gathering at the foot of the tank. After the water dancers, expectations were high . . .

WB heard the curtain fall the last few feet to the floor . . . the music stopped . . . he stared at the bewildered faces . . . the room was dead silent . . .

The guests were baffled and waiting. WB turned around . . . the tank appeared to be empty.

WB started to sweat visibly. Speechless, he waited. He had a backup plan if Epyphany decided not to cooperate, but he was hoping he wouldn't have to use it . . . he waited, silently questioning the sanity of his own plan . . . these powerful men would not tolerate anything less than amazement . . . he was forced to act . . .

Thurrow was in the front row. He knew WB's backup plan. When Warrain verified the rumors of WB's strategy, Thurrow was appalled, but when Sadjah relayed the information to Epyphany it turned out be another lucky break.

Still watching WB, the guests remained frozen in their seats.

Suddenly they heard a large splash. A cloud of air bubbles frothed and swirled in the back of the tank. The audience gasped in unison as a great white shark swam swiftly out of the cloud and, confused by its own reflection, raced toward the front of the tank, slamming its open jaws into the thick glass. It bounced back stunned, then turned and battered the glass repeatedly with its tail.

Though he knew WB's men could trigger an implant and disable the shark with the push of a button, Thurrow was the first in the group to stand, shouting at the top of his lungs, "How could you be such a fool?" As he stormed off the platform and headed toward the door, the others began to shout questions and threats, warning WB that he had better have another trick up his sleeve because they hadn't flown halfway around the world on a moment's notice just to see a shark.

Then, just as WB turned back toward the angry crowd, they stopped yelling. Slack-jawed and wide-eyed, each man in turn sank slowly back into their seats, anesthetized by the incredible scene.

The shark was still trying to attack the glass when Epyphany slowly moved out from the shadows. She wasn't afraid. Sadjah and Thurrow had warned her, and she reassured them that she had been dealing with sharks her entire life. They weren't mean, they were just always hungry and very, very stupid.

Wild Bill looked back at the aquarium and felt the fist around his heart unclench. A big smile blossomed on his face and his ashen skin began to regain the familiar ruddy complexion of a man who loved his scotch.

Meanwhile, Thurrow leapt down the steps three at a time. The guards instructions were to keep people out, but there were no instructions to stop anyone from leaving. He waved off the valet, ran past the Tesla and hopped on Warrain's motorcycle. Within minutes he had driven the short distance to his ship, boarded Samu, activated the monitors, and tuned into Warrain's designated frequency. The screens popped to life and Thurrow breathed a sigh of relief, thankful for Warrain's expert hijack of the distortion field override cameras. Samu immediately headed out of the channel to open water while Thurrow nervously watched the bizarre spectacle unfold. He hoped Sadjah's instinct was right when she convinced him that she should stay behind to serve as a liaison between himself, Epyphany, and Warrain.

The Shark

The shark was so intent on fighting its own reflection it didn't notice Epyphany approaching. In order to communicate with less intelligent species, she found sound more effective than thoughts. Hovering less than six feet away, Epyphany parted her lips slightly and began to emit a very low frequency tone. It was not unlike the purring of a cat, but for the fact that it was several octaves lower. The shark stopped thrashing, turned, and circled Epyphany. Rotating slowly, keeping the shark in view, she stretched her arms out in front of her with her palms raised and her thumbs pointing straight up.

The audience was stone quiet . . . mesmerized.

The shark moved in toward her until its snout rested in her hands. Still purring, Epyphany gently rubbed just above its mouth, inducing a catatonic state. The killer was like a baby in her hands. Maintaining that position, they floated to the top. Epyphany surfaced for air and the shark swam listlessly out of sight.

The duly impressed guests had recovered their voices and were talking excitedly amongst themselves. WB signaled the musicians to play softly while he mingled on the platform with his guests. It was just as he had imagined—each one vying for his attention, showering him with questions and offers. They praised his discovery and thanked him for the privileged viewing . . .

Then one by one the men stopped talking as they gazed at the tank. WB turned to see Epyphany floating in the center of the tank with her arms crossed and her head tilting down slightly, staring at him in a posture of pure defiance. The lighting within the tank cycled to an eerie twilight. A cold shiver of fear ran up his spine and his hand started to shake. WB dropped his drink.

The musicians, again baffled by yet another strange mood swing, stopped playing. This time they conferred quickly and packed up their instruments. They had no idea what was going on, but based on the vibe, they knew they wanted no part of it.

Before the last instrument was in its a case a new sound began to fill the room. It started with a very low note, lower than humanly possible, a reminder to WB that he had absolutely no idea what this creature was capable of. Captured in her gaze, he realized the source of his animal fear. There was no hate in her unrelenting glare, it was just the unbridled power of her being.

Some of the men were looking back and forth between Epyphany and WB, thankful to be outside her focused beam of intention. One by one, men were slowly edging off the platform.

Epyphany opened her mouth wider and closed her eyes. She began to string notes together into an ascending scale layered with an occasional tri-tone harmony. Another human impossibility. As the pitch rose, the guests were startled by a loud high crack. Seconds later, another . . . then another, until suddenly some of them were being sprayed with powerful jets of water . . . within seconds it was a deluge. WB broke Epyphany's gaze and looked up just as the first of the tall cylinder aquariums cracked open, sending torrents of water and jellyfish everywhere. A gush of water sent WB flying off the stage just as a couch floated out from under the platform cushioning his fall. He clung to one of the cushions as the destruction continued to raise the water level. Now the guests were scrambling off the platform, tripping over each other in a selfish dash for the exits. The band and their priceless instruments were saved by their early retreat, and most of the guests made it to the exits, but a few stragglers were floating around on cushions with WB.

The initial flooding had forced the entrance doors open but the exterior doors were locked, turning the atrium into a glass-walled swimming pool. Thankfully, two interior exit doors were jammed open, relieving the pressure. WB had a brief moment of relief when the last of the smaller tanks emptied and the water level began to fall. Just when he felt his feet touch the floor, he heard Epyphany's powerful melody increase in volume. He thought, "My god, she's being amplified."

It was true. Warrain engaged the two small sonic concentrators and they were doing their job. Not only were they amplifying Epyphany's sound waves throughout the room, but they were also concentrating a triangulated sonic beam to intersect within the giant tank, exactly at the interior front center of the two-foot-thick wall of glass, where it was creating a destructive cavitation field. According to Samu's calculations, this would in turn weaken the massive wall the way a tiny pebble might crack a windshield.

The sound became unbearable and the direness of the situation suddenly became clear. WB signaled the remaining men to swim as fast as they could toward the entrance. At first they balked, seeing the front doors blocked by a tangled mass of floating furniture caught up in a maze of giant tentacles. But when they saw WB climbing the wreckage they understood.

Thurrow couldn't have been more pleased with the results so far and he was glad no one had been seriously injured, but as he stood in the safety of his ship waiting for the wall to burst, he realized how much he and the rest of the planet had to lose if this plan failed. As much as he loved Sadjah, his love for Epyphany was something beyond romantic love. It was akin to having faith in a higher power, in God, the Buddha, or Jesus, then one day facing this higher power, only to find it even more magnificent than imagined. Epyphany was an affirmation of all that is good and all that is possible. The fate of the planet hinged on her survival.

In those seconds of painful anticipation, Thurrow fought down the impulse of self doubt. A lifetime of both considered and careless decisions had all been steps up a ladder leading to this crucial rung . . . this one last hasty decision to blast a hole in a two-foot glass wall.

The Wave

The men caught up with WB and joined him where he clung to the mantle of the giant bronze squid. The singing stopped. Epyphany swam to the back of the tank and held tightly to a large boulder. A small bullet of glass popped out of the front of the tank and flew across the room, striking the interior atrium wall with a loud ping and causing a small crack to form. Then several more glass bullets in quick succession pinged the entrance wall and ricocheted around the room. WB flinched when a shard whizzed by his head. The deadly glass bullets ceased. The room filled with a sound like hail on a tin roof as the tank wall suddenly filled with a thousand tiny cracks spinning out from the weakened epicenter into a web so thick it obscured Epyphany from sight.

Glued to the screen, his face shiny with sweat, Thurrow felt his heart skip a beat when he lost sight of Epyphany. Samu maneuvered as close to the waterfront as possible, and Storm and Dali waited several hundred feet on either side. Reefer circled above, ready to swoop in if necessary.

With a deafening, thunderous explosion of water and glass, the entire two-foot-thick wall of glass exploded and crumbled into the room. One of the men lost his grip on the statue. WB reached out, and with lightning reflexes and surprising strength, managed to grab the man and pull him back to safety. The pressure of two million gallons of water instantly blasted through both the atrium and exterior wall, taking everything in its way as it carried its precious cargo to the open sea. Epyphany's strength and instinct kept her from harm. She managed to struggle against the initial surge, giving herself to it at the exact moment that would allow her to stay near the top and center of the brief tidal wave. The wall of water duplicated Samu's computer simulation precisely, pushing the debris ahead and off to the side while she swam safely inside the wave. By the time it crested the marble steps, Epyphany was practically laughing with joy as she body surfed the dwindling surge into the bay.

Thurrow and the tribe were transfixed, it all happened so fast. However, from the time Thurrow lost sight of her to that joyous moment he spied Epyphany splashing into the bay, it felt like the longest minute of his life. He knew they weren't home free, but the worst was over.

Thurrow glanced at his screen and chuckled. He thought, "This would make a great promo shot for the 'Support the Arts' campaign." He imagined the poster: WB and his cronies flailing their arms, stranded on top of the giant indestructible Kraken sculpture, framed by the hollowed-out ruin left in the aftermath of the colossal jailbreak. The caption might read, "Set your imagination free—great art saves lives."

Blyss

Having spent the best part of two days sitting perfectly still on top of the tower, linked to Epyphany and Thurrow simultaneously, Blyss was elated and exhausted. There was little she could have done from such a distance, but she had been prepared to burn herself out trying.

Blyss was impressed and proud of the way the whole team pulled the plan together on such short notice. She was also intrigued by Thurrow's choice to add another member to the team. Blyss climbed slowly down the tower to inform the Tribe and wait patiently for the reunion.

HOSTAGE

The second Thurrow knew Epyphany was safe, he gave Samu the order and they sped out to sea. The rising sun lit up the morning sky with translucent layers of pink and fiery orange. They followed the reflections of the amber rays, a sparkling path of gold led them safely through the quiet bay. Reefer swooped down close and gently brushed the back of Epyphany's head as she surfed over a wave to greet him. Soaking up the warmth, swimming at full speed with her friends, Epyphany was in heaven. She felt a renewed connection to her ocean world and finally understood her purpose. Epyphany would fight until death to preserve the glorious sea.

When they reached a safe distance from shore, Samu came to a stop. Thurrow was already in his sub preparing to head back to pick up Sadja and check on Warrain. In the interim, WB had been rescued from his embarrassing perch. He wasted no time springing into action, ordering his men to search the town for any signs of Sadjah and to round up all the key personnel associated with the Aboriginal Sea. WB assumed Sadjah was with Thurrow, but he wasn't taking any chances. He also figured Thurrow must have had people on the inside.

At the very beginning of his outrageous plan, Thurrow understood that success would very likely precipitate some kind of retribution. He made sure to cover his tracks and create solid alibis for everyone on his team. Warrain chose to stay behind until Sadjah was safely aboard the sub. He effectively erased any trace of his own history, not only from the aquarium's database but from Fremantle's archives as well. The minute he was sure the sonic concentrators were doing their work, he continued with his mission to deliver Sadjah to the secluded dock.

While the glass walls at the Aboriginal Sea were crashing down, Warrain and Sadjah were scurrying out an emergency exit on the opposite side of the building. The dawn was breaking and they had lost the cover of night, but with all the distractions taking place in the Harbor Wing, they assumed they would have a clear shot to the parking lot.

They were wrong. Since WB had doubled up on his security, there was still a patrol scouting the perimeter. The chaos had only served to make the guards more vigilant. The men yelled to the two suspicious strangers, and when they were ignored they fired shots in the air and called in the security breach. The guards were heading for their vehicles just as Warrain and Sadjah jumped into the Tesla. Fortunately for them, the access road was unguarded and they sped out of sight just as the ambulances, fire trucks, and local police were arriving, effectively blocking their pursuers.

The Tesla was a great getaway car for speed but its unique appearance made it easy to track. Warrain compensated for their conspicuous vehicle by taking advantage of his knowledge of the area and navigating the most circuitous route he could manage under their time constraints. The early hour of the day worked in their favor and they encountered minimal traffic as they followed the winding road to the rendezvous. The roadster slid to a halt at the foot of the dock. Warrain started to get out to help Sadjah, but she insisted he leave at once, explaining there would be no mercy for him if he got caught. She thanked him with a kiss on the cheek and waved him off as she ran to the end of the dock.

Up to this moment, Sadjah had no idea if the rescue was a success. She ran to the end of the dock trying not to fear the worst. Waiting in the misty dawn, she was reminded of a similar scene so many weeks ago when she stood frightened and abandoned on the secluded pier in the Maldives. So much had happened since that time.

She was staring into the mist, lost in the memories of her recent past, when the phone startled her. "Thank God." She answered and just listened while Thurrow filled her in on the events. Sadjah sighed in relief, then related the unfortunate circumstances of their escape. Thurrow assured her that he was pushing the Sub to its limits. He told her to just sit tight and to stay on the phone. He was close now . . . the sub rose up into the mist a short distance from the dock. Sadjah couldn't see it but she could hear the familiar gurgle. Then Thurrow heard gunshots over the phone. Sadjah screamed in surprise.

"Sadjah! Sadjah! Are you alright? Have you been hit? Sadjah! Speak to me!"

". . . Sorry, yes . . . yes . . I'm alright, but they've seen me. You should dive. Right now! It's too late for us! Thurrow, you have to leave. Go! There's nothing you can do. There are two trucks full of armed men. I have to throw my phone away. I know you'll find me. I feel it! We still have so much to do. Good bye for now."

"But Sadj . . ."

Sadjah hurled the phone into the mist as the guards rushed up the dock and carried her roughly away.

Thurrow submerged reluctantly. He knew Sadjah was right. There was nothing he could do now but get Epyphany back to safety. He just couldn't believe it. His heart filled with regret and self recrimination. A long list of "if only" scenarios came to mind, but he stopped himself from going down that road. He forced his mind's eye to look forward. Regrets were a waste of time. He was a man of solutions and he vowed to get her back. In an attempt to remain optimistic, he thought, "Hell, if we could rescue Epyphany from WB's clutches, we can certainly do the same for Sadjah." In the past he'd been guilty of underestimating the lengths to which WB was willing to go. Thurrow hoped he wasn't kidding himself once again.

CONSEQUENCES

WB wracked his brain trying to figure out how to spin the disaster. He thought, "It's going to take an incredible amount of money to keep my name out of this. It will be a miracle if no one snapped a shot of me hanging from the giant squid like a circus monkey."

When WB finally arrived back at his suite, he found Sadjah waiting there with two of his men standing guard. WB dismissed them with a wave. Sadjah stood up and started to speak, but her father cut her off and motioned her to sit down. He was so angry he could barely look at her. Turning his back, WB walked over to the mini-bar and poured himself a scotch. He didn't bother with ice for the first one and just gulped down a shot. Then he took his time and poured himself a proper drink. Minutes passed and they both remained silent.

Sadjah was no longer afraid of her father, nor was she conflicted. She detested him, but she wasn't stupid. Knowing her recent tactics would no longer prove effective, she thought perhaps she might try to create some doubt in his mind. She could plead ignorance, or she could tell her father how she had tried to plead with Thurrow not to take any chances with Epyphany's life. But she knew any story she might come up with would be full of holes. There was no way around the fact that she had been caught trying to escape. The more she considered her situation, the more she became convinced there was little she could do. She was at the total mercy of WB.

It was pointless to try to reason with her father when he was angry, no matter what the circumstances. She was sure in this case the degree of his current outrage was unprecedented. Sadjah remained silent.

As she sat quietly waiting for WB's tirade, her thoughts turned to Epyphany and she had to suppress a smile. On the dock during the short moments between her last words to Thurrow and the rough grasp of WB's goons, she had silently called out Epyphany's name. It wasn't a conscious call for help but a simple reflex. Much to her surprise, Epyphany responded, and in the midst of the pain and drama of the situation they actually carried on a brief telepathic conversation. Given the distance and the circumstances, they were equally surprised at the clarity and ease of their communication. They had been conversing silently for weeks but those conversations only took place when they were in close proximity and controlled settings. This was something new, something very special. It was different from the "Thought Bundle."

With a drink in his hand and a curious smile on his face, WB walked back across the room and sat down next to Sadjah. In a plaintive tone he began.

"My own daughter, my flesh and blood, are you blind? Can you not see? All that you are, all that you have, your riches, your power, your fame . . . everything, ev-er-y-thing you now possess . . . I have laid at your feet. You were my princess. I paved your path to success with gold and gave you the key to the palace. When finally, after years of searching, I find the one thing in this world that fills me with awe, that brings me pure joy to behold, that completes my quest . . . "

WB buried his head in his hands and sobbed . . . "I had such plans for all of us . . . united at last . . . the circle complete . . . Sadjah you have stolen my muse." Raising his head and wiping a tear from his eye, his voice hardened with contempt. "And now I will use you to get her back . . . you are no longer my daughter . . . you are my hostage . . . and you won't walk free until Epyphany is mine once again."

Sadjah met his cold blank stare and paused before she spoke. She was struck suddenly by the blackness of his gaze. He was like a shark—those same deathly vacant eyes of a born predator looked back at her—but she didn't turn away. All these years she had never known the depth of his madness. He had fooled her and most everyone around him. Sadjah vowed that she would do every thing in her power to save Oojai and its miraculous inhabitants from his egomaniacal destruction.

Speaking calmly and softly, Sadjah replied, "You gave me nothing of value. I have been your pawn since the day I was born. There is no excuse for the indecent, immoral methods you have employed to manipulate my choices and use me to further your ceaseless quest for power and riches. I have been just one more addition to your trophy shelf, another work of art to hang neglected in your gallery of souls. I have no love left for you, only pity. There is so much you could do to make this world a better place for every living thing. For all your treasures and power, you remain weak and alone. You think you can rule the world while we both know you are brought to your knees daily by a bottle of scotch. But for your bank account, you are no better off than any other sad hapless mumbling drunkard. Thurrow was right when he called you blind. If you could see beyond the blinding glitter of your gold you would be rewarded tenfold with the all the beauty this planet has to offer.

I haven't stolen your muse. Epyphany is not a thing to be owned, she is a unique and special being. Epyphany was never yours. And if she was truly your muse you would have honored her existence and supported us in our fight to save her world."

Unaffected by Sadjah's words, WB stood to leave and replied, "My men will be here in ten minutes to escort you to your penthouse. You can pack two suitcases. You'd better choose your belongings wisely because you may be gone for a very long time."

THE QUEEN

The mild breeze was predictably warm. A small flock of delightful white terns were perched in the scraggly branches sticking out of a massive stone overhang that shielded her from the relentless sun. Standing naked in the comfort of the shadow, she curled her toes slowly on the cool smooth stone. The terrace was carved into the solid rock face of the tallest and thinnest peak on the island. She remained motionless as the shadow lengthened; her dark tanned skin rendered her virtually invisible while the sun moved slowly overhead. Staring impassively out over the infinite horizon, she was neither happy nor sad.

For much of the past twenty years, this is the way she had felt and this is where she had stood, for hours each day, trying to remember. She sauntered out of the cool shade and approached the high perimeter wall, a safety barrier for a person of average height. She was anything but average.

The stone wall rose up in front of her to just below her shoulder height. She leaned forward, comfortably placing her elbows flat. She rested her chin on her intwined fingers. Her nipples grazed the polished stone, setting off a vertical tingle that looped down between her legs and back up her spine. She shivered in spite of the heat penetrating her long gold and silver-streaked hair. The gentle warmth of the setting sun caressed the back of her head and massaged her shoulders, spreading it's comforting rays down her back and over her firm buttocks and strong thighs. She felt the wind tickle her long lashes, and blinked the sensation away.

The Queen wondered if she would ever cry again. She wondered if she would ever have a real friend to laugh and joke with, someone to both console and confide in. The most she would ever give William was a thin Mona Lisa smile. She had exquisite teeth, but he was seldom privy to her gorgeous, captivating smile. Though he tried his best to win her affection and catered to her every need, he had stolen her freedom and so much more. She would continue to let him use her, but she would never give herself to him freely. The Queen could never forgive him.

She turned and walked slowly along the wall, one hand sliding along the silky smooth curves. Where the barrier met the interior wall of the enclosure, she entered an arched opening and walked slowly down a narrow stone stairway that wound down the face of the cliff to one of the channel caverns. About half way to the bottom, the stairway intersected another small terrace that protruded several feet out over the deep channel. She sauntered out to the end of the balcony and stepped up on to the low wall.

The last light of day threw her long, slender shadow against the opposing sheer rock wall. She tilted her head back and raised her hands straight in the air. Washed in the scarlet golden rays of sunset, her body appeared to fly up into the tangerine sky as she leaped out and over the dark channel. The breeze spread her long hair behind her like a flaming yellow cape and her body twisted in flight as she danced in thin air, performing multiple somersaults and acrobatic twists. Straightening out like an arrow at the last moment she pierced the water with barely a splash.

The momentum of the astounding cliff dive propelled her deep into the channel, and even in the low light of sunset she could see far down into the ancient ravine. For millions of years, the tides and the intense ocean storms had worked together to smooth the walls and grind channels into this island of solid rock. As she swam swiftly to the surface, a pod of dolphins joined her.

It was in these moments she felt the most alive. The dolphins swam close, and while they danced with her in the crystalline waters of the channel, she released her captive smile. She was transformed. When the Queen surfaced she was grinning like the child she once was. A twinge of sadness caught her off guard. Memories of Spinner crossed her mind and she instinctively raised one hand to her breast. Her heart ached for those days, growing up with a such an unusual friend—a friend beyond any young girl's dreams.

Her smile faded. She recalled her days with Spinner fondly, but tied to those images were the unwelcome memories of her parents.

Plagued by an aggravating gap in her memory that never ceased to haunt her, she felt as though a piece of her soul was adrift, floating unseen, just out of reach in a choppy sea. Something extremely important belonged to her but was lost, and she was powerless to search.

After her short swim, the Queen walked up the ramp into the giant cavern and, waving off her inescapable steward, made her way slowly to the stairs leading back to her rooms far above. She could have taken the elevator and arrived in seconds, but she was in no rush. The climb had the twofold benefit of killing time and keeping her fit.

When she reached the top of the stairs, her steward was already there waiting for her.

"Stew, I'm fine, really. My needs are met. Why don't you take a break?" She called him Stew because William rotated the stewards frequently and she couldn't keep track of their names. They didn't seem to mind.

The young man smiled, bowed slightly, and removed himself to the back of the room.

William called her his queen but she had been his prisoner right from the start. Over the years, she had gotten used to his overprotectiveness and his unwarranted jealousy. She found she didn't need the company of humans. Her ocean friends fulfilled her needs for companionship better than any of William's guests.

With so much time on her hands, the Queen made an early decision to devote herself to art, science, and literature. Though she was restricted from communicating with the outside world, William agreed to supply her with a comprehensive library and the digital equivalent of any degree program she chose. In addition, his team designed a beautiful art studio and a fully equipped modern laboratory. She had become a very accomplished painter, and she was qualified to teach in several disciplines at any university in the world. Her life was rich albeit solitary.

The Queen had accepted her destiny long ago, and except for the occasional spells of melancholy, she reasoned her life to be as good as anyone had the right to expect.

QUIET WHISPER

As soon as Thurrow docked the sub, he headed to the swimming platform at the stern to tell Epyphany and the others the bad news. They were already there waiting for him. The moment he saw them, he could tell they knew. He wondered if his mood was that obvious? Epyphany spoke first, "Sadjah told me."

Thurrow was confused for a minute, then asked, "You can communicate from this distance?"

"So it seems. In fact, I have a feeling that distance is no longer a factor. I'm almost as surprised as you are."

"That's incredible. Can you locate her as well?"

"Not yet, but I'm hoping Blyss can help us with that."

"Well . . . things aren't as gloomy as I thought. I have to check on Warrain. Will you meet me up at the pool in a while? We need to figure out our next move."

Thurrow went back to the control room and asked Samu to find Warrain. Thurrow proceeded to the bar and poured himself a glass of rum, plunked down on a bar stool, and put his head in his hands. He felt overwhelmed, burned out—his brain was tired and overworked. He had been looking forward to a relaxing journey back to Oojai. He was frustrated, and his hopes of sharing the wonders of that peaceful island with Sadjah were dashed. He missed her already and he feared for her safety. Thurrow was worried. WB would no longer fall for her act, and her credibility at Pisces would be completely shot. Thurrow was sure she'd been replaced by now. He tried not to imagine how WB might take out his anger on Sadjah. She would be a liability to him at this point, and in spite of their kinship, WB would likely show little mercy. The destruction of the Harbor Wing and Epyphany's incredible escape was no doubt one of the biggest public defeats WB had ever suffered. He had lost his ill-gained treasure, millions of dollars from potential investors, and most of all, he had lost "face" with his peers.

Though he was remorseful about the devastation of such a magnificent and well intentioned facility, Thurrow understood that in war, beautiful things must often be sacrificed for the greater good. He was fully aware that WB would view the attack on his aquarium as an act of war. Thurrow also knew that WB and his relentless corporate machine had to be stopped. Without the help of Blyss, Epyphany, and the Tribe, Thurrow and Sadjah would stand little chance of saving the oceans from plunder and pollution.

Samu interrupted Thurrow's serious introspection, reminding him that Epyphany was waiting in the pool. He forced himself to his feet, took a deep breath, and said, "Thanks, Samu. Tell her I'm on my way."

Waiting patiently in the pool, Epyphany used the time to put the recent events into perspective. The days in captivity were a harsh but enlightening experience. She finally understood what Blyss had been trying to impress upon her for so many years. Her life had meaning now. Her sense of purpose was finally clear and she welcomed it. All the things she'd learned recently from Thurrow and Sadjah had become more than just words. Epyphany had survived the test and she was stronger in many ways. With the support and collaboration of her friends, she felt emboldened and empowered. Epyphany could see a glimpse of hope for the planet.

In her heart she felt the future would hold much suffering and the successful formulation of a sustainable society would come at a very high price. But she was reassured by a vision of a planet shared equally by all the species with balance and respect for each other.

Epyphany sensed Thurrow's presence and looked up to see him smiling down on her. They hadn't been alone together since he rescued her from the Water Kingdom. Looking deep into one another's eyes, they let their gaze linger in the comfortable silence . . .

Epyphany was first to speak. "Thank you, Thurrow. Thank

you for everything. My life is enriched beyond words by your friendship and your truth. I love you far more than I could have thought possible. I have come to fully understand why you allowed Blyss to convince you to leave me. I have learned so much about the world as it really is, and even more about myself. I am convinced that you and I and Sadjah are destined to serve a higher purpose. The odds against us are overwhelming, but I sense the possibility of victory. We are the potential, the genesis of a new paradigm. Our task is to reach beyond our own imaginations toward the alternative solutions yet to be imagined."

Just hearing her voice filled Thurrow with joy. Epyphany's words validated and inspired him. He was awestruck by the change in her. He could feel the energy surrounding her. She glistened in the fading light of the day. She glowed with a translucent life force, and her love was palpable. He was not predisposed to religious doctrine, but the incredible creature before him certainly qualified for deity status. He was speechless.

Epyphany swam closer and beckoned him to join her. Thurrow shamelessly removed his clothes and slipped into the pool. She reached out her long, slender hand toward him. His memory flashed and he was back in the fateful moment when they first met. He remembered seeing her hand as a threatening webbed claw and how he had pulled away from her gentle gesture of rescue. Thurrow realized now what that gesture had cost her. With that simple act of faith, she chose to put her future and the future of her Tribe, Blyss, and Oojai itself in his hands.

He took her hand and they swam closer together. Epyphany led Thurrow to the deep end of the pool. He pulled her close and felt the hardness of her nipples press against his chest. It seemed like her entire body was pulsing with heat. She tilted her head and opened her mouth. As he moved in for a kiss, her long tongue licked his lips then slid inside his mouth. The setting sun threw long shadows on the deck behind them, and though his eyes were open, the sky and the shadows blurred. Thurrow gave up trying to focus and gave into the sensual delight of Epyphany. Locked in deep embrace, they sunk beneath the water and began swimming in slow spirals. Epyphany shared her oxygen with Thurrow much the same way she had brought him through the tunnel into the Cavern Temple during their first encounter. They were lost in the moment, immersed in the sensations—cool water flowing over warm flesh, the swirling current sending tiny bubbles dancing around tangled limbs, weightless bodies skin to skin, sweet caresses like silk against silk. They surfaced, gasping and laughing, euphoric, released from rationality and drunk with passion.

Thurrow pushed Epyphany against the side of the pool and pinned her arms above her head. She arched her back and the hidden crease of her soft mound parted. He grasped her more firmly; she used her powerful tail and thrust her hips forward. They both screamed in ecstasy as he entered her. They fell back into the water clinging madly to each other, horrifyingly beautiful animals thrashing and thrusting in the twilight, following their true nature and defying the arbitrary rules of humanity . . .

Sadjah was sitting in the back of the limo with WB heading back to his sub. He was completely ignoring her while he busied himself making calls and issuing orders. He abruptly dropped the phone and silently turned to Sadjah. Her head was relaxed against the head rest. Beads of sweat were gathered on her forehead and upper lip, her eyes were closed, and she was smiling. WB asked, "What just happened? Are you alright?"

Without opening her eyes she whispered softly, "Yes . . . yes . . . quite alright."

At that same moment, two special women simultaneously serenaded the heavens. The Queen stood high on the parapet, her voice ringing joyously out over the rocky shore, while many hundreds of miles away Blyss sat at the foot of the Chrysylyss and improvised a haunting melody on the swhorl . . . and in that moment . . . the world grew silent . . .

nothing was ever going to be the same . . .

Breathless and speechless, Thurrow sat on the edge of the pool with Epyphany. Finally, Epyphany broke the silence. "So, was that the next move you wanted to talk about?"

Thurrow laughed loudly and said, "To be honest, that was the last thing on my mind until I saw you glowing in the last rays of sunset with that look in your eyes. I hate to roll out the cliches, but I think that we might have stopped time. I feel so calm and at peace . . . Epyphany, I can no longer imagine this world without you. I agree with everything you said. The word 'love' has new meaning to me since I met you. It describes feelings much wider and deeper than I have ever known. I have lost my fear of being misunderstood when I say "I love." It simply describes a singular feeling that transcends categories. Perhaps the meaning of 'love' is still subject to degrees, but even that seems pointless. I have a growing list of the souls that I love, none of which are in competition for my heart and mind. Does that make any sense to you?"

Epyphany nodded in agreement. Now that her heart rate and her breathing were back to normal, she found herself wondering about the fallout from their impulsive act. She was not feeling a shred of regret, but she was curious about what Blyss might have to say. Epyphany smiled as a sweet tingle ran through her from her tail to the ridge of her head, the sweet aftershock of their seismic coupling. Her joy had been magnified by her subtle consciousness of a shared experience. She doubted if Thurrow had been aware of the third party, but at the moment their lips touched, Epyphany heard Sadjah's quiet whisper of approval.

They managed to keep the conversation light, but there was no denying their actions would have consequences. Unlike any other encounters of love and passion taking place around the world at that very moment, their situation was unique in the truest sense of the word. Theirs was a pure love combined with an animal passion between two different, intelligent species. Epyphany was the single link between human and dolphin, and Thurrow the only man on the planet worthy of her love. It was their fate. They couldn't know this, but Blyss made the discovery many years before. Their magnificent union was depicted in the ancient silver tablets. Oblivious to the profound evolutionary significance of their love, Epyphany and Thurrow willingly and joyfully accepted their destiny no matter what the consequences.

BACK TO OOJAI

Samu was speeding along, navigating the course Epyphany had provided. As they drew closer to Oojai, Epyphany received a transmission from Blyss and relayed it to Thurrow. He directed Samu to slow down. Just before Epyphany slipped into the exit tube, Thurrow grasped her shoulders, pulled her close and kissed her gently on the lips.

Samu requested Thurrow's presence on the bridge. The instruments were going haywire and the GPS signal was fading fast. Unconcerned, Thurrow switched to manual override, and explained that the location of Oojai was securely blocked from the outside world through the mystical power of the Gold Tower. He took over the helm and followed Epyphany the remaining distance to the island. In spite of his total focus on Epyphany and the distant horizon, Thurrow was taken completely by surprise when suddenly the island appeared before him not more than a mile away. It was as if it had popped up out of the sea.

As they entered the the bay and headed toward the lagoon, Thurrow could feel his whole body relax. He said aloud, "We did it. We made it back home." Thurrow was surprised how "home" just rolled off his tongue so naturally. Even though his time here had been brief, it felt like the place where he belonged. A cascade of memories flooded his consciousness—waking up under the Gold tower, meeting Blyss and the Tribe, the barrage of information as Epyphany shared the wonders of Oojai, and that incredible first kiss . . .

Thurrow anchored the Samudra Hantu near the Chancel and dove into the bay. He joined Epyphany and Dali and swam the rest of the way into the lagoon and through the tunnel.

When they surfaced inside the Cavern Temple, Blyss and the rest of the Tribe were there to greet them. Blyss was standing at the foot of the Gold Tower. Before a single word was spoken she unsheathed her Swhorl and began to play.

Epyphany took Thurrow's hand and led him closer until they floated together alongside Dali near the tower. They looked up at Blyss, captivated by the music.

Blyss played for several minutes, using music rather than words to express all she felt and to celebrate their safe return. She wove a comforting tapestry of rhythm and melody, enfolding her audience and renewing their bond.

She placed the Swhorl back in its case and the Tribe drew nearer. Blyss spoke. "Welcome home. It would be a refreshing luxury to just give my congratulations, to expound on the success of your dangerous exploits, and to get back to the joyful life we have enjoyed here on Oojai for so many years. But the world is a different place than it was when you left. Your actions have set the stage for the final act, and like brave actors, we wait in the dark wings with a blank script. We know the plot and we know some of the players, but we cannot predict the outcome. We must give ourselves to the notion of success and improvise the rest. My heart tells me we are on the right path, and I am hopeful. Let us swim together, gather allies, win over our enemies, and enter this transition with open hearts and minds. Take some time to catch up and rest, then meet me here at sundown in two days. We have much to consider.

The tribe followed Epyphany and Thurrow back out to the lagoon, where they swam lazily and listened to stories of the big adventure. When the questions were all answered and the satisfied tribe slowly drifted away, the couple swam leisurely out to the chancel. Sliding onto the warm, smooth stone they fell asleep arm in arm as they watched the fiery sky grow dark.

REVELATION

As WB's submarine approached the Retreat, two guards entered Sadjah's cabin and placed a blindfold over her eyes. By this time she had learned it was useless to object and offered no resistance. They guided her to her father's quarters and sat her down next to WB.

"Well Sadjah, our destination approaches. I think you'll find it quite to your liking. I spared no expense in the design and construction. It's too bad your friend Thurrow can't be here to join you. I'm sure he would appreciate the art and science involved in my labor of love. There's nothing like it on the planet. I want to emphasize the remoteness of your new accommodations. It is literally off the map. It is an inescapable and impenetrable fortress.

Sadjah barely acknowledged his words and they waited in silence while the sub maneuvered into the narrow channel. They disembarked quickly and Sadjah was surprised by a strange loud whistling sound when she stepped out of the sub. She could tell by the reverberation they were standing in a very large cavernous space. Irritated, Sadjah raised her voice above the noise and asked, "What is the point of this blindfold? I have no idea where we are."

WB replied, "Just a little while longer, my dear. I have a wonderful surprise for you, and you know how your old dad likes to add a little drama to his surprises."

When the elevator door opened onto the terrace, the pair stepped out. Sadjah felt a gust of warm wind on her face. WB walked her to the center of the terrace, removed the blindfold and said, "Welcome to your new home."

The midday sun was in her eyes, so Sadjah held her hand over her head to block the sun. Squinting, she was surprised to see the silhouette of an incredibly tall woman, her long hair flowing down the length of her back. The mysterious figure was leaning on the wall facing out to the sea, a beautiful gossamer-thin gown of golden silk furled around her like a brilliant blazing cape.

WB continued, "You may be staying at the Retreat a long time but you won't be alone. There's someone I want you to meet."

They stepped closer and the statuesque woman slowly turned to face them.

Sadjah grasped WB's arm to steady herself. She felt her heartbeat quicken and she barely kept herself from fainting. The two women looked one another up and down, both of them speechless.

"Sadjah, I'd like you to meet your mother . . . my Queen . . . Your Highness, may I present Sadjah . . . your daughter."

The magnificent woman seemed to float toward Sadjah. She clasped both of Sadjah's hands in her own. Sadjah tried not to stare at the woman's large unusual hands, and so directed her attention to the warm smiling face looking down upon her. Sadjah thought, "She is so tall, so regal . . . such breathtaking beauty, she's not of this world . . . I have her eyes . . ."

Her thoughts were interrupted by the most mellifluous voice she had ever heard, and she thought she would completely melt away when she heard these words . . .

"Henceforth, consider yourself my honored guest. Though I often have reason to doubt his words, I believe William this time . . . I . . am . . . your mother . . . Sadjah, I am so very glad to meet you. My name is Chrysylyss."

The End of Book One - The Mermaid Story: Epyphany

Slated for a 2014 release:

Book Two - The Mermaid Story: Chrysylyss

visit www.TheMermaidStory.com for more information. Please "like and share" The Mermaid Story Page

Thanks,

Sev

ABOUT THE AUTHOR

"There has always been some level of narrative in my work, in the form of a song, a short animation or even within the frozen moment of an engaging pose. The Mermaid Story is a welcome opportunity to relax and take the time to develop a story, to sing in the varied voices of my characters and to imagine and design entire landscapes. Art should be fun and I'm having fun as I continue to build the magical world of The Mermaid Story."

Sev is a musician, sculptor, 3D graphics designer, and mermaid enthusiast living with his imagination near the New Hampshire Seacoast, USA.

Find out more at www.sevhead.com

CHARACTER GLOSSARY

Epyphany: The unique, powerful and strangely beautiful Mermaid.

Blyss: The mystical and magical spiritual guide and mentor to Epyphany.

Thurrow: The genius inventor/scientist, the first human to discover Epyphany.

Sadjah: The beautiful precocious billionaire corporate tycoon. Thurrow's lover.

Wild Bill: The playboy multi-billionaire. Sadjah's father.

Chrysylyss: The Queen - The Mother

Samu: Short for Samudra Hantu [Indonesian meaning - Ocean Ghost] Thurrow's ship.

Warrain: Thurrow's young Australian multi-talented assistant.

Ondina: Seattle journalist, Warrain's love interest.

The Tribe: A varied group of evolved species devoted to Epyphany.

Dali: Artistic Dolphin

Storm: Quiet giant Blue whale

Reefer: Oversized pelican

Magnum: Extra large mutated alligator

Speed: Giant leather backed sea turtle

Zip: small flying fish

Irie: extremely fast sailfish

Hue: manatee

Cheeks: manatee - Hue's mate